THE MOON SISTERS

ALSO BY THERESE WALSH

The Last Will of Moira Leahy

Crown Publishers
New York

THE

MOON

SISTERS

A NOVEL

THERESE WALSH

Copyright © 2014 by Therese Walsh

Published in the United States by Crown Publishers,
an imprint of the Crown Publishing Group,
a division of Random House LLC,
a Penguin Random House Company, New York.
www.crownpublishing.com

CROWN and the Crown colophon are registered trademarks
of Random House LLC.

Library of Congress Cataloging-in-Publication Data
Walsh, Therese.
    The moon sisters : a novel / Therese Walsh.—First Edition.
        pages   cm
    1. Sisters—Fiction. 2. Mothers and daughters. 3. Forgiveness—
Fiction. 4. Families—Fiction. I. Title.
PS3623.A36617M66   2013
813.'.6—dc23   2013018032

ISBN 978-0-307-46160-5
eBook ISBN 978-0-307-46162-9

Printed in the United States of America

Book design by Barbara Sturman
Jacket design by Kimberly Glyder Design
Jacket photograph by Stephen Carroll/arcangel-images.com

10 9 8 7 6 5 4 3 2 1

First Edition

This book is dedicated to Riley, for one hundred read-throughs and one-hundred-and-one sage comments; and to Liam, for one thousand rounds of laughter.

And to my sisters, who are as different as the moon and the sun.

THE MOON SISTERS

What one commonly takes as "the reality" . . . by no means signifies something fixed, but rather something that is ambiguous. . . . There are many realities.

—*Albert Hofmann*

✳

Action is the antidote to despair.

—*Joan Baez*

FEBRUARY

The End of the Beginning

✷ OLIVIA ✷

The night before the worst day of my life, I dreamed the sun went dark and ice cracked every mirror in the house, but I didn't take it for a warning.

The day itself seemed like any other Tuesday at the start. Papa made pancakes, then went to the bakery to prepare for deliveries with Babka. My sister, Jazz, followed behind him shortly after that. Even though it was one of the coldest stretches we'd had that February, I chose a button-down shirt from the pile of clothes on the floor of my room instead of my wool pullover, because I planned to see Stan.

When I went to say goodbye to Mama, I found the door to the kitchen closed from the living room. She'd have the oven on to battle back the chill in our house. The kitchen, at least, could be warmed quickly this way, a small room shaped like a stubby number 7 that doubled as Mama's office in the wintertime.

"What's out there?" I asked when I stepped inside to find her staring out the room's lone window. She wore her frayed blue robe, thick socks, and a ponytail that was just to the right of center. It was still cold in there; the oven had yet to warm the room.

"Nothing," she said. "A gray sky."

I was hardly aware. Even though it was the middle of winter, my nose filled with the scent of clothes right off the line on a summer day, like sunshine itself. That's what seeing Mama always did to me; it was my favorite part of having synesthesia.

"If you live your whole life hoping and dreaming the wrong things," she said, "what does that mean about your whole life?"

Her voice sank low, looked like roots descending in a slow and seeking way into the earth, which told me she was in what she called one of her "up-and-downs."

I sat at the table, littered with manuscript pages, a plateful of cold pancakes, and a typewriter older than my mother. She'd been working on a fairy tale called *A Foolish Fire* nearly my entire life but had yet to finish it. I knew this was what she was talking about.

"There's nothing wrong with your dreams, Mama," I told her. "Believe, believe."

"Not everyone has your courage, Olivia."

I might've suggested she take the trip she dreamed of taking, go to the setting of her story—a bog in our state of West Virginia called Cranberry Glades. But I knew a mention of the ghost lights she hoped to see there could send my mother's mood up or further down, and that maybe this wasn't the time to risk it.

"Maybe you'll feel better after you take a nap," I said, because Mama called *sleep* her personal tonic.

She said, "I take too many naps as it is," which is when I pulled off a boot.

"I'll stay home with you today. If you're up for it, we can dream together for a while. We haven't done that in a long time."

When I was younger, we called it "the dream game." Sometimes I'd describe life through my eyes—like the way thunder filled the air with a mustard-gold fog—because she enjoyed hearing about it. Sometimes we'd both poke our heads through the clouds, especially after math, when we were worn out from too much thinking. She'd lie on the couch with her eyes locked shut, and I'd fling myself over a chair with my eyes wide open, and we'd unloose our wildest imaginings. Trees rained soft white buds the size of platters onto our shoulders and into our hair, covered us until we looked like exotic birds. We'd fly to Iceland or France or Russia or Brazil. Visit creamy blue pools and limestone cliffs and waterfalls that went on for miles.

Sometimes we'd visit the bog and see the ghost lights, which Mama said were like a vision of hope itself, and she'd have a revelation about the end of her story.

But it was all just dreaming.

She told me she wasn't in the mood for that and urged me to go on with my plans. I took it as a positive sign that she sounded calmer when she said it, that the downward trek of her voice had stilled. I half expected her to say something about Stan—*Don't let that boy into your knickers*—even though I was nearly eighteen and we lived in the middle of nowhere.

"Will you write today?" I asked, when she stayed quiet.

She nodded but never turned around. I pulled my boot back on. I told her to stay warm. I told her I loved her. And then I left.

I was the one who found her later—not moving, not breathing, dead with her head on the kitchen table. The gas on and the pilot light out, the windows and doors closed, sealing the room as tight as the envelope sitting beside her.

I have a hard time recalling what I did in those next minutes. Screamed. Felt for a pulse that wasn't there. Called 911. Pulled her to the floor. Held my mother, and rocked us both, the way she'd rocked me over endless hours when I was a child.

"You're not dead, you're not dead," I chanted, rocked harder, hoped harder, as cold air from a window I must've opened poured over us both. "Mama! Mama, please, wake up!"

She did not wake up. The ambulance came and took her away, and I saw no colors or shapes from the siren—the beginning of a landslide of change.

I hid the letter in the torn lining of my coat, where it dug at my heart like a spade, and I told no one. It was not a letter meant for us—me and my father and sister. It was not *Goodbye, life wasn't what I thought it would be. I've lived and dreamed the wrong things, and I no longer believe, so I am gone.* Mama had turned on the oven, and the pilot light flickered out because it was an old stove in an old house, and she'd fallen asleep with the door closed, because that's what she did all the time.

An accident.

Ghosts sometimes visited from the other side, Babka always said; they breathed on glass as a sign of their discontentment. It was only later that I noticed frost on the bathroom mirror.

JULY

FIRST STAGE:

DENIAL

Hope is the denial of reality.

—*Margaret Weis*

CHAPTER ONE

The Foolish Fire of Olivia Moon

∗ JAZZ ∗

My sister began staring at the sun after our mother died, because she swore it smelled like her. For me, it would always be the scent of oven gas, since that's how Mom went—fumes pouring out, her breathing them in. Like Sylvia Plath, my father said, because my mother was a tortured writer, too.

Olivia's actions were just as purposeful. Burned her retinas out over a period of months, made it so she couldn't drive or even read. Well, she could've, if she'd used the glasses the doctor gave her—those big things that look like telescopes on her face—but she wouldn't. So no reading. No driving. Instead, she lived with her head always tilted to the side, with an oil smudge in the center of everything she might want to see.

My sister's reality had always been bizarre, though, with her ability to taste words and see sounds and smell a person on the sun. So when she decided to toss our dead mother's ashes into a suitcase and go off to the setting of our dead mother's story to find a ghost light, I wasn't all that surprised. She'd never been the poster child for sense.

There were dozens of tales about ghost lights, or will-o'-the-wisps, as they're sometimes called—those slow-blinking lights that folks claim appear over bogs and swamplands. Some say they're the spirits of dead Indians or disgruntled miners, even unborn children. They're lost souls trying to find their missing parts. They're mercurial sprites who'll lead you to hidden treasure or danger if you follow, which is why they're also called *Foolish* Fires; trusting in them is not a sensible thing. Scientists say they're just swamp gases blinking to a strange pseudo-life now and then. A reasonable explanation, if you ask me.

Olivia did not ask me.

She woke up one day determined to find them. As if she might see with her blind eyes just when she needed to see—notice those lights hiding in a mushroom ring, or hanging alongside a thousand leaves in a hickory tree, or drowning with a bunch of cranberries in a bog. As if finding them might matter somehow, when our lives had been upended and nothing could ever be the same again.

I knew better.

"I'm not a cripple, Jazz, and I can see well enough to walk around without falling into a ditch. I'll be just fine."

Olivia stood at the end of the lane, a small tattered suitcase in one hand and a bag lunch in the other. Dirt swirled around her ankles when Old Man Williams rattled by in his pickup.

I pulled as close to the curb as I could and glared out at her from the small window of the biscuit bus. The shame I'd felt having to drive the ancient red-and-rust beast, which my grandmother and father didn't even use anymore but which seemed unwilling to quit, had been worth it in the end. I'd won the job in Kennaton. I'd won it, and I couldn't even enjoy it. Not when my eighteen-year-old, legally blind sister was about to do another stupid thing.

"And what happens when you get thirsty?" I asked.

"I'll buy water." She rattled her pocket. Coins jangled from within.

At least those denim shorts were hers. The bleach-streaked blue

V-neck she wore—like so many of the things she wore now—had been our mother's. Taking her things was Olivia's latest obsession, as was trying to braid her hair the way our mother did for her when she was young, when her hair was an artful mix of curls and waves. The opposite of the nest of neglect on her head now, with braids wound so tight they jutted from her skull like worms with rigor mortis.

"What if you're not near a store?"

"There are streams all over the state," she said. "I'll find water."

"You'll get giardia."

She didn't blink.

My fingers dug into the cracked plastic steering wheel as the bus coughed. "And what happens when you're tired?"

"I'll sleep."

"Where?"

She shrugged. "Wherever I am."

"And where are you going to find these ghost lights, Olivia? Do you even know?"

She looked sidelong at me with big, blue, broken eyes set in a pale face, and said, "Cranberry Glades," as if I'd asked her the time of day.

I was sicker than I could say of hearing about the bogs and ghost lights of the Monongahela Forest. Our mother had talked about them a lot over the years, always in relation to her book. *One of these days I'll visit that bog, see those wisps, and figure out the ending—you'll see*, she'd say.

I might've asked her how that could matter, tried to impress upon her the impossibility of finding the end to a fictional story out in the real world and that she didn't need a trip so much as dogged determination and hard work to finish. But logic wasn't my family's strong suit, and my mother had never been one to actualize a dream—even one as straightforward as *Visit Cranberry Glades*.

"That trip isn't for you to worry about, Olivia. It isn't anyone's to worry about anymore," I said, giving logic a try despite what I knew about my blood. "We need to let it go."

"It's unfinished business," she said, and sounded for a moment like my grandmother—a woman I respected for being both a dreamer *and* a doer, even if she was far too superstitious for my taste.

The dead remain when there's unfinished business, Babka had said after the funeral, reciting one of her Old World beliefs and covering the mirrors in our house lest my mother's spirit reenter our world through a looking glass. They were still covered, too, even though it had been five months since my mother died. *The business is still unfinished*, Babka insisted whenever I pressed her on it.

Maybe my mother's ashes were scattered in my sister's suitcase, but I had no doubt that my mother's spirit had long since moved on. I'd seen the way she looked through magazines, planning trips we'd never be able to afford. I'd heard her gasp with longing over any number of things in *People* magazine: the latest red-carpet dress, elaborate mansions with manicured lawns, even a lobster drowned in a pool of butter—things you'd never find in our hometown.

Dreaming. Always wanting what wasn't.

No, my mother's spirit wasn't hanging around Tramp. She was gone. Free, finally, of the cement shoes that had always been of her own construction. She might've worn those shoes right out to the deepest part of the stream running through our town, let nature take its course, but that wasn't the path she chose when at last she chose.

I knew something was wrong with me.

I should've felt something about her death, more than I did—something that I could label and understand, instead of the knot that I couldn't. All I knew for sure was what that knot *wasn't*. It wasn't what I'd believed grief would be. And it wasn't the desire to memorialize my mother in marble or the stars, or make good on any of the dreams she'd abandoned along with her family.

At the other end of the spectrum lay my father, whose grief was so evident that it hurt to look at him. Sometimes he stood in the bathroom with a portion of the mirror uncovered—staring into his own vacant eyes, his face half-shaved—hoping, praying maybe, that my mother would sneak back through the glass. He blamed himself for her death, I knew, though I didn't understand the *why* of that; it's not like he'd turned on the gas.

A few weeks ago, I came home to find her favorite chair gone. I couldn't begin to guess the number of naps my mother had taken in that seat, or the number of library books she'd read there, either. Maybe my father thought he'd miss her less if he didn't see that empty dented cushion every day. But if that was the reason he would've done well to get rid of all her things instead of leaving the most significant reminders of her right where they'd been.

The typewriter in our tiny kitchen.

Her manuscript tucked under that.

The makeshift desk in their bedroom.

Maybe it's time the rest went away, too, I told him just yesterday, hoping we could be rid of it all, quick and done. But spontaneous, dramatic gestures weren't his nature.

A dog's bark brought me back to the present.

"Olivia!" I shouted, when I noticed her start to walk away again—noticed Mrs. Lynch, too, on her porch across the road, staring at the two of us. I pulled the door handle, a snakelike metal bar angled up and out of the dashboard, until the squeezebox doors creaked open. "Get in, Olivia. Right now."

"Goodbye, Jazz. Try not to worry," she said, and continued down the lane.

Our hometown of Tramp, West Virginia, had about a hundred homes, all of them old firetrap constructions, and only six businesses: a post office, a liquor store, St. Cyril's Church, a gas station, a corner store, and my grandmother's bakery. Everyone in town called the business Susie's—even though its real name was Sušienka, a Slovakian word for *biscuit*—and they called my grandmother Susie—even though her real name was Drahomíra. She didn't mind. Not so long as they came in every morning and bought a bag of her warm small cakes. I tried to steer clear of them myself, since most of my neighbors could probably attribute their potbellies to Susie's biscuits.

Everything was a stone's throw from everything else in Tramp, so I drove a stone's throw and left the keys in the ignition. My grandmother was inside, cleaning a countertop. She stopped when she saw me, her face full of animation and an unspoken question.

"I got the job," I said.

She pressed her thick lips together and narrowed her wrinkled eyelids. "When will you start? Tell me everything."

"In a minute, Babka. Is Dad here?"

When she looked over her shoulder, I ducked under the counter and walked past her, into the kitchen, where the scent of bread had long ago been baked right into the walls. Now early afternoon, appliances sat cool and settled from the morning's work. My father was also settled—bottom in a chair, top slumped over a desk in the corner. There was an open bottle of something beside him—an increasingly common sight this summer.

"Was he drunk for deliveries? When did he start?"

"After lunch. He is just sad," she said. "Give him time. It has only been five months."

It felt more like five years.

I took the bottle. Vodka. Walked it over to the wide porcelain sink.

"Don't," she said. "He'll just buy more."

More of what we couldn't afford to begin with. Still, I knew she was right. I screwed the cap on the bottle and put it back beside him, then gripped his shoulder and shook.

"Dad. Dad, wake up." He didn't stir. "Dad, come on. It's about Olivia. Olivia's in trouble."

One eye squinted up at me. "Liv?" he said. "What?"

"She's halfway down the street, heading out of town with Mom's ashes in a suitcase. She's keen on walking them all the way to the bogs, but with her miswired senses she'll probably end up in Canada."

Or dead. Flattened under someone's tires. Dead. Picked up by some hitchhiker killer. Dead from dehydration, from being lost or—

"You have to tell her to come home," I said. "She won't listen to me."

Vodka poured off him in sheets as he righted himself. *Three sheets to the wind.* Maybe that's where the saying had come from.

"Ready?" I asked.

He pulled himself upright, his hands on the desk, his left cheek coated in flour, his mass of dark, wavy hair—something Olivia and I had both inherited—in desperate need of a trim. His eyes looked a little screwed up. If my mother were suddenly brought back from the grave, she'd die all over again seeing him like this; she'd always thought him the handsomest guy on the planet. At least he never threw up on himself.

"I can't drive," he said.

As if. "I'll drive. Come on, she can't be too far." I pulled at his sleeve, but he didn't budge.

"I should've taken Beth to the bogs," he said, almost moaning the words. "Why didn't I take her?"

Another replayed topic. But you couldn't turn back time, or halt it, no matter how many clock batteries you chucked out the window. I felt the presence of the three ovens behind me as if they'd come to life and nodded their heads, mouths snapped shut.

"Because she didn't want you to take her," I said, hoping my pointed words cut through his fog. "Remember how she always had an excuse whenever you brought it up? Remember how you tried that one time and she couldn't bring herself to get in the car?"

What an ordeal that had been, what a disappointment for us all, but especially my father, who'd taken great pains to try to make it happen.

"She didn't *want* to go," I continued. "Not really."

"You'll have to take her down there, Jazz," he said. "In the bus."

"You can't be serious."

"Drive her down to Monon—Monongahela. Go on and find

those berry bogs for your mother." His eyes came into focus when he said it, too, which made my pulse race in a fight-or-flight kind of way.

"Can we take a moment to ground ourselves in the reality of the situation here?" I said. "Olivia doesn't just want to visit the bog, have a moment, then turn around again right after. She wants to play hide-and-seek with a will-o'-the-wisp. She wants to find one. That could take an eternity, if they even appear down there, and for what purpose? It's not like seeing a light is going to bring Mom back. It's not like her ashes are going to care, either."

My blood pumped harder when my father's expression didn't change.

"All right," I said. "What if we find a ghost light but it's not the good sort of spirit Mom imagined? What if it's a trickster goblin who'll charm us right off a cliff edge?"

His eyes lost their clarity, and I knew I should've taken more care with my words. But was it my fault that I had to sink to the level of superstitious bullshittery in order to make a point?

"It's such a small thing to do for your father, to bring peace," Babka said. "Such a small thing for your sister, to keep her safe."

My grandmother had such a wise way about her; that's what made her guilt trips especially potent. But driving around the state in an ancient bus searching for ether was not how I wanted to spend my time. Not when my life was about to change so dramatically.

In one week and one day, I would start my job at Rutherford & Son Funeral Home in Kennaton, working directly with Emilia Bryce. I would be there four days a week as a rule, though my official start date—August 1st—was a Thursday. Emilia liked the neatness of the idea: new month, new staff member. I couldn't use my job as an excuse, though, because I hadn't told my father about my interview yet; I didn't know how he'd feel about me taking work in the same funeral home Mom's body had been laid out in.

Babka had asked me at least a dozen times if the job was what I wanted, if something more than money motivated my decision.

I knew she asked for a bigger reason than being sorry to lose my dough-rolling hands at Susie's, too. It was hard for her to accept that I was a twenty-two-year-old doer who was not a dreamer—that such a thing could exist with the involvement of her DNA—or that my choices didn't have to satisfy a deep need of any sort. And, if they did, I didn't know about it; self-analysis was anything but my talent. The bottom line was that I wanted the job and wouldn't risk it on my sister's whim.

Babka seemed to read my mind. "It will not take long to drive there, little *macka*." *Much-ka*. Cat. An endearment as well as a reminder to use my claws for good, to scrabble on behalf of my family, toward and not away from them. "You know your mother would want you to go after her, to protect."

Oh, yes, I knew. I could almost hear her voice.

Find your sister and bring her home, Jazz. She's off wandering again.

When wasn't she? Following her impulses, regardless of sense. As predictable as smoke in the wind. But I could not live my life as my sister's keeper. I wouldn't.

Please, Jazz. Be good.

I was sick of being good.

"Thank you, Jazz," my father said.

I stomped my foot—"Wait a second!"—but he'd slumped down again, his head already returned to the desk.

Babka led me out of the back room by the hand. "I have a map for you," she said, also assuming.

I kept up my end of the argument, but I knew I was finished when she started to pack a bag full of biscuits for me, when I realized that's what Olivia had held, too—not a bag lunch but a sack from Susie's—that Babka had been aware of Olivia's plans all along. She handed it to me along with a jar of peanut butter and a dull knife, and said, "You never know. Maybe you'll find the end of the story." An inside joke I'd never found funny.

Any doubt that I'd been bamboozled evaporated when she told

me she'd put the sleeping bags in the storage room and reminded me how to unstick the tricky latch on the back of the bus—the cheapest motel one could find, as the bus was all but gutted. Once home to racks of biscuits, the wide floor now housed only dust.

She tucked money into my hand, if I needed to call or buy more food.

"I thought you said this would take just a few hours."

"A few to drive. A few to look. A few to sleep. A few to look again. A few to drive back. Just a few." She landed a wet kiss on my cheek, and her features turned serious when she said it: "Keep your sister safe. Keep *you* safe. And do not worry about Miss Emilia Bryce. Some dead can wait with patience. Some dead cannot."

The air that rushed out at me when I opened the door to the house nearly melted my skin, and that's saying something, seeing as I was coming from the hottest bus ever manufactured. But, along with covering all our mirrors, Babka had insisted we keep the windows closed. Those spirits—you never did know how they might slip in. And, of course, there was no air-conditioning in our house—or in any house in Tramp. There were no cordless teakettles, either, or iPads or flat-screen TVs. We knew they existed, out there in another sphere, but they were not a part of our world any more than was the water found recently, supposedly, on Mars. A lack of money had a way of repressing a life, turning it back a few years—sometimes a few centuries. I suspected that it had a way of taking the dream out of you, too, that you cashed it in at some point in exchange for a few dollars.

It was while I rushed around, grabbing what I thought we'd need for an overnighter, that I noted the latest change: My mother's desk had been moved out of my parents' room and into Olivia's. There it sat—two tall crates bridged with a plywood worktop—butted up against the end of my sister's bed. In the warmer months, my mother would spend hours there, writing longhand and typing and staring off into space.

On top of the desk's usual tablecloth covering were Olivia's rejected glasses—exhumed from a small drawer filled with other things I was probably never meant to find, including an unopened pack of condoms. Sitting beside the glasses was the framed photograph that had always been on the desk—a picture of a man with steel eyes and a thin smile, his hand held in the air in the manner of a wave, or the waving off of a photographer. My grandfather. My mother's father.

Sometimes my mother called this desk her *altar*, though I never understood why. She didn't exactly believe in God, though she wouldn't admit that and risk an eternity in hell; she'd always preferred purgatory to making a real choice. And now there it was— desk or altar—taken by my sister the way she took everything else.

Everything except what had lain hidden under the loose floorboard in our mother's room. Twenty-two letters, and they all began the same way.

Dear Dad.
Dear Dad.
Dear Dad.

"Must be nice to always do whatever the hell you want," I muttered, taking one last look at the desk before zipping up my mother's old Kennaton State backpack, where those letters lay snug under food and water bottles.

The pack was tucked away under the bus's dash when I reunited with my sister on the road, about half a mile from where I'd last seen her. This time, when I swung open the door, she stepped up and in.

"You can be dangerously passive-aggressive," I told her.

In an unusual display of good sense, she said nothing. Just settled into the seat behind me as we headed out of town.

CHAPTER TWO

Blue and Chocolate

✶ OLIVIA ✶

I was seven years and seven months when my father said he could hear music in the box fan that sat on the floor of our living room. It was fiddler's music, he said, well bowed and true. Mama, Jazz, and I couldn't hear anything but the sound of blades cutting into the hot summer air, but he hummed the tune for us and it was nice. I was so excited that maybe he was like me, but it only happened the one time.

Back then, everyone but my family thought I was either crazy or had the wildest imagination they'd ever heard expressed. They didn't know that there were others who could smell sights (Papa was fresh-mown grass, the sun was Mama) or taste words (not every word, and not the way regular people taste, either; *freckle*, like the dots all over Mama's face, tasted like togetherness). They didn't know that others could see sounds (Babka's voice looked like a tumble of soft flour). They didn't know that I wasn't the only one who could see a calendar in her own head, with days and numbers that lingered in the background, like a hungry dog when you're eating a sandwich.

They didn't know there was a word for what I had.

synesthesia (n.): the stimulation of a sense other than the one receiving input; sensory areas with faulty wiring

That's what the dictionary might say, my doctor explained when he figured it out. After that, my mother told the school they needed to stop using colored chalk and ink in my classes, because if a letter was written in the wrong color (like *A* written in sky blue instead of cranberry red, which was the color it always was to me) it made my brain stall. But they didn't change, so she took me out of there in the sixth grade and taught me at home after that. Taught me everything I needed to know and everything she'd learned in three years of college besides. She always used black ink on white paper, which left my letters free to be themselves. *D* was a superior sort of hot orange, standing beside C, so modest in her buttery tones. O was my favorite, like water shooting out of a hose in summertime.

My mother liked hearing about my letters about as much as Jazz *didn't* like hearing about them. Maybe that's because my sister had to stay in school even after I was taken out of it, and I was able to finish my twelfth-grade requirements early. The trouble between us began before that, though.

The year I turned six, Jazz got a lava lamp for Christmas. It transfixed us both from the second she plugged it in, with globs of oily crimson that rose and fell like sleepy dancers in a pool of green.

That's how "Silent Night" looks! I'd said, excited to share what I saw every time I heard the song. I grabbed the lamp, but it slid out of my hands and broke, spilling all those little dancers onto the kitchen floor.

When my parents walked into the room seconds later to find Jazz boring holes into my skull with her eyes like some medieval torturer, Papa covered one of his own eyes to remind us that there were two ways to look at everything.

It's not the end of the world, Mama said. *Maybe Santa will bring you an even better lava lamp next Christmas.*

Jazz's eyes flicked away from me and to my parents, where they stayed for a long second before she stormed away. *I hate your synesthesia. And there's no such thing as Santa Claus*, she said, already halfway up the stairs.

I might've cried for a week over the death of Santa, but my mother pulled me onto her lap and reminded me of one of her life truths: It was okay to believe in things that others didn't believe in. It was okay not to believe, too.

I leaned my forehead against the rattling window as Jazz merged onto the highway on the way to the glades, my nose raised to catch the slim breeze sneaking in through the permanently stuck window. The world was still an interesting place to see, even now that I was blind in the legal sense of things, unable to clearly make out expressions on faces or my colored letters. Being left with only the periphery made you look at life in a unique way, consider its exhalations and auras—like the deep, deep green of the forested hills on either side of us and the secrets it might hide. And in many ways I could still see more than most: The red-streak sounds left by passing trucks and cars looked like rubber eraser bits on paper, and a clear blue sky always smelled of warm chocolate and adrenaline.

If I'd been in the bus with anyone else, I might've shared that the day was like a cup of chocolate coffee, but I knew better than to bother with Jazz, especially when everything down to her clothing choice of gray shorts and a black T-shirt revealed her storm-cloud mood. She was driving us to the glades against her will and better judgment, she'd said, which meant I would get the mostly silent treatment from her for the duration, with a few snippety snap comments thrown in for good measure. How was I supposed to know she'd come home today with a job in her back pocket? It's not like my sister told me anything. And now I couldn't get it out of my head.

A funeral home. *The* funeral home.

I recalled my mother in her casket with her eyes closed, how

I'd stood beside her with my hand on her hair. They'd covered her cinnamon-sugar freckles with wrong-colored makeup, and I wanted to rub it off her face.

I want to see Mama's eyes one last time, I told Missy Finnegan, one of Babka's oldest customers from Tramp, who'd stepped up to pay her respects.

She'd lifted her glasses off her nose, looked at me with her tiny black eyes, and wiggled her teeth. *They take the eyeballs out of 'em before now, child. Hang on to your memories.*

"Will you have to do the eyes?" I asked the back of my sister's head.

"What?" she said, the word like a bite.

"They take the eyes out of corpses, don't they? You won't have anything to do with that, will you?"

"We don't remove the eyes, only the tongues."

"Really?" I asked, before my brain kicked in.

Maybe it was because Jazz always treated me like a five-year-old that I sometimes felt like one with her. She was the only person who'd ever made my mouth run off out of nerves. Sometimes I wished I were still five when I was around her. My five-year-old self never cared what my sister thought of me, or knew that what she thought of me didn't amount to much.

I twined my fingers through a section of hair, started another braid, as Jazz ended our not-quite conversation by turning on the radio. A familiar lime static appeared as she searched in vain for a station. I was glad to see that static—glad to have it back.

Grief had turned everything black as coal for weeks after Mama died. Even my inner calendar shut down then, when everything tasted like ashes and dust. No one knew. Not about that, and not about my eyes. Not until late May, when Jazz made me go with her to the bakery and asked me to list what was low on the pantry shelves but I couldn't, because I couldn't read the labels.

Maybe Jazz wanted to be with dead people because she was in a dark place—so dark you sometimes forgot yourself and did things you normally wouldn't do. Like drink half a bottle of vodka in the middle of a workday. Like stare at the sun.

I turned my head, tried to see the sphere of fire in the sky, catch a hint of Mama's scent, but it was too far over the bus and I would never see it straight on again anyhow. The dark blot was there, though—to remind me of what happened, what I'd done. The eclipse of my central vision.

The lime static disappeared as Jazz turned off the radio with a curse. Papa had put that radio in the bus years ago, when it was still used for deliveries, but he'd learned pretty quick what we all knew now. It wasn't the quality of the receiver that mattered in our neck of the deep woods; nothing ever sounded quite right near Tramp. I tried to make my voice light as I quoted a saying as well worn by our father as his shoes.

"The mountains of West Virginia—can't live with 'em, can't imagine living without 'em."

"How could you when they're all over the damned place, crowding around us like buildings ready to collapse?" Jazz said, which made me think of dead folk again, hollow of their organs and crowding the ground with their bones.

"Will you have to do anything at all with the bodies at the funeral home? What will you have to do there, exactly?"

"I'm in charge of the glitter nail polish."

Not even my inner five-year-old could miss that sarcasm. I asked the question that got to the heart of the matter.

"Why do you want this job, Jazz? Why now?"

She flung the question back like a grenade. "Why do you want to drag us to the glades, Olivia? Why now?"

I lost track of where I was in my braid, started another.

Why now? Because this was something I could do in a sea of things I couldn't.

Last night I'd found Papa disassembling Mama's desk in their bedroom, the tablecloth stripped off the crates and plywood, like flesh off old bones.

Don't throw it away, I said. *That was her altar, remember? It gave her so much hope.*

I was glad not to be able to see the details of his face—the grooved lines near his mouth, the shallow pools that made his eyes, once deep puddles of blue. It was hard enough to see his voice, its edges frayed like butchered thread.

There's nothing to hope for anymore, Liv, he said. *Your mother's gone, and there's no undoing that. No way to wish or hope or pray it undone. She killed herself.*

She didn't kill herself, I said, as my insides twisted in my chest—my heart pulled over my lungs, my liver tugged up and turned, a braid of organs. *It was an accident.* And then I hugged him, kissed the top of his head, thick with the scent of alcohol and unwashed hair, and he buckled over and began to cry.

Maybe it's because my mother's altar sat beside me all night that I dreamed of the bogs. I stepped over a wriggling and saturated earth until I found one: a will-o'-the-wisp, full bright, darting here and there.

It smelled so strongly of hope that I could taste it.

Hope that Mama hadn't killed herself.

Of course I wanted to catch the wisp. I wanted Mama's dreams to have meant something, couldn't bear the thought that she'd died believing the opposite about that or her very life. But when I turned to tell my family, who were nearby but in that weird way of dreams also in a long, dark hall, they would not run with me to follow the wisp. And they smelled atrocious—like a stew of alcohol and unwashed hair, sadness and fear and confusion, and ellipses that went on forever, circling them and rattling like a snake. I ran from the ellipses, because running eased the pain of the letter jabbing at me through my coat. I ran for three days before I found the light again, and I swear it looked like someone smiled at me from within all that bobbing bright.

Mama.

I woke before I could reach for her, opened my eyes to find a light still dancing like a grin in my blind spot. Impossible; I would never see anything in that spot again, Dr. Patrick had said so. Yet there it was.

The sensation faded within a minute, but for the first time since my mother died I felt glad. Expectant. It had seemed like a sign.

Talking to Babka about it decided me. I told her of the dream, how vivid it had been, like it was speaking to me, and how I didn't want to make the same mistake twice.

Twice? she asked.

I described the visions I'd had the night before Mama died, with the sun dying in the sky and mirrors turning to ice.

Maybe my dreams are trying to tell me something, I said. *But I'm not sure what they want me to do.*

Babka nodded. *Maybe you won't understand it until later, but here is something I know for sure: Dreams like feet better than knees. What do your insides tell you?*

That's when I packed my bag.

That's when I decided I wasn't going to take the trip alone, either, though my thoughts weren't on my sister. I found the blue jar with a small portion of Mama's ashes—the part of her we hadn't buried—next to my father's side of the bed. Mama had always loved the jar's vibrant hue, a match for Papa's eyes. Now it leaned against the wall beside an empty bottle of vodka.

We'll do this together, I told her. *You'll get to the bog yet, and we'll finish some business. Believe, believe.*

I leaned my leg up against my suitcase, where Mama's ashes now lay inside a sealed plastic bag. "Jazz?"

My sister grunted in reply.

"You're not doing the cremating, are you?"

"Oh, for God's sake!" she said.

That marked the end of her mostly silent treatment, when she let me know what she was really thinking. This trip was ridiculous. If I thought we'd stumble upon a will-o'-the-wisp when they were the definition of unpredictable, then *I* was ridiculous. Waste of time. Driving around in this stupid bus. Daddy would drink himself into oblivion while we were away, because Babka wouldn't do a damned thing about it, and I knew it. One night. One night at the most, because we were going to be back in Tramp by Thursday, and then I was going to sit at home and behave, because she had a new job to worry about. Real money. Stop haranguing her about the funeral home. She knew I didn't like it, and that was too bad. And if I thought she wanted to sleep in this friggin' antique when it was so hot and unventilated, I had another thing coming.

Thursday tasted like disappointment, like dry Cheerios without the sugar.

She swore then with more conviction, and I could tell it wasn't at me. The bus buzzed, and my ears filled with the sound of tired brakes straining to slow, to stop, of tires riding over the rumble strips on the highway. I thought I saw a green sign to my right, the kind that tells you the name of the town off an exit ramp, but then it was gone and I couldn't have read it anyhow.

"Hang on!" Jazz said, too late.

The bus lurched, and somehow I landed on my belly, the floor heaving beneath me.

"Are you all right?" I felt her beside me, her hand on my back. "Move something."

I lifted my head. "I'm all right."

"Good," she said, her voice thready with adrenaline. "I've got to check the bus. You stay put."

"What happened?" I asked, but then I heard the door open in a shimmer of amber starbursts, and knew she was already gone.

I flipped over and opened my eyes. Decade-old flour motes floated all around me, shook up like the rattled specks inside a snow globe. It was beautiful, the way they coated my inner calendar of numbers, days of the week, months of the year. There was a veritable blizzard of motes over July. July, which was now, this month.

Catch them, Olivia, I imagined my mother saying, as I lifted my palm and smiled.

August 13, 1990

Dear Dad,

What can I say? That I miss you? Because I do. So much. That I'm sorry? I am. I'm sorry for getting into trouble out of wedlock. But I would never have quit college. I would never have chosen one over the other: you or Branik, college or motherhood. Those things were your doing. It's not too late to undo them. We can raise this baby between the three of us, can't we? We can raise him or her to appreciate music and dance and literature and fine food. Under your influence, this child will strive for greatness.

I will do better with your grandchild, Dad, than I did with myself. I promise. I promise I'll be a good daughter from now on, the perfect daughter. Just take me back into your life. Let me have another chance, and you'll see. I'll prove to you that I can do this, do it all! If only you'll open your heart and let me try!

Who will water the bamboo? You always forget. Who will pet Fat Lizzy when she cries, wandering the halls and looking for attention? You will never dust—you know you won't—and your eyes will turn pink and watery because of it. And what will you eat? You will have to hire a cook if you're ever to eat anything but canned soup again. You need me. You may not want to admit it, but you need me, and this has to hurt you as much as it is killing me.

Did you hear that, Daddy? I am dying. I will die here in this town, without my life, without you, without college and my future! You have no idea what it's like in Tramp. I am crying again, so hard that I am ruining this letter! I will have to fetch a clean piece and start over!

CHAPTER THREE

Square Pegs

* JAZZ *

The quirks in my family weren't easily swept under the rug, and not just because of Olivia and her synesthesia or her burning her eyes out. Our father liked to play his fiddle on the roof—or did before my mother died. Yeah, like the Broadway show and the movie. He'd stand out there, on the flat part above the garage, and fiddle around sunset. His name is Branik. His nickname among my peers at school was Breakneck, for obvious reasons. He had a passion for peanut-butter-and-jelly sandwiches, and considered the grilled version one of his specialties. (I'd never understood my mother's pledge to work a mention of a PB and J into the end of her book. Was it a bizarre sort of dedication? I didn't bother to point out that the characters in her tale—witches, warlocks, will-o'-the-wisps, and a sun fairy—probably wouldn't have access to modern-day convenience foods. Why waste my breath?)

When she was alive, my mother used to fall asleep at random moments, and couldn't drive for as long as I could remember. After the fifth accident—plowing over Sherry Wilson's mailbox because she'd fallen asleep again—her license had been revoked. She couldn't work like a normal person, not even with my grandmother—the only baker in West Virginia who refused to make pepperoni rolls, even if they were as much a part of our state as black bears and brook trout, because it wasn't a recipe from the Old Country.

Babka's obsession with the Old Country, even though she came over from Slovakia in the early 1960s and was in truth far from an Old World immigrant, had marked our family life for as long as I could remember. Recipes from Slovakia, traditions from Slovakia, superstitions from Slovakia. How was I supposed to know that not every family in the world celebrated Christmas by setting a place for the dead or throwing walnuts into the corner of a room? How was I supposed to know that not every family ate pierogi the way most ate fries?

The kids at school had asked often enough, *So, Jazz, what's wrong with you?*

I decided early on that nothing would be wrong with me.

I strode around the front of the bus to find a dark streak of blood across one of the headlights, then looked at the tree line beyond the highway. No sign of the deer I'd clipped, which had come careening at me from some unseen periphery. I hoped it was all right. Not in too much pain. Not carrying broken bones. Not dying somewhere. The bus looked fine, not that that was any surprise to me, as it seemed to have been granted eternal life. I recited a prayer for animals that Babka taught me long ago, then touched my bent fingers to my forehead and kissed them, let them go. It seemed like the right thing to do.

When I stepped back inside the bus, I found Olivia still on the floor, curled on her side like a spent bug. "Why aren't you up yet?" I said. "You hit your head real hard or something?" I put my hand beside her face, where I knew she could see it, and made a peace sign. "How many fingers?"

"Two," she said.

"Well, are you hurt?" I asked.

"No, just . . . hanging out," she said, running her index finger through the flour residue around her before flopping onto her back. Between the old bleach stains and the new coating of bus grime, her shirt looked like a molding blueberry.

"There's dirt in that flour, you know. Probably spiders and mites, too. Might not be your smartest choice to play in it."

She shifted her face, which could've been an attempt on her part to see the grit I mentioned. A failed attempt. I stood there for a few seconds more before finding my seat again, suddenly exhausted.

Blind. For months she'd been partially blind and said nothing, and I hadn't noticed. *I hadn't noticed.* My father—her parent—should've noticed. My mother would've. Babka would've, too, if she'd seen more of Olivia, if Olivia hadn't stopped going to Susie's.

What could I have done about any of it? Was I supposed to take on all of Olivia's issues with my own head in a whirl? Was this my responsibility now, my charge? Because I didn't think I could do it. I felt gorged on life and death and drama. Stalled out over processing it all.

I waited for Olivia to take her seat, then restarted the bus. As I eased us back onto the highway, I watched carefully for deer, for all the animals that might come crashing out at me, reckless or wanting.

Some people were in tune with their feelings. They watched self-help TV shows, bought *The Oprah Magazine*, talked with their girlfriends and therapists. I was not one of those people. It was difficult enough for me to name my anxieties under the best of circumstances—when all was quiet, when I was alone and might come close to an answer when asking myself, *What's the problem here? Why the lump of discomfort in my chest?* It was all but impossible in the midst of one of my sister's jabberfests.

Olivia was like a CD with only three tracks. My job at the funeral home, track No. 1. Ghost lights and the bog, track No. 2. And the latest track in the Olivia Moon collection, track No. 3: the trip itself.

"Jazz, what's the last town we passed?"

"I don't know," I told her, as I began to shift the bus into another lane. A horn blared out at me, and I pulled back, wondered when the car had surged into my blind spot.

From behind me I heard, "Careful."

"I *am* being careful," I snapped, as my anxiety ratcheted up another notch and a pain was born in my forehead. I rubbed it with two fingers as the driver of the car drove past and graced me with a finger of her own. This wasn't what bothered me.

Why do I feel this way?

My apprehensions increased with every mile, as we continued our drive south, past small towns, and back and forth over switch-back roads. When we rounded a bend, the sun stabbed at my eyes. I tried turning my face to avoid it, sat taller, but it was no use. I couldn't even wear my crappy sunglasses—the ones with the lens that popped out at random times—because they made it harder to see through the bugs splattered all over the windshield. White bugs, yellow bugs, green. The wipers didn't help; they just spread those bugs around the glass like insect frosting on a cake inscribed "Jazz's Shitty Day." I was out of wiper fluid.

"What do you think the bog looks like?" Olivia asked as my eyes watered.

"I don't know. A bog."

"I wonder if it'll taste like cranberries."

It hurt to roll my eyes.

Olivia stayed on track No. 2 for a while ("Did you know bodies don't decompose in bogs? There might be a two-hundred-year-old corpse under a dozen feet of soaked plant bits out there, perfectly preserved!"), then skipped back to No. 1 ("Will you be in charge of ordering things like the makeup they use on dead people?").

"Please shut up," I said, trying not to think about my mother. The Velveeta-toned foundation on her skin, the pink lipstick and the slash of blue shadow. The deep-green blouse, the black skirt barely visible beneath the shut lower half of the coffin. Her hair straightened, arranged in a smooth fall of chestnut over one shoulder. That day I had to remind myself that she was laid there; she didn't lay herself there. She was not asleep.

Why would I want to return to that place?

Why? Olivia had asked. *Why? Why?*

Are you sure this is what you want? Babka had asked. *Is it what you need?*

I'd driven back one cold, rainy day in late spring—taken the bus without telling anyone, without honestly knowing where I was going. I drove to Kennaton, past the university that always made my skin itch—the scene of my mother's liaison with my father, and her disownment from her former family—until I found myself outside Rutherford & Son. I parked on the street, right behind a hearse, and didn't care how it looked. Sloshed through a wide puddle on the walkway, and strode up stairs framed by tall bushes. Stalled at the front door with my hand on the old-fashioned knob.

Need help?

A man stood a few paces away, on a wraparound cement patio. He smoked a cigarette, and wore a fluorescent orange T-shirt coated in short white animal hairs. He didn't strike me as a cat person.

You here to set up a service? he asked.

No, I said, *I'm not here to set up a service.*

He opened his fingers, and his cigarette fell. He crushed it against the cement with one booted foot. *You here for the job, then?*

What job?

He smiled, his brow quirked in confusion. *Why* are *you here?*

I don't know, I said, and sniffed. My nose had begun to run. I bounced on my feet, tried to disguise a shiver as the man in the T-shirt looked at me and shrugged.

All right, he said. *Let's go inside. Maybe you'll figure it out.*

His name was Rat, and I followed him into the house. Music seeped out at us from unseen speakers, as somber and low as the music that had played at my mother's wake. When we neared the room she'd been laid out in, empty now, I stepped into it. The air smelled vaguely of flowers, though there were none to be seen, unless you counted the blue flowered fabric on each of the three couches. Scattered among them were chairs of green and gold thread. Tasseled lamps and boxes of tissue adorned every side table, and art decorated each wall—paintings of trees and butterflies, and more flowers. All of it in place to be a comfort, I guess, to counter being left to face the thing that made everyone so uncomfortable. Death. It struck me then that this was death's home, this house of illusion and faux control.

I asked about the job.

"Was that a town sign, Jazz? What did it say?" Olivia asked as I felt the change; all of a sudden, we had no power. An indistinct rattling sound emanated from all around us, like a beehive full of angry life. I pumped the accelerator pedal. It didn't matter. We'd been traveling up a hill and wound down real fast. I pulled onto the shoulder for the second time that day and, out of sheer disbelief and frustration, slammed the heels of my hands against the steering wheel, eliciting the bus's warbling goose-honk warning. We slugged to a complete stop.

"Jesus Christ, we're cursed!" I hollered. And for the first time all day there was a quiet behind me so comprehensive that I could hear my own breathing.

It was almost worth it. Almost.

We waited in the bus for ten minutes, and when no one stopped to help, and the heat got to be too much, we left to walk alongside the highway. I set myself closest to the white line, between Olivia and the trucks and cars that passed, and settled the pack on my back.

There were no arguments. We were going to the nearest town to find a phone. The bus—was it even towable? How much would it cost to fix? It wasn't like we had AAA. Whatever it was, I would have to cough it up, because that bus was my ticket to Kennaton.

We were calling for help. And then we were calling home. Eventually our father would be sober again, and then he could pick us up.

Olivia remained silent, her shoulders slumped as she hugged her suitcase to her chest. A crow dropped twenty or so feet from us to pick at something dead or dying.

"Some things aren't meant," I said, knowing she had long shared my mother's trust in fate and ready to lean on that to make a point if I had to. "Things that are meant slip into place like the missing puzzle piece in your life, right? You get the job, you ace the test, whatever. Your car doesn't break down, you know?"

It was a rabbit, I think. Ten feet away now. Hard to tell, but that looked like flattened rabbit ears. The air buzzed with bugs.

"It's not the right time," I continued. "We need to go home and reassess this whole thing."

There were no arguments, but for some reason I still felt the need to defend the obvious, sensible course of action, the path we were taking.

We followed the shoulder to an exit ramp as cars poured off the highway along with us. Buildings created an irregular skyline in the distance; a city I'd never visited before—Jewel—lay just ahead. And maybe my luck was changing, because there, tucked between a diner and a dry cleaner, was a mechanic's shop. JIM'S, the sign read. There were only a few cars in the lot, too, which seemed promising—an old Chevy, a Jeep with some serious rust issues, and an antique car missing two of its tires.

"There," I told Olivia, pushing my sunglasses farther up my nose, the tricky lens staying in place. "The setup couldn't be better, see? You can sit in the diner while I talk to whoever is at the shop, all right? You can order a Pepsi and a sandwich, and even have a piece of pie."

She slanted her head, looked at me with her dead eyes, then let me lead her into the diner, where the thick scent of greasy bacon slammed into us like a heart attack. Speakers from the far end of the room blared country music. A song I couldn't name morphed into one I did: "Jesus, Take the Wheel," by Carrie Underwood.

No offense, Jesus, but I think I'd like to keep the wheel, thank you very much.

I left my sister in a booth, then stepped back outside to find the stairs newly blocked by a sixtysomething with a full head of white fuzzy hair and a doughy face. Beside him sat a leashless dog.

"Got the time?" he asked, as if telling him that would be the secret password to unlock his butt from the stair and let me by. His camouflage pants were cut at his calves, and his rust-colored T-shirt was ripped at the neck. He wore big boots that lacked laces, held together instead with wound pieces of rope. There was a discomfiting intensity to his expression.

"It's ten after twelve," I told him, taking a second look at the dog—a mutt that might've had sheepdog somewhere in its lineage but whose appearance was made ridiculous by a large dose of mini-mutt genes. It barked at me, and a goop of drool landed near my sneaker.

"Thanks," he said, and moved just enough so that I could brush by him.

Maybe it was because I never credited those sorts of feelings, thought them too much in the realm of superstition that was my grandmother's, that I ignored a hint of unease as I walked away from him and his dog, and the diner that held my sister.

CHAPTER FOUR

Hope and Mirrors

✳ OLIVIA ✳

I was twelve when Mama and I had the only significant conversation we ever had about Jazz. We were together in the kitchen with the door closed and the oven on, because it was a frigid January day. Later we'd make pizza, so I was busy on the sauce, swirling a wooden spoon through a pot of crushed tomatoes laced with garlic and oregano. Making sauce was one of my favorite chores, even back then, because I loved both the smell and the look of it. Shimmering, iridescent circles formed in time with burbling stovetop noises, each new circle appearing outside the older ones, which grew smaller and smaller. They were ten times more transfixing than what I might see in a regular pot of boiling water, which is why I never volunteered to make pasta. Jazz was in charge of that and other cooking chores.

I hate winter, Mama said, gazing out the kitchen's single squat window. *Sometimes it feels like we'll never see the sun again.*

When I told her that her voice sounded like a tunnel that went on for years, Mama let go of the curtain clutched in her hand and let it fall free. We'd made that curtain ourselves, out of an old sheet, and dyed it using a package of coloring called Sunbright, which we hoped would inspire her writing.

I'm sorry, Olivia, she said. *I'm just worried about your sister.*

A glance at the clock told me that Jazz was an hour late, and for the third time that week. I knew Mama thought that something was going on with her, especially since Jazz wouldn't tell anyone where she'd been or what she'd been doing. It wasn't like my sister to be secretive. Usually she was honest, and sometimes too honest. Just that morning, she'd said I was more annoying than slush in a boot.

She told me she doesn't want to go to college, Mama said, lifting a blanket from the chair where she worked. She wrapped it around her shoulders before stepping beside me and easing the oven door open a hair more. *Careful you don't get burned, sweetie.*

I abandoned the spoon in the pot and turned toward my mother as heat rose around us in waves, asked her why Jazz didn't want to go to college.

She said, *Probably because she knows I want her to go.*

I didn't know what to say to that. Even at that age, I knew college didn't sound like a good choice for me. Besides, Mama needed me at home for dreaming. She'd always tell me how much it meant to her that we did that together, said I was like the sky to her sun— even though the sky was always there and my feet itched to wander more often than not. Still, I could make a decent life for myself in Tramp. One day I'd convince Babka that a marriage between my sauce and her dough could make a perfect pizza. I'd get to travel then, as I sold my pies all over the country. I listened more intently to my bubbling creation.

I blame myself, Mama said after I'd counted twenty-two circles. *I should've spent more time with her when she was growing up. I should've gotten to know her as a person and not just as a child. I should've been a friend to her as well as a mother. Children need their parents to be both, I think, but not all parents know how to be both.*

When I told her that she was the best friend any girl could want, Mama gave me her sunlight-in-the-rain look, with her lips upturned but her eyes sad.

You made me your friend, Olivia Moon, because you wouldn't take no *for an answer when you asked me to play. You pulled me down to the ground and shoved a doll in my hand, and that was that. Not that I didn't enjoy myself,* she added, when I felt my own smile begin to slip. *I just didn't know I would enjoy myself until you showed me the way. With Jazz, I was a mother only. And sometimes not a happy one.*

Why weren't you happy? I wanted to know, and she lifted her hands, palms down, into the path of the oven's rising heat.

Sometimes people get sad after having a baby. Women's bodies are like that, she said. *Maybe that was it, but I don't know.*

It was difficult to picture—Jazz alone with her toys on the floor. I asked Mama if she was sad after I was born, but she said that she didn't think so, that I'd kept her too busy for that. And then she looked again at the clock above the stove.

Are you worried because you think she's with a boy? I asked, but Mama didn't answer. I stirred the sauce.

I went rambling a lot, too, but I always told Mama where I'd gone if I forgot to tell her where I was going, which was most of the time. Back then I was too young for boy trouble, but I still thought about it. Nuzzling up to someone and kissing in a car somewhere, making more heat than a hundred stoves. That's where I'd want to be, I decided then, if I were as pretty as Jazz and fifteen and had such a great chest. But I wasn't about to say that to my mother.

Maybe I should've homeschooled your sister, too, right from the start, Mama said, her voice like an expanding balloon. *Then she would understand the value of education and communication. She wouldn't be so closed off and rebellious and—*

Disappointing?

The blanket around Mama's shoulders dropped an inch from the oven when she spun around to face my sister.

Jazz stood with a set jaw right outside the kitchen, her bare hand clutching the doorknob, her hair coated with tiny balls of ice. She sniffed, but I thought it was because her red nose ran from cold and not because she was going to cry. Jazz never cried.

Where have you been? my mother asked, and Jazz snapped right back.

Does it matter?

Yes. It matters.

I wasn't sure if I should leave the room or stay, so I listened again to the sauce and stared at a spider I found near my foot on the slate floor. Circles closed in around that spider, like one lasso after another. The spider stayed still.

Finally, Mama said, *I'm sorry, Jazz. I shouldn't have said those things.*

Did you mean them? Jazz asked.

Yes, Mama said. *I suppose I did.*

Jazz ran up to her room after that, and Mama ran after her, though it wasn't any use, because Jazz slammed her door and locked it straightaway. Later, she told Papa that she'd been staying after school to help tutor a student in math, making some money so she could buy presents for my parents and my grandmother, who all had birthdays coming up. Mama cried a lot after that, and she slept a lot, too. Jazz didn't speak to her for at least a week.

Mama told me later that she was sorry, that it wasn't good of her as a mother to talk about Jazz like that in front of me. I told her she didn't have to apologize, but she did it again anyway.

You're such an old mirror, Olivia Moon. But your sister is a mirror, too. Just harder for me to look into.

I didn't understand, and told her so.

I see myself in both of you, she explained. *Different parts.* She put her hand against my cheek. *Here's what I want you to remember, my old-mirror daughter. You should always think about what you say before you say it, always mean what you do before you do it. Always be sure of yourself, and consider the repercussions. It's not something I'm good at, Olivia. I never have been.*

I had a sense of it then, but later I knew it for sure: Thinking ahead to the repercussions of any given choice wasn't something

I was good at, either. The big difference between me and Mama, though, was that I didn't let it bother me.

I wished there was a way to convince Jazz that a stalled-out bus was something we could overcome, that it didn't have to mean the end of the road. But she'd said *going home*, said *period*, said *end of story*, and even I knew a brick wall when I ran into one. I leaned against the window beside me, but although the sky was as blue as ever, it smelled like failure.

"Here you go, sugar," said the waitress, settling a tall glass on the table.

It was easier to perceive her if I looked toward the side of her face, so I did that, and tried not to care that she might think me shy or rude or just plain weird for not looking her square in the eye. She was tall, with a mass of blond hair, and wore a purple apron that said something I couldn't read.

"Did you have a chance to look at the menu?" Her voice was as light and frothy as the root beer I'd ordered. "Our buffalo burger with cilantro mayonnaise is on special today if you'd like to try that."

Buffalo? Cilantro? I wasn't even sure what those things would taste like. Maybe chicken. Everything was supposed to taste like chicken.

"Or maybe you'd like a slice of pie," she said as I chewed my lip. "We've got some real nice lemon meringue today."

"I do love pie," I told her.

"Smart girl," she said. "My name's Rocky. Whistle if you need anything."

I wished whistling would work. I'd whistle for a week. The thought of going back to everything as it was—to my father drinking and my sister about to start work in a funeral home, to my mother's ashes stuck in a jar and a letter stuck in my pocket—made my dark spot twitch with the threat of growth. I sent a silent question up to the universe.

Do you want me to go home? Can you give me a sign?

I waited. Listened to the conversations of people around me. Talk of taxes, of road work, of not trusting a babysitter and buying a surveillance camera. Listened to the restaurant's swinging doors whoosh open-closed-open in a spray of maroon rectangles. Breathed in the greasy smell of burgers and fries, the sweet underscent of pie. Felt the cold table beneath my fingers, as smooth as stone. Saw Rocky rush here and there, saw others come and go, saw black-and-white floor and red seats, saw—not enough. Not nearly enough.

If not for my eyes, maybe I could've made this trip alone. If not for my eyes, maybe I could've borrowed the bus and driven myself to the glades. Even with my eyes, I could've driven myself—after getting the permit for folks who required special glasses. I thought about those glasses, how I'd told my father and sister that I'd lost them. I hadn't. But I couldn't use them. Not yet.

"No dogs allowed," someone said at a distance, and I peered over my shoulder to spy two men standing beside the entrance. I couldn't see a dog.

"You need to turn yourself around right now, so we don't cause a scene," said a man with a voice like a bad muffler.

"Come on, I'm dying for a coffee," the other man said. "This isn't even my dog." His voice reminded me of our driveway back home. Full of stones.

"Rules are rules. Out with you now. And stay away from our dumpsters."

"Now, that's just plain insulting."

I strained to get a better look, as the man and the dog I still couldn't see were ushered outside.

"Gonna sprain your neck doing that, sugar."

I whipped back around as Rocky set a plate in front of me.

"Who was that?" I asked her.

"Train hopper, I'm sure," she said. "They come in every once in a while, sometimes with their dogs. But, dogs or not, Den doesn't like them—they're not the right sort, a real weird mix." She pointed toward the window. "See that out there?"

I couldn't make out any details and told her so, that I had bad eyes. When she didn't ask me any questions about that, I decided I liked her all the more.

"There's a train down there, stopped with some Levi Pike cars at the tree line," she said. "They're empty now, going back to Levi to restock, which is why the hoppers were in them, taking advantage of a free lift."

"People still do that?" I'd heard about that sort of thing but thought it was an old-fashioned fad, something that had stopped a long time ago.

"They sure do, right under our noses and within eyeshot of a whole restaurant full of people. It's close to the yard down there, but not in it, so those cars are away from the bull." She laughed when my eyes went wide. "Not the animal, sugar. The bull's a person. He's the one who tries to prevent hoppers from catching out in the first place."

"So it's illegal?" I asked, and Rocky laughed again.

"Only if they get caught."

She left me there to stare out the window, struggling to make out the train. Levi Pike cars. Levi. A town that lay southeast of where we were. Southeast, and close to the bogs. Closer than we were, at any rate.

I plunged my fork into the lemon meringue, then took a bite. It might've been the best pie I ever tasted. It tasted, I thought, like second chances.

Second Stage:

ANGER

The intoxication of anger . . . shows
us to others, but hides us from
ourselves.

—*John Dryden*

August 2, 1991

Dear Dad,

*Your granddaughter, Jazz Marie Moon, turned six
months old today.*

*Yes, she was born—pink, healthy, crying as she
should, and with a wickedly misshapen head. Labor
was hard. Thirty-six hours. I passed out once from
the pain, when the doctors had to push at my legs
to make more room for the baby. But time passes,
doesn't it? She came. The pain ended.*

*She had no name at all for two days. I didn't even
call her "baby." In the end, I named her after the
music the nurse played for me while I labored; it was
either Jazz or Wynton Marsalis.*

*Jazz is a good baby, I guess, in the way of babies.
She eats well; she is growing. She's a good baby,
but when I look at her I feel nothing. She coos and
laughs, and I can't even smile back. I know I should
feel something more than I do. She's a baby. She's*

*my baby. But all I see when I look at her is what
I've lost. How could I not? She has your mouth, the
downturned lips that make you look so serious. She
has your eyes.*

*I still miss you, Dad, but I try not to think of you—
how you are, your health, whether the house has
fallen around you, what you feel. Because I am more
mad at you than anything. Furious sometimes. So
much so that it verges on hatred.*

I just thought you should know.

Beth

CHAPTER FIVE

Boiled Poet

* JAZZ *

Anger and I had a strange relationship. It claimed me more and more often, and I understood it less and less. Sometimes I worried about this. Why was I so angry? I never landed on a complete answer. I felt it, though, simmering inside me, ready to go off at any second, and had become all too familiar with the cycle. Boil over. Shut down. Steep in guilt. Return to a simmer. Repeat.

It wasn't always like this. I remember being happy.

What do you want to be when you grow up, Jazz Marie Moon? my mother asked when I was little. *An architect? You're smart enough. A model? You're pretty enough. How about a rocket scientist, or an artist, or the president of the United States?* I'd shoot her a knowing look, and she'd smile, because she knew what I liked best. *Or you can be a writer! You'll become a brilliant novelist, or a playwright, or the next poet laureate! Be a good girl and listen to Mama, and you can be anything you like, anything you put your mind to.*

I believed her then. I did listen to her. I was a good girl. And I dreamed. I'd wake up before the sun and write a new constitution, or I'd stand in front of the bathroom mirror and practice poses. I'd draw pictures of big houses and include an office for my mother;

never again would she have to work on a plywood desk or in a cramped kitchen in a house with poor heating.

And I'd write. I loved to write plays best of all, though most were nonsensical. Once I wrote a play about a girl named Candice Kane, a name I thought to be exceedingly clever.

I wrote poetry, too. Long, windy things that went on for pages. Short haikus that were displayed on the refrigerator:

> Alligator ham—
> eating you up with mustard,
> and a glass of milk.

One day I'd try a bigger project, write a story that could become a book, just like my mama.

Things changed as I grew, as I learned how life worked.

The message never wavered—*listen and dream and good things will happen*—but neither did anything else. My father went to work and came back again. My mother rarely left home. When I asked if I could do something—like go into the neighborhood to see if I might find some kids to act in a play I'd written, back when I was younger, when I had a friend or two who hadn't yet decided that my family was too weird to associate with—my mother always found a reason to keep me planted beside her. There were things to do (cooking, cleaning, watching my sister) or things to avoid (the rain, the snow, the mud, the unleashed dog or the bully down the road).

The unreasonableness of this situation became more glaring to me as time passed. How would I ever become anything at all without real world practice, and not just an ability to imagine a greater existence? Because I *could* imagine it: a unique life, boundless and full of color, in stark contrast to the browns and greens of West Virginia and the stagnancy of our days. But as I grew it became clearer that there was a gap between what my mother said she wanted for me and what she expected of me, and that the only thing full of color at my house was my sister's head.

I envied Olivia's altered perceptions, but not as much as I envied her freedom. I told myself it was because she was younger that things were different, and that my mother was probably as permissive with me as she was with my sister when I was her age. But that was not the case.

You will not be able to manage Olivia the way you try to manage Jazz, Babka said one day, in a conversation with my mother that I wasn't meant to hear. *But she will bring a new perspective to your life if you see life through her eyes.*

It was a perspective I would never share, never could. And eventually it occurred to me that Olivia's perspective was the reason my mother was so different with her. My sister was, intrinsically, genetically, more creative. All she had to do was open her eyes to see the world in fine pastry layers of color and flavor. Everything that came from my mind, and all that went onto my pages, seemed gray when compared with my sister's reality. The surreal art that began to dominate the surface of the refrigerator was not anything I could ever compete with. My mother knew it, too; she didn't have to say it for me to feel that from her every day.

Hope hardened for me like an overbaked biscuit. My grand drawings became doodles. My plays became brief, drafted on the backs of my papers at school, on tests and quizzes. I tried not to write at all, though I was once made to write a poem for a junior high English class. It was about black claws and the bleeding guts of crow men. I liked writing it and thought the poem had a good flow. My teacher gave me a D and said I should talk to the guidance counselor if I felt troubled. That was the last poem I can recall writing down.

Olivia became my mother's muse. I became the cook.

My headache bloomed as I stood talking with Jim—a tall, skinny man with oil-smeared gray coveralls and less oily gray hair. He needed to *see* the bus before he could diagnose the problem, he said several times as I quizzed him on what could be wrong, stressed

how important it was that my bus be all right and that he make it
so as soon as possible.

"It'll take a bit, no matter what it is," he said.

"Do 'bits' run into hours or days?" I asked, and he surprised me
with a full-fledged guffaw.

"Well, this here's no fast-lube joint, but it'll get done. You have
the key?"

I appraised him, tried to guess what sort of mechanic he might
be by the lines around his eyes, the creases on his forehead. Back at
home, we'd used the same guy for as long as I'd been alive.

Then again, what choice did I have?

He and my key disappeared inside an orange tow truck that
seemed not to have a speck of rust anywhere on it, which was at
least some sign of a strong work ethic. I waited until it disappeared
beyond my sight, my heart turning over like a failed engine. The bus
had to be all right, otherwise what would happen with my job?

Inside the shop's bathroom, under the watchful eyes of a blue-
and-green graffiti cat, I tossed cool water over my face. A small relief
until I accidentally inhaled some of it. In the midst of my cough-
ing fit, I made the mistake of looking into the mirror. Dark half-
moons lay on their backs under my eyes, water dripped off my nose
and chin, and my hair looked as ill-kempt as Olivia's. For a second
I wondered if my mother's spirit would come crashing out of the
glass, rake me over the coals for worrying more about my respon-
sibilities to Emilia Bryce than to my own sister. My head pounded
with a newfound intensity when I realized I hadn't packed any pain
relievers.

I developed the only migraine I've ever had the year Olivia's
homeschooling began, on Christmas Eve. My eyes had been funny,
my vision not quite right during our traditional holiday dinner at
Babka's.

It is not velija, *but it will have to do,* my grandmother said, refer-
ring to the five courses spread over her table, gracing her best white
china plates, instead of the traditional twelve courses for the holiday.

I could barely eat a bite. The candle she lit wavered until the white fish swam on my plate along with the *holubky*.

I shouldn't have said anything to Olivia.

Sounds like synesthesia was her reply.

I took another *kolači* for my plate, and ignored her attempt to find common ground between us.

I was fifteen, and Olivia was eleven. Our mother had made the decision to homeschool her just three months before, so life at home wasn't much fun. Books lay all over the place. Every spare dime seemed to go into buying them, too. That meant there wouldn't be a lot under the tree for us, and we knew it going into the holiday.

When the headache came, my mother worried it was because of all that. No big presents. Olivia at home. Jazz wasn't feeling love, or something like it. I told her she was wrong—it's not like I would've held out any hope for an iPod—but she still sat with me most of the night. Gave me medicine. Brewed tea for me, and watched to be sure I drank it. Offered her pillow when the ice bottle leaked water all over mine.

Good daughter, good mother, I thought, remembering something I never should've read, my teeth ground together.

I tried to ignore her, turned the other way, but I could still feel her there—a warm, worried, and resented presence. *Don't be here. Go away. I don't need you, don't want you looking at me, examining me, trying so hard to care.* My forehead felt balled into a knot over the whole thing, which might be why I was sick in the toilet, my head exploding over the porcelain. Mama stood behind me during all that, rubbing my back.

This, too, shall pass, she said.

Would feeling like my mother's personal atonement pass?

How about the way I hated her right then, my *good mother* who never wanted *me* but wanted to control my every move and thought and dictate my future to prove that she was a *good daughter*? Could I purge that emotion into the toilet, too? It's not like I wanted to feel that way, any more than I wanted a puking headache.

It won't pass, I said between heaves.

Of course it will, she said. *You'll feel right as rain tomorrow, sweetie.*

Don't call me that, I said, and she stopped rubbing my back. *I don't want to go to college.*

She didn't say anything.

She helped me back into bed a few minutes later, then reached for the warm ice bag. Time to dump the water.

I won't change my mind, I said, when she was halfway out the door. *Don't bother trying.*

She pretended not to hear me, but I know that she did.

Long minutes passed as I waited outside for Jim, but I didn't hear the rumbling return of his truck with my bus in tow. Maybe he'd had a problem. Maybe the bus was too big for him. Maybe . . .

I walked back across the lot and toward the diner, settling my pack over a shoulder. Coffee might, at least, help my headache.

The place was called Ramps, I noticed, and was nicer inside than I'd processed fifteen minutes before, with a polished black-and-white tiled floor, vinyl red booth seats, and a ceiling of ornately pressed tin. Central to the main room was a Snapple beverage cooler, butted up against a wall covered with old doors and knobs. The other walls were stripped to reveal brick and housed a display that reminded me of something from an Early American art exhibit, with everything from tin animal cutouts to signs advertising the cost of live bait (CRICKETS—$1, 50/COUNT). On a large chalkboard, a list of specials mentioned things I thought existed only on TV shows and in places like New York City—things like marinated chicken on focaccia bread with sun-dried tomatoes and pesto. And, I noticed with a sinking feeling that originated in my wallet, the people around us wore blouses and jackets, looked more like business professionals on a lunch break than travelers from Tramp hoping for a cheap seat.

Set before Olivia, though, was no more than a drink and a piece of pie, which eased my throbbing head—but not for long. I'd been in the booth less than a second when she blurted out an idea as absurd as the dog I'd seen earlier on the stairs.

"We can take a train to the glades."

"Olivia, please let's not do this now. I need coffee," I said, using one of my father's favorite escape lines. Sense trouble? Delay. It had worked for him for most of my childhood. This, however, was Olivia, and with Olivia the rules had always been different.

"No, Jazz, really. We can take a train," she said, her eyes wide and her body tipped so far toward me that she seemed inches away from sprawling over the table.

"That's the worst idea you've ever had, and I'm including the time you wanted to dye the dog blue to match his name."

"I was six. This will work. I—"

"Stop. I have a headache," I said. "Jim isn't back with the bus, and I have no idea how we're going to get—"

"But it's the answer to all our problems," she said, looking somewhere in the vicinity of my left ear. "The train down there is heading to Levi, and Levi's close to the glades."

I followed the direction of her thrown-back thumb and noticed the train in the distance, the line of baby-blue Levi Pike cars. "Jesus, Olivia, that's not a passenger train. It's a freight train."

"It doesn't matter," she said. "People can ride and—"

I shushed her, shut down her jabberfest before it could begin, then waved my hand when I spotted the waitress two tables away. "Coffee, please," I said when she arched her brows in question. "Black." She nodded, and was off.

I tried another of my father's favorite tactics: diversion. "I don't suppose you have anything sensible in that bag of yours, do you? Aspirin? Tylenol? Anything?"

"No," she said, then veered back to the track of her choice. "It's fate, Jazz, don't you see? Why else would the train be right there, pointing in the right direction, going right where we need it to go?"

Obviously my father's techniques weren't going to work; I'd have to do it my way.

"First of all," I started, "it isn't 'right where we need it to go.' Levi is not Cranberry Glades."

"Rocky said it's real close, and—"

"Second of all, why the hell are we having this conversation? The answer is no. I can't and won't let either of us be carted all over the state in a dirty freight train. I won't chase after you, either, and you have to stop doing things that mean someone *does* have to chase after you. I mean that. I can't do it anymore, Olivia, I have a real job now. And Dad wouldn't have a clue how to rein you in." I watched with satisfaction as the light in her eyes faded away, then for insurance added, "You think harping on things that meant so much to Mom is good for him? He needs to let it go."

"There's more than one way to let something go."

"Yeah? Well, this isn't one of them."

Her gaze shifted from my ear to the window.

"There you go, sugar," said the waitress, setting a steaming mug of coffee in front of me, only one of her blond curls out of place. "Can I get you anything else? There's a menu right over there." She indicated where the menus lay, wedged behind a chrome napkin holder.

I didn't want anything, I told her, and seconds later she disappeared through a set of swinging doors. Mad, maybe, that I wouldn't be adding substantially to the bill or her tip.

I regarded my sister again. Pale skin—too pale for summer. Cracked lips. Thick black lashes I'd coveted for the better part of a decade. Unruly eyebrows. Fingers busying themselves with a new braid.

"Olivia, listen."

"I get it, all right?"

"No," I said. "I don't think that you do. You're talking about doing stupid, dangerous, illegal things here."

"It's only illegal if you get caught," she said.

I leaned closer, lowered my voice. "I'm going to pretend I didn't just hear you consider becoming a criminal over this bullshit trip."

"It's not a bullshit trip," she said. "It means something to me. And it was everything to Mama."

"Why does it seem that you can't hear me? Maybe those braids of yours are too tight."

She dropped her hands, made small fists on the table.

I took a breath. "Listen, Olivia, I think even Mom knew life wasn't going to imitate *Field of Dreams*—'If you visit the glades, the end of the story will come'—even if she wanted it to. And even if she didn't, we know better, right?" I said, including her as a person of reason despite her nature, hoping she'd like feeling part of the club. "It's pointless, taking a trip like this for a woman who's no longer with us."

"A woman who is no longer with us?" Her crazy brows jammed together. "What is that, funeral-home-speak? How can you be so cold? That's Mama you're talking about. Mama."

Right. But one of us had to be practical. Sober.

"Look, I know things have been hard since she died," I said, "especially considering *how* she died, but—"

"She didn't kill herself. Don't say she did."

Heat spread through my spine at this—my sister asking again that the world bend to her perception of things, even if she shut her eyes to reality.

"Olivia Moon, you need to check yourself," I said, struggling to keep my voice down. "It's time to grow up, right now. It's time to be what Mom would've wanted you to be. If you're not going to do it for yourself or because it's the right thing to do, then do it for her."

"I am doing it for her," she said, with a rare edge to her voice.

We stayed like that, mentally circling each other, until the sound of an overburdened vehicle made it past my black fog. I burned my mouth chugging down the coffee, then slid out of the booth gripping my bag, the backs of my legs sticking a little to the seat.

"Stay here," I said, looking down at my sister. "I have to tend to the bus, all right?"

She stared off into the seat I'd vacated without a word of acknowledgment.

"Olivia?"

Silence.

"Fine, be a bitch," I said.

I strode toward the door and somehow slammed right into the waitress, which loosed the metal coffeepot in her hand. It fell as if in slow motion, raining acid all over the pristine black-and-white floor.

I took a seat in Jim's office to wait for the official word. The stone-and-glass room was air-conditioned, which might've made it easier for me to cool off, figuratively as well as literally, and think through what to do next. My bus sat in the lot outside. Though Jim hadn't had time for a full diagnosis, he thought the problem might be a bad axle shaft caused by the collision with the deer.

But you never know, he'd said. *Sometimes a thing—after it's been around the block a couple hundred times—gets tired.*

I'd nodded and looked at the bus—long since the bane of my existence—but my mind was on my mother.

My mother, bent over her story in the kitchen.

My mother, fallen asleep while making dinner, while driving.

My mother, in the casket at the funeral home.

I remembered the day the ambulance arrived in Tramp, how I'd followed it a stone's throw from Babka's to find it stopped and silent in front of our house. Olivia sat near it on the withered grass, not wearing a coat despite the season. There was something about her fractured expression and the way her eyes twitched around that told me all I needed to know. That's when the earth began to spin the other way on its axis.

And not just for Olivia.

Was that what was bothering me? Was Olivia's need to deny our mother's suicide another example of her highlighting her experience, as if her grief was deeper and more significant than anyone else's? I pressed my palm hard against my forehead. It did feel sometimes—compared with her and my father—that my grief was nothing, that there wasn't any time for it. Just because my feelings were complicated, though, didn't mean they didn't exist. I'd lost her, too. Sometimes I felt that I'd lost the most when she died. Another thing I might not understand.

Not suicide?

What would've made Olivia say that? Did she believe it? Denial was a part of grief, I knew. I'd read all about that in a pamphlet I picked up at the funeral home the day I accepted the job from Emilia Bryce. But still. I eyed the bag at my feet. There was something inside my canvas sack that would put an end to my sister's delusions, if I cared to share it with her. If I cared to share it with anyone.

No, I didn't think that was the answer, even if I didn't know what was. I couldn't avoid her forever, though. And I knew I should probably apologize for calling her a bitch.

Good daughter.

As much as I didn't like it, as unfair as it might be, as difficult as it would remain, I'd have to find a way to do better. Olivia was family, my legally blind sister. I would need to be there for her and try harder to identify with her. In many ways, we were all each other had left.

The phone rang, and I leaped up, but Jim was inside by the second ring.

"How's the bus?" I asked, before he even reached the phone.

"Hang on," he said, then picked up the receiver. "Jim's."

I walked over to the window as he made cursory remarks to the caller—"Yepper. Huh, that's odd. Sure, gotta pay"—and stared out at the bus.

Let it be all right, I thought to whoever might be listening. *Send some good luck my way.*

"Well, sure, I'll let her know," Jim said, and I spun around. He hung up the phone, then scratched at his head with the same hand that nudged aside his cap. "Your sister left a note on a napkin at Ramps saying you were here and would pay for the pie and drinks."

"She's gone?" I asked, but I knew already, felt the truth of it churn in my gut with all that coffee.

In the distance, the train whistled.

CHAPTER SIX

On Fate. Or Luck.

✳ OLIVIA ✳

We didn't have a computer at home, not even an old one like they used to have in the health office at school, so whenever Mama and I needed to look something up online we had to walk a few miles to the next town over, which was just as small as Tramp but had a free library. We always had a great time there and were able to answer a lot of the random questions that filled my head when I was younger—like how fish have babies, why salt melts ice, and if worms sleep.

I wish I could drive, Mama would say sometimes. I'd give her a hug and tell her I was glad we couldn't drive, because that meant more time for us to talk. She didn't have a license because of a series of accidents she'd had while I was still in public school. I didn't miss her not driving, but it was true that the weather wasn't always ideal for walking, and I knew that lost license bothered her.

One chill fall day, we had to walk to the library. I had a test to study for, and neither of us knew how to divide algebraic expressions. Midway between Tramp and the library sat a lone house, where an old woman lived with her seven dogs. She was always in her rocking chair on the front porch, and never shushed her pack when they barked at us, either. As we passed on this particular day, the dogs barked as usual, but the woman wasn't on the porch. It was sort of weird, but everyone has to go to the bathroom now and then, so we didn't think much of it until the dogs started going crazy the farther we got down the road.

Something was wrong.

We turned back, and though Mama was nervous about the dogs, I told her there was no reason to be. The barks of angry dogs were black karate chops in the air, but these dogs weren't mad; the high notes of their barks were blue with anxiety. Once she knew that, Mama went with confidence onto the woman's property and up the porch stairs. I followed, even though she said to stay put near the road.

Turns out the woman who lived there had been trying to reach a photo album at the top of a bookshelf and had stepped onto a low shelf to do it, toppling the whole thing—books and all—onto her legs, both of which had broken. She'd been trapped there for two and a half days before we found her. Two and a half days without food or water, and not having a bathroom except for the floor. Mary Lee Wilson was her name, and we found something out about Mary later on, after she got back from the hospital and felt better. Mary was a retired teacher, and she was nice, too, once you got to know her. She died a year later, but not before teaching me everything she knew about algebra and in a way that I finally understood.

Things happened for a reason, Mama always said, even when you couldn't see the why of it right away. Mama lost her license. I couldn't stay in public school. Tramp didn't have a library. We had to walk miles from home to get to a computer. They all seemed like inconvenient things. But Mary Lee Wilson may have gained an extra year of life because of all those things, and that was saying a lot.

The distance from the ground to the floor of the boxcar was more than I'd thought it would be. The bed of the car I'd found—a blue one with an open side door—was even with my armpits. I rested my hands there along with my bag, feeling flecks of rust against my skin and the hard slap of reality.

I couldn't do it.

Alone and handicapped and without direction.

The absolute certainty of this, knowing that getting into the train would be a giant mistake, was the opposite of how I'd felt five minutes before, when I'd scrawled a message that may or may not have been legible on a napkin and left it on the table. When I'd stood with my bag in hand, and opened the door and walked through it. Just beyond the shade of the restaurant's rooftop, I'd lifted my face. Even though the sun slipped into the dark space of my vision, I felt it on my skin and sensed Mama long enough to be sure.

I was going on alone, leaving Jazz, because doing anything else would mean failure. And despite what she thought—what she argued—this did mean something to me. Everything. I needed this trip, maybe more than I'd needed anything in my life.

The tang of something musty stirred in the air, as I followed along the brick building, trying to better my view of the tree line I'd seen inside, but still unable to make out the train. When I would've begun inching my way down the hill, a low hiss came from the direction of the tracks, announced to the world just where the train lay. And that it was leaving.

Now. Last chance.

I ran toward the sound, toward the tree line and the train's cars, clearer now, through long grass and weeds that brushed against my bare legs like a thousand fairy fingers, scratched like a thousand fairy nails. One car caught my attention with its open door, but before I reached it I fell on the stones lining the track and landed hard on my forearms. They stung now, as I laid my hands inside the car's vibrating body and realized . . .

I couldn't do this. It was stupid.

Why didn't I stay with Mama that day? We could've been together; I could've made her feel better. Dreamed her through her up-and-down and back to a better place. Taken her on a trip with wings as soft as flour, into a canyon on a summer day, or to a gur-gling stream or bog full of will-o'-the-wisps. If I'd made that choice, the sun would've risen the next morning smelling like my mother, and with my mother in her bed instead of a morgue, instead of dark and death and grief and everyone broken.

I hadn't made that choice.

Instead, I'd pulled my boot back on and left to meet Stan, because I wanted him to get into my knickers while I got into his. Mama died while I was getting busy with a boy who'd never meant more to me than a diversion, who'd disappeared like a puddle of rain in a hot sun after Mama died anyway, because this sort of thing was too hard. Too real.

Most everyone did that. Retreated. Jazz. Even Papa.

I didn't want to go back to that, and if I didn't go forward how would anything ever change? I gripped the car's metal edge and leaned my forehead against the back of my hand as the train groaned and the hiss grew louder.

"Shit. That one!"

I froze. The male voice came from behind me. Was it the bull? Would I end up in jail now?

A dog barked.

"Run up, jump in, hurry." A different voice.

"Hey, there's a ladder right there. You gonna use it or—"

Hisssss. Pop.

Grung-grung-grung-clank.

"Well, help her, you asshat!" someone shouted, and I was pushed over the rusty lip and into the car—despite cries that I'd changed my mind, despite trying to propel my body back outside again.

All effort was lost as a rush of bodies piled in after me, as my head went light and a dog's growl crystallized to my left. The world clouded over with darkness as the train bucked under my feet and we started to move. Someone corralled me into a corner and yelled, though I only caught pieces of it.

"What do you think, you—get us caught? Bull . . . yard . . . stay there . . . you blind?"

"I *am* blind," I shouted back. And then I repeated it in a whisper—"I *am* blind"—as noises poured over us and creaks turned into squeals, squeals into screams, screams into a banging, trembling, thudding tumble of asymmetry, explosions of shapes and colors—the darkest of browns and greens, reds and blacks, purples and blues—assaulting me like hail in a wild storm.

I covered my ears with my palms, clamped my jaw to keep my teeth from rattling, and planted my head against the rocking steel car as wind snatched at my hair and threw it back into my face. I began a chant to my family, told them one hundred times that I was sorry.

Urine with a hint of French fries and hamster bedding. That's what the car smelled like. Every part of me felt as trapped as my toes against my shoes, as I cried along with the train. With my eyes closed, I could envision my sister: the grim line of her mouth, the sharp jab of her gaze. She'd be back at the restaurant by now. What would she feel, finding me gone? Probably relief at being rid of me.

Someone tapped on my wrist. I opened and adjusted my eyes to find a redheaded girl there. Her voice rose above the noise. "It's all right. We're away from the yard now, and my brother's got the dog. Kramer's bark is way worse than his bite, anyway, trust me. If anything, he'd lick you to death."

I hugged my left arm, felt a slick of blood and the stick of slivers under my fingers from the fall I'd taken earlier.

She whistled. "Fuckadoodledoo. You're bleeding. Hobbs?" A true shout. "She's bleeding. Do you have a bottle?"

I tried to make out the others on the train—three more strangers, and the dog. Someone stood. I turned my head, still not sure that I was safe, but there were no options there; beside me lay stacks of things, a big wooden structure of some sort.

"Pallets should stay put, if you're worried about 'em," said a male. He leaned over the girl's shoulder, a hood pulled up around his face. "Only one died on this rail because of pallets, and the way the story's told he wasn't too bright. Glad to see you looking at them, though. Jop wanted to toss you off if you really were blind."

I dropped my forehead to my knees and sobbed again.

"Niiiiice," said the girl.

"Well, she *can* see, right?"

"How am I supposed to know?" she said, and rubbed my shoulder. "No one's going to throw anyone over the side. Jop is king of the dipshits. I know that because he's been my brother for the last eighteen years." She sat beside me. "Listen, we can either leave you alone or help you clean your cuts. Whatever, though, right? It's your call."

A line of warm blood trickled down my left elbow. I had no idea how bad my cuts were, if they were deep and dirty and could become infected. I'd have to decide: trust or not trust, risk or not risk. Or maybe there was nothing to decide at all.

I held out my arm.

"You do it, Hobbs," she said.

Something was passed between them, and even I could make out the bold black-and-white label, the blur of "Vladimir" on the bottle of vodka. I'd seen plenty of that around my house over the last few months. This was going to sting.

"You want a swig first?" asked Hobbs.

"No, thanks," I said, my voice a sandpaper rasp.

My doctor told me years ago to avoid liquor or drugs stronger than aspirin, that my mind was altered enough by nature and there was no telling how heightening that would affect me. Maybe he saw a spark of curiosity in my eyes, because he spent the next ten minutes going on about drug-related disasters, like kids on LSD who'd leaped out of windows thinking they were pools of water, which scared me enough that I listened for the most part; I'd had a few sips of beer here and there with no dramatic results. But, even though I'd already left my better judgment behind me, I didn't think drinking myself into oblivion with a group of strangers would help any.

Hobbs said, "You're not a snob like this one, are you? A girl who needs her liquor strained through a Brita before she'll drink it?"

"What's a Brita?"

"Never mind," he said.

"Trust me, girl, it doesn't help," she said. "I'm Ruby, by the way."

"Surf," said Hobbs. "You know the rules."

"It's not like she's going to—"

"You know the rules," he said.

"Fine. You can call me Surf," Ruby said, a second before Hobbs poured the vodka.

I felt the moan in my chest, but not even I could hear it over the relentless clang-clatter of the train.

Ruby guided me down the car, until we sat closer to the others but not too close, with our backs against the wall across from the open door. The world beyond blurred in greens and browns, familiar to me but causing an unfamiliar pinch of anxiety along my spine. Colored shapes tumbled around in my vision like earlier from the noise, but they were more polite now—not covered in awkward points or raining into my face like a child's tower of tumbledown blocks.

"It's primo seating, unless you really can't see, and then who cares, right?" Ruby said, and the strength of her high-wire voice put me at ease.

"My central vision's gone," I said. "I can tell you're a redhead but could only guess the color of your eyes." Blue, maybe. Green. "I could tell if you stuck your tongue out, but not the exact expression on your face." I smiled when Ruby stuck out her tongue. "I saw that."

"So what's a partially blind girl like you doing on a train like this?"

"Trying to reach Cranberry Glades of the Monongahela Forest. My mother was writing a story set there when she died. I brought her ashes."

"To scatter?"

"To see a ghost light."

I expected questions, criticism, but Ruby just said, "That's a new one."

We spent the next hour talking about everything and nothing. I told Ruby about home—Babka's shop and Papa's talent with the fiddle. I told her about my synesthesia, which she said sounded like taking peyote, a Texas whacky plant that, in Ruby's words, "makes you see some seriously weird shit."

I didn't mention Jazz.

Ruby, who insisted that I not call her Surf, told me she'd once lived on the West Coast in a house with a five-car garage that no one used because the door opener had broken. How her parents decided to abandon the family on the same day, leaving notes for each other in different parts of the house, and leaving Ruby alone with her younger brother. It wasn't a shock. She'd prepared herself for them to leave at various points throughout her childhood; her folks were second-generation hippies with happy feet who shouldn't have tried to settle down in the first place.

When they took off, Ruby and Jop decided to follow suit, hop trains like their parents and grandparents before them. Living on the rails was, Ruby said, a "totally unique and harmlessly rebellious way to get out from under the oppressive thumb of the real world, and say a big *F you* to the parents if they ever decide to phone home." She had no regrets, she said, and had learned more during a few months on the road and rail than she had through four years of college.

"So, I have a question for you," she said, and her tightrope voice swayed. "Traveling alone on the rails isn't always safe, especially for women. Does your family know you're out here? Are you meeting anyone on the other side?"

I dug my hand into my hair, drew a clump over my shoulder, and separated it into three pieces. "I'm not meeting anyone. But my sister knows I'm here. I have a sister. She thinks our mother committed suicide," I said without meaning to.

"Did she?" Ruby asked, as if strangers spilled their sorrows to her every day.

"No." I pulled one section of hair over the other—right over middle, left over middle—and felt the stretch of skin beneath the bandages on my arms. "She didn't."

I remembered, then, things I'd forgotten about that day. I'd turned off the gas. I'd opened the window and the doors. I'd pushed at my mother's chest, pounded the skin over her heart when nothing happened, when she didn't breathe.

Mama, Mama, please wake up!

Later, I threw up in the bathroom sink—a sink that had often been littered with my mother's hair. Less than a year ago, I'd found her staring into the mirror above that sink, holding such a mound of strands that they looked like a dead mouse in her hand.

I'm getting old, Olivia, she told me. *Sometimes I feel as ancient as a tree with a thousand rings.*

I stopped myself from saying, *I still need you, Mama*, because maybe it was coincidence that I'd finished my high school requirements a week before that, and I didn't want to set off an up-and-down. But I did hug her, and she didn't say anything more about it.

"It's too bad we didn't hook up before today," Ruby said, bringing me back. "I would've liked hanging with another girl."

"Yeah, it's too bad." Things happened for a reason, Mama always said. "You're not headed in the direction of Cranberry Glades, by any chance, are you?"

"Where's that?"

"South of Levi, where the train's headed."

"Gotcha. But nope." Her voice contracted like a shrug. "Jop and I are leaving West Virginia today, as a matter of fact. It's time. We've never seen the East Coast."

"Oh," I said, deflated.

"But, hey, Hobbs said he's walking on to see a friend after the next stop. He might tag with you if I tell him about your eyes."

"He has a thing for handicapped girls?"

She laughed. "I think he has a thing for challenging Darwin."

I wrinkled my nose.

"You know, helping with the survival of the weakest—like trapped dogs and lost travelers."

She told me the story, then, about how they'd met Hobbs. They'd just crossed into West Virginia and were looking for a jungle—a sort of home base for train folk—when they found him trying to free a dog's leg from a trap. The dog had belonged to a guy named Ran, a hopper who'd decided not to help his dog, because that morning the mutt had stolen his last package of cheesy crackers. Ran called it karma, and abandoned his faithful friend in order to catch the next train. Jop figured out how to open the trap, and the dog latched on to him after that. Jop and Ruby latched on to Hobbs, who had helped the right side in a desertion scenario and had a good heart, despite what you might think about his looks.

"What's wrong with his looks?" I asked, and she leaned close, told me that most of Hobbs's face and body was covered with tattoos—swirls of green and blue running along his cheeks and near his lips in thin lines, like a network of rivers. They traveled down his neck, giving wide berth to his eyes and nose and forehead. That might explain the hood, I thought, but what I said was "I don't care about looks," and meant it.

"Cool," Ruby said, "because I'm telling you, he's *the* person to know out here. He's taught us more in two weeks than the three months we had on our own before that. Dude might have a past—I mean, who doesn't—but whatevs. He gets it. He's, like, everything my parents wanted to be and never were. Free."

I wondered if such a thing was possible—to give up your past, start something so new there was no trace of what you were before. Erase it all. Be free. My mouth watered.

"Too bad his walls are so high up, and I'm such a lazy climber," she said with a silver-rain sigh.

I smiled. "You like him."

"Mad crush. Not reciprocated. This," she said, "is the story of my life. I've always had a thing for inaccessible men. Maybe if I had your lashes." I fluttered them at Ruby, and she laughed. "Yeah, do that when you ask him for help. You know, this could work out. You can't stare at him, which he'll totally love, and hanging with you will give him an excuse to ditch Red Grass, which he'll consider a huge bonus."

"Who?"

"Older dude over there. Pushy and, I don't know. . . . With Hobbs, you have to be real. It's like he can smell pretense or something."

"Be real," I said, as if I was taking notes, committing something important to memory, though in truth I was always pretty real. It was one of the things my sister disliked most about me.

"I'll go ask now. I may not be able to feel him up for me, but I can feel him out for you," she said, and moved over to the rest of the group.

There were always two ways to look at things.

Either I'd made the worst mistake of my life, getting on this train, or this was right where I was supposed to be—closer than ever to the glades, and about to get closer.

The feeling in my chest might be anxiety over the whooshing world outside this car, or it might be excitement.

Every part of me felt as tight as my toes against my shoes, or maybe that was just a sign that I needed to loosen up a little.

What was it Jazz had said? Things that were meant to be slipped into your life without a lot of effort. Sort of like being tossed onto a train.

I took off my sneakers and flexed my toes.

*

As it turned out, Hobbs's trip wasn't going to take him close to the park, and there wasn't another train I could hop after this to get me any closer, either. But if he could take me nearer to my destination by foot, that would be a lot better than me wandering around alone. I'd worry about the rest of it later—a strategy that had worked for Scarlett O'Hara most of the time. The challenge would be to get him to agree.

"Why Cranberry Glades?" he asked, sitting an arm's length away.

"Because the glades inspired the setting of my mother's story. It's where she wanted to see a ghost light," I told him. "You know about ghost lights, don't you?"

"Course I know wisps," he said, and I nodded. Sometimes I thought West Virginia must be the ghost-story capital of the world. "But why do you want to go with me? You can't trust me."

One of my braids caught the wind, hit me in the cheek, as the train rumbled on. "Why can't I trust you?"

"Because you don't know me, and you can't go around trusting people you don't know. Not on trains."

There was a scent to him that I couldn't place. I might've thought *earthy*, but this wasn't any earth I'd known. His hood was still raised up around his cheeks, and I found myself wanting to push it back, put my face right up to his and see those tattoos. Strange to hide something you'd done to adorn yourself.

"I could be a serial killer, waiting for my chance to cut you into chunks," he said. "You don't even know my real name."

I liked his voice, the way it turned up at the edges.

"So Hobbs isn't your real name?"

"Train name," he said. "Can't trust anyone with your real name out here, Wee Bit."

I smiled at this. "Well, I doubt a killer would try to warn me off. Besides, you've been with Ruby and Jop for weeks and they still have their limbs. And Ruby had plenty of good things to say about you. You helped rescue Kramer over there from a trap, right? It sounds like you're a natural hero, which is what I need. Without you, I'll be lost in the wilderness."

I resisted the impulse to bat my eyelashes.

"I'm anything but a hero, and I'm not going where you're going," he said, introducing me to that wall Ruby mentioned. "Just how blind are you?"

For a second, I thought about painting myself as blinder than a bat and the very definition of Darwin's weakest creature. But it was a slim second. I knew I couldn't live with that picture, and I didn't want anyone to see me that way, either. So I told the truth.

"I'm not *blind* blind," I said, then tried to describe what I could see—life as a smear—and what I could do, which included walking just fine. It wasn't like he was going to have to carry me around or anything.

"Maybe *I'm* blind here," he said, "but it doesn't look like you're decked out for sleeping in the woods. I've got a tarp and blanket, but I'm used to this life and—"

"I can sleep anywhere," I told him, and it was true. "But we shouldn't need to, right? The waitress I spoke with said the glades are just thirty-five, maybe forty minutes away from Levi."

Hobbs had an uncommon laugh, a ho-ho like Santa that made the curve of his voice ripple like a wave. "It is, if you've got a car stuffed in that suitcase or if you're planning to hitch a ride. That's not for me. I use my feet when I'm not on a train, and it'll take three days of hiking to get down to the park."

"Three days?" I may have gulped.

Why hadn't I asked Rocky to clarify her estimate back in the diner? But then I realized it wouldn't have mattered; I was so mad then that I would've run to the train anyhow. And, at this point, what else could I do? Throw myself at the mercy of the bull, beg for a phone and call home? What did I have to go home to? More arguments about what I should and shouldn't think, what was worth my time, what was stupid or not? More lectures from Jazz on *the work of a woman who's no longer with us, it's time to grow up, bitch?* More watching my father drink and cry and forget about us? More stagnancy and unanswered questions and feeling like I'd burst if something didn't change? More dreams of the death of the sun, of frosted mirrors, and lights beckoning, beckoning me on?

More *suicide, suicide, suicide.*

Hobbs had started to talk about hitching, how I could head up near the highway with Ruby and forget all this walking-and-sleeping-in-the-woods business, when I interrupted.

"I'm in," I said.

"You're what?"

"I'm in," I repeated. "I'll walk with you."

He was silent for a minute, and then he did something I didn't anticipate. He pulled back his hood. I knew he expected a reaction of some kind, that I'd see his face full of tattoos and call the whole thing off. Truth was, I couldn't see much besides a blur of color, swirls or patterns without detail. What did it matter?

"I'm still in," I said. "I can't go back home. Please don't force me to do that by taking away my one other choice. Please."

Something shifted in him after I said that; I could feel it like a substantive thing.

"You're ready for a three-day hike?" he asked.

I nodded, said, "I am if you are, if you'll have me. If you'll help."

"I don't know," he said. "I might have to—" He looked up and around, like he had a calendar in his head, too, and was checking to see if he had any appointments, any previous engagements, if he could spare the time. He was quiet for so long that I felt my hope wane again. Truly, I couldn't succeed alone. I needed his help.

"I stole something from my father," he said out of nowhere. "Something valuable. Now you know something to protect you."

"Protect me?"

"You have something on me."

"I don't need anything on you."

"Of course you do," he said. "You have something on a person and they act trustworthy even if they aren't, since they don't want you calling them out over whatever it is you have on them. Don't be stupid."

"I'm not stupid," I said. "What did you steal?"

"Does it matter?"

"Not if we have a deal."

He didn't say anything, which I took for a *yes*. In my mind's eye, I circled today on my calendar in fluorescent yellow. Somehow it would be important in the long scheme of things. And because trust meant a lot to Hobbs, and because I wanted to seal the deal, I held out my hand.

"I'm Olivia Moon," I told him. "Looks like you have something on me now, too."

And then I batted my lashes.

March 22, 1993

Daddy,

It is three in the morning, and I just woke from a nightmare. You know the one—the same old one. I don't know why I'm here writing to you when I swore I never would again, except that the dream gets to me every time, and it's about us, you know.

We were camping at the lake again, and again I was lost, as I truly was lost back when I was six— the year Mom left us. You remember that summer, how mad you were, always, how you couldn't even look at me. Then one day you said it was enough, that you were still my father and we'd have to learn to make it work between us because we were stuck with each other. You pulled our stuff together and decided we were going to go camping and I'd learn to like it (goddamnit) if it was the last thing you did. The drive was long, longer because it was so quiet, I think. I was scared. I remember wondering if you might take me out into the woods and kill me. I don't know why I thought that! Maybe because I was Suzanne Howell's daughter and she'd been so horrible, and maybe I felt that you wanted to kill her, but because you couldn't I would be the next best thing.

That's not what happened, of course. We arrived, and you set up the tent, and we ate Dinty Moore out of a tin pot and drank root beer. You'd just asked if I wanted to roast marshmallows, melt them over thick slabs of chocolate, when I said I had to go to the bathroom. And I guess you didn't think about it, that I was six and had never been off on my own before, because it was something Mom always took care of—back when she was taking care of me, of us, before her secret pregnancy and Henry and desertion. I thought it was a sign that you trusted me that you let me go off on my own, and felt tall in my shoes because of that. You gave me a silver flashlight and pointed the way. Follow the trail, you said, and you'll see it; you'll run right into the outhouses.

My flashlight died before I got there. Maybe the batteries were old, or maybe something shook loose,

I don't know. But all of a sudden I was in the dark, the trail disappeared. I should've called your name, but I thought, I'll find it. I thought, I don't want to lose Daddy's trust. I thought, I don't want to get into trouble, even though I hadn't done anything wrong; it was just that our nerves then were so raw, and I was confused about everything that had happened—more scared about that than about the forest. So I walked on in the dark, and hoped I'd find the bathroom or make my way back to camp. I wandered for I don't know how long. Twenty minutes, maybe, before I cried your name, screamed your name, ran and ran. I thought, I have failed my father in every way, that you'd think I'd left you, too, just like Mom. I was afraid then—more afraid than I'd ever been in my life. I curled into a ball alongside a berry bush and wet myself.

I saw your flashlight in the dark before I heard your voice. I told you later that I thought the dim glow was a ghost and that's why I'd stayed hidden and didn't walk toward it or call out to you when I could have. You found me, anyway, somehow. You hugged me close, damp pants and all, my clothes stained

with the smilax berries around us, and said you'd
never let anything happen to me again.

But that's not how it happens in my dreams. Tonight
it was a bear who found me out in the dark, who
chased me up a tree, his white teeth gleaming like
false promises. From my place on a long branch I
could see a bobbing light below, but when I called
your name the light disappeared.

Branik woke me. I didn't realize I'd been crying
in my sleep, calling for you. How embarrassing. A
grown woman, in bed with her husband; a married
mother, crying for her father. I told him, my good
husband, that I was all right—of course I was—
and left to get a glass of water but found myself
sipping Scotch and writing this letter to you instead.
I don't know why, when it isn't any use at all.
Maybe because it still feels as if I'm lost in the dark
sometimes and the trail has disappeared.

You do miss me, don't you? You must. I have to
believe it, that you remember as well as I do how
special that moment was—like a commitment

ceremony of our own. We would make it without Mom, we would thrive by holding on to each other. I promised to stay close to you and be a good daughter, a good girl, to always listen, and to never wander again. You promised to try harder to be a good father, because we were all the other had left. We stayed awake and ate s'mores until dawn, and you told me silly stories to clear my head of lost mothers and ghosts and darkness.

That was the start of our ghost stories, wasn't it? And the start of our joking, too. Broke a glass? Blame a ghost. Slam a door? Damned ghost. And who knew ghosts could belch while watching television? We kept it light, because I still had nightmares that the light was there but you were not, and I couldn't move because of the ghosts. You told me that one day, when I grew older, you'd take me to see a true ghost light on a bog, and show me that they were nothing to be afraid of, that maybe we'd chase one down and find a pile of treasure.

We never did that, did we? Because I ran off with a man like my mother did, got pregnant just like her,

too. Didn't listen to you when you told me to stay.
Turned into a bad girl in your eyes, who deserved
her wet pants as well as her fear. I wonder if you
blame yourself for not controlling me better, for
not taking the wild out of the child, or if you tell
yourself that there was nothing that could've stopped
Suzanne Howell's daughter from ruining her shot
at a respectable life.

There are two ways to look at everything, my wise
husband says, but you never did see that. And now
I am drunk and tired, and I still hate you, Daddy.
Nearly as much as I love and miss you (goddamnit).

Beth

CHAPTER SEVEN

Good Daughter

* JAZZ *

For as long as I could remember, my mother had called on me to look after my sister, find and rope her in when needed. Only once did I almost lose her for real.

We were children in a department store in Kennaton. My mother was off looking at something in the kitchen section, so I stayed near the large appliances to look after Olivia. One minute she was there, the next she wasn't.

What do you mean, lost? my mother said when I told her. I could tell from the quirk of her mouth that she thought Olivia had hidden well and I had given up too easily.

I opened every refrigerator and freezer, and every oven and dishwasher, I explained, my voice rising to convey significance. Strangers turned to stare. *What if she's out on the street? Will she find her way home like that dog and dog and cat in* The Incredible Journey? *Maybe she has a map inside her head along with that calendar of dates.*

That reached my mother. Her eyes stumbled over the store as her voice cracked. *You were supposed to watch her! This is why I say . . . this is why!*

We found Olivia, of course, on another floor of the store after a woman called my mother's name over the loudspeaker. And though we all mostly recovered from the moment via a rare session of retail therapy, I couldn't let go of the look in my mother's eyes at the thought of losing my sister—as if life without her would lack something vital. For a handful of seconds after seeing that look, I hoped my sister might be gone for good, that my family would be all mine again. This made me a bad girl, a bad sister and daughter, a bad person. I didn't tell anyone.

If the shame I felt then could translate the way it did for my sister, morph into one of the five known senses, it would have sounded like a train.

I left Jim's and my bus, ran down a long rutted hill and toward a train that seemed to be vibrating, creating an unreality of noise, a slam of sounds that drowned out my shouts as if they were nothing. From a distance I could see that a domino effect of movement had begun, each car jolting to attention, pulled to attention by the car in front of it, as sections of the train began to inch away, foot away, yard away, away.

But not the car my sister leaned against. Not yet.

She stood too far from me at the base of the hill, looking tinier than ever in our mother's shirt. Before I could reach her, though, faceless strangers with enormous backpacks emerged from the surrounding woods. Pushed her into the car. Hauled themselves in after her as that section of the train began to move.

Men. Men, and a dog.

Bad girl, bad sister, bad daughter, said the blood in my veins. *Your fault. Do something. Stop her.*

What else could I do? Go home? Tell my father and grandmother, I'm sorry, I lost her. Sorry, I wouldn't stay with her. Sorry, I don't know where she is, when she'll be back, if she'll wind up dead somewhere.

I couldn't catch them, though I tried. Instead, I roared along with the train, ran until I reached another car. Not a boxcar. A car that was enclosed except for a rail-edged platform on the end, and a ladder I might catch if I pushed myself and didn't trip on the stones nearest to the train, if I—

I leaped, surged forward against the ladder, and somehow landed a foot on the lowest rung. No small feat, considering the pack on my back. The train accelerated as I moved with careful steps—one foot to the left, then the other—until the opening to the platform was right there. I stumbled through it, onto something mechanical—not hot, at least not yet. All around me were things I couldn't name, cylinders and curved pipes. Behind me were the ladder rails I'd traversed—and all that stood between me and the tracks. There was no way inside the car itself that I could see; I would have to stay on this half-guarded rim.

I grabbed hold of the ladder and shouted my sister's name, threatened to kill the men if they hurt her, to kill them even if they didn't. But I couldn't even hear myself above the tremendous scream of the train.

Sometime after the second hour, as we snaked through the back-sides of towns decorated with adolescent weeds and yesterday's appliances, I vomited. The pain in my head had grown until my entire body ached. My fingers from gripping the ladder. My ears from the noise. My back and thighs from maintaining my balance as the car joggled from side to side. My eyes and face from the whip of wind and dust, which I couldn't escape, because standing with my back to the airstream left me dizzy.

I was afraid to lean against anything behind me.

I was afraid to lean against the ladder in front of me.

I was afraid, most of all, of what might be happening between my sister and a group of strangers. I couldn't know, couldn't control, what happened out of my reach and sight.

The fear made me hot, made me shake, swelled my brain.

They were train people—vagrants—and desperate, I was sure. Stabbed. Filleted. Robbed. Assaulted. Raped. Murdered. Dead. Dead. Dead.

I vomited a second time.

Hours passed like a slow torture, until my headache ran its course. I did what I could for myself. Drank water from my bottles. Ate half a biscuit and managed to keep it down. Wrote haikus in my head about how a normal-seeming day could turn into a nightmare in a matter of hours, how sisters were the most distressing creatures on earth, how I would make it my life's goal to repay Olivia for all this stress if we got through this. *(Please let us get through this. Let her be okay.)*

I didn't realize the end had come until it was on me, and even then I didn't realize it was a normal end and not a disaster of some sort. The brakes wailed like a banshee, random crashes could be heard all around, we slowed. In the near distance, I saw groupings of barrels, stockpiles of wood, pieces of old railroad cars, and a tall building overlooking it all; we were in a train yard.

My car jolted when the train came to a stop, knocked me forward and then back onto one of the pipes. I eased one hand off the ladder rail before me, stretched my fingers, touched my face. Numb. Coated in sand or silt. My gaze snagged on a single flip-flop deserted in a sparse grass in the distance, and I swallowed hard. *Let her be okay.* And then the air cut from the train, and I knew it was over.

After hauling the pack once again onto my back, I found my way off—at first edging along the railed perimeter, then stepping down the ladder. My limbs felt like ghosts of my normal limbs, but eventually I put both feet on the rocky ground beside the train.

I saw Olivia right away, ten or so feet away from me, carrying her red bag. Alive and whole and fine.

Not filthy and exhausted. Not sick and numb and terrified.

Fear morphed into anger, an exact transfer of emotional energy, part for part.

And amplified when I saw *him*.

A stranger, holding one of those huge backpacks I'd seen earlier, stepped out of the gloom alongside the tracks. Most of his face dyed in a labyrinth of tattoos. Free-flowing brown hair. Angular jaw. Tall. An expression that said, definitively, *Bite me*. He gripped my sister's shoulder, steered her toward the woods beside the train.

No way.

I dropped my bag, rushed at them. Struck the stranger's left shoulder with one hand, swivel-turning him to face me. Waited for our eyes to connect. Punched him in the face. His jaw didn't just look hard; it was rock solid. My knuckles screamed. So did Olivia.

"What the fuck?" he said, eyes blazing.

Olivia sounded frantic. "Hobbs, wait! That's my sister!"

He touched the corner of his mouth. Looked at the blood on his fingers, then back at me. Fierce eyes, lighter than the markings on his face. My age, probably.

"Sister? Well, sister, if you weren't a woman—"

I squared up with my still tingling arm, ready to hit this Hobbs again, but an echoing shout stilled me.

"Bull!"

A duo materialized out of nowhere and took off with a dog. Hobbs followed.

"Hurry," Olivia said. "Jazz, let's go!"

In the distance, a white pickup approached. I guessed from the way the others had run that the truck held an official of some sort. I walked to where I'd left my backpack in the grass, picked it up, and made my way out of the yard like a civilized human being who'd just punched a guy in the face. Olivia stayed by my side.

A voice crystallized behind me—"See you here again, I'll have you fined!"—and I ignored it.

As soon as our feet hit a forest trail outside the yard, Olivia said, "I'm glad you're here, but also"—she pinched the inside of my arm—"I'm really mad at you."

"Stop it!" I said, nudging her away.

"How?" she said. "How did you even get here?"

"How do you think? I sucked fumes and dust for six hours, clinging to a train ladder. You should try it sometime," I said, as we stepped into a large clearing where the rest of the group stood at a distance. I put my hand out to stop my sister's advancement, shushed her.

A woman—a twentysomething with a disastrous tangle of red hair and several face piercings—stood on tiptoe inspecting Hobbs's mouth, her hands on either side of his jaw, tilting his head one way and then the other.

"Where's Red? Was he caught?" said a rail-thin boy who seemed overwhelmed by a mass of blond dreadlocks and his own colossal backpack. A familiar dog panted at his feet.

"No idea," said the woman. "I'm more worried for—"

A series of staccato barks pierced the air.

"Kramer!" said the boy, and the dog aborted his run to greet or eat us, and returned to his side.

Hobbs's eyes turned dark and slitlike when he saw me, and I had to admit he looked ominous in the shadowed woods. Pissed off. Almost as pissed off as I felt.

"Maybe we should start over," the woman said when Hobbs threw down his pack—a good indication that he was ready to forget I was a female. "Olivia, maybe you can introduce us to—"

"Touch my sister again and die," I said, pointing right at him with one hand and wrapping the other around Olivia's arm.

She yanked it back. "What is wrong with you?"

"What's wrong with *me*? What's wrong with *you*, Olivia Moon? It's like you're hell-bent on setting yourself on a path of destruction! How can I take care of you if—"

"You don't have to take care of me," she said. "I'm not your job."

"How typical of you to be delusional."

For the first time, I took a hard look around and realized there wasn't any sign of a town, just woods, woods and more woods. A finger of fear returned to trace my spine. We were in the middle of nowhere. Lost. Outnumbered by the sort of strangers you'd see decorating a police lineup on the evening news. A knife hung from the boy's belt.

I averted my eyes, worked to control my voice. "Which way is town?"

No one responded. I looked at the woman in need of a brush.

She shrugged. "Not my state," she said. "Hobbs?"

With reluctance, I regarded the ink-dyed freak. "Which way is town?" I repeated.

He tried to stare me into dust, but I refused to blink. Finally, he said, "That way," and pointed back in the direction of the tracks. "About half mile north of the yard, not that there's much to it."

There'd be a phone. That's all I needed.

"Perfect," I said. "Let's go." I made to grab Olivia's arm, but this time she evaded me.

"Which way to Cranberry Glades?" she asked.

"In the opposite direction," said Hobbs. "You coming?"

"I am," she said, and took a step toward him.

"You're not." This time I did grab her, pulled her back with my cold hand. "This game ends now."

"Game?" Her shoulders squared, and her wide blue eyes narrowed. "I know what I'm doing, Jazz, and I'm a legal adult. I can and will do what I want."

"I don't care how old you are on paper, you're reckless!" I said. "You're irresponsible! You're—you're like a two-year-old out here, devoid of any sense of logic or reason, and this—" She squeezed my shoulder until I let go of her arm. "This proves it! Riding a train? Running around in the wild with strangers? Are you trying to kill yourself?" I hadn't meant it literally, but now the words hung in the air between us, dangling like a noose. Made me even more afraid, even angrier. "How can you just blindly trust him?"

"Trust *me*? You see me going around punching strangers?" said Hobbs. "But at least now it all makes sense. Why she'd rather stay with the likes of me than go back home. Why she'd choose anything else over having to return. No one would want to have to deal with the likes of you."

"I'm her sister," I said with a snarl.

"You're a bitch," he said.

"Doesn't feel so good, does it?" Olivia said quietly, as a crow cawed high above us. "Listen, Jazz, you never wanted to do this in the first place. I get that—how you think this is a waste of time, stupid, how you have a job to get ready for, all of it. That's your point of view, but I have a point of view, too, and it's just as valid, even if it's different. I need to keep on and finish what I set out to do. It's what *I* need. Hobbs has said he can take me closer to the glades, and I'm going to let him. I'm going to trust him, and I'm going to trust *me*. I have to trust *me*."

A breeze blew up when she dropped her hand, and my panic spiked. This was a change. Not a jabberfest. There was something different about my sister, as if she wasn't trying to bait me to follow. As if she'd grown an inch taller, her skin a millimeter thicker. As if her heart had become sufficiently calloused, and now she was not only ready but determined to walk on without me.

"I will take you once the bus is fixed, okay?" I found myself saying. "I'll take you and Dad and Babka, and we'll scatter Mom's ashes together so she can see whatever wisps she wants whenever they decide to come around. Isn't that a fair compromise? We'll do it on a weekend, when I'm not working."

"Working at *Rutherford and Son Funeral Home*, you mean?"

I felt the others' eyes on me but kept mine on my sister, my voice even. "You know that's what I mean."

"Dreams like feet better than knees," she said.

"Am I supposed to know what you're talking about?"

"It means I need to do this now. And I'm going."

This time I couldn't hide the quaver in my voice. "Do you realize I left the bus—just left it—at Jim's to chase after you? We need to find a phone and call home so they know where we are and—"

"I have an iPhone," said the redhead.

I glared at her. She didn't look like she could afford a plastic spoon.

"What?" she said, with a hint of defensiveness. "Just because I'm out here enjoying a hippie moment doesn't mean I can live without my cell any more than the next American. I charged it in the last town, too, so as long as there's service—"

"You'll have to sleep in the woods, Jazz," my sister said. "If you come. If you decide to go with me now. We won't be able to get there today."

The air felt like fire in my nostrils as my desperation rose. "Olivia." I gripped her shoulders again, fighting the urge to shake her into submission, and played the last card I had to play. "I will hate you forever if you do this."

But, as always, my sister held the ace.

"Oh, Jazz," she said, and her eyes turned sad. "I think we both know that you will hate me forever anyway."

I called Babka using a cell phone that looked more expensive than any I'd ever seen. The reception wasn't perfect, but it was good enough. I was able to say what I needed to say, even if I didn't hear what I wanted to hear.

She was glad I'd called, glad we were still on the way to the glades. She would take care of the bus, as I would take care of my sister. I was a good girl.

I wasn't a good girl, I told my grandmother. I was a stuck one.

CHAPTER EIGHT

A Fortunate Thing

✳ OLIVIA ✳

The story of how my parents met is a tale of love at first bite. Papa was at Kennaton State, taking a trayful of Babka's biscuits and rolls down a flight of stairs and to a campus grocery store. Mama, a junior there, lingered behind him with some of her friends, admiring his cute butt and strong shoulders—until she tripped, somehow, on her own heels. She couldn't catch herself; her feet wouldn't land right on the steps, her hands couldn't snag the railing no matter how she tried. She said it was like being a bird flung out of a nest to learn that it had no wings, and that she was lucky someone was there to break her fall. She plowed into Papa's back, which threw him off balance, too.

There were ten steps, maybe, to the bottom, which didn't sound like much but was a lot when you were out of control. I picture them rolling, cartwheeling down the stairs, baked goods everywhere, biscuits raining over them like falling stars. When they reached the end of their tumble, my mother's body landed over my father's back in an ungainly sprawl, and her shrieking mouth pierced his shoulder.

When he turned himself over to face her, like a half-cooked griddle cake, Mama kissed him—despite her throbbing teeth and sprained ankle. Her friends thought maybe she should see a doctor because she was acting so funny, but Mama said the only prescription she needed was the delivery guy's phone number, which he gave her.

I asked her once what made her kiss him, and she said it was two things. The first was his eyes; they were big pools of blue, bright and happy to meet her. The second was the taste of him when she bit into his shoulder. He tasted, she said, like tomorrow.

If that's not love, I don't know what is.

The train rattled on in my veins long after we were off it and on the ground, which might explain why my feet were slow to do as I asked—like they'd turned to clay and clay didn't have to listen to me. The clearing we'd argued in, the one we'd said goodbye to Ruby, her brother, and his dog in, was the last we'd seen of a wide-open space in the forest. The brush became thick as we walked south, the air heavier, *greener*, the weeds tickling my ankles.

My stomach cramped with hunger as we moved in a single line, but I wasn't about to ask for a break when we'd just gotten started. Still, everything I saw and heard seemed to remind me of food. The crunch of leaves and twigs underfoot drifted from the upper reaches like overturned potato chips, while the bag that bumped with regularity against my leg created a staccato of orange splats, like melted cheese dripping onto a counter.

I'm sure Jazz noticed from behind whenever I tripped over a root or rock, though she never said anything. Hobbs, who led the way, didn't speak, either, unless I spoke first, like the time I realized I couldn't see Jazz behind us when I stopped to look.

"Don't go too fast, or we'll lose Jazz," I said.

"Right." He shifted his backpack. "We wouldn't want to lose Jazz."

I should've been happy, because we were on our way; we'd get to the glades. But it was hard to be happy when the day smelled like a big pot of I-hate-your-guts.

When I was five, there was a storm cloud over Tramp that had the eye and tail of a monster, and brought the loudest thunder I can remember, filling my head with black icicles along with the regular burst of mustard-gold fog. Some in town swore that it brought a tornado, because it ripped limbs off trees and knocked the power out for a week. Whatever it was, it became a source of childhood nightmares for me. I'd wake after being chased by black icicles, and Mama would bring in a damp washcloth to soothe my skin and wipe away my tears. Oftentimes she'd fall asleep on the covers with me still attached to her like a barnacle, and I'd drape the washcloth over her nose and eyes to try to wake her. But not much bothered Mama when she was sleeping.

If Jazz were a storm, she'd be a storm like that. I could feel the pressure of her sometimes in the small spaces behind my cheeks— a promise of hard rain and wind and darkness, a willingness to rip limbs from branches. Whenever I'd felt that pressure from her at home, I'd left the house. Gone for a walk or a swim in the stream that ran through town, or headed across the road to see if Mrs. Magee's cat had more babies. Something about Pippin's purr always put my head back in the right place, the deep sounds spindling from ear to spine, relaxing my muscles as I pet her and admired her wee ones. I couldn't do anything like that now. I couldn't leave. I needed my companions, was dependent on them both.

I tried to remember that there were two ways to see even this situation. I would be stuck with a pair of mad and quiet people for three days. But being stuck would give me time to practice using my peripheral vision. Maybe I'd get better at everything. Maybe I'd prove that I didn't need those glasses after all. It was the last thought I had before I tripped and fell on my forearms again.

In retrospect, I'd say the fall was a good and fortunate thing, but in that moment it seemed like anything but. Jazz helped me up with a tug of hands, and called Hobbs back to us with a sharp word. He pulled out his bottle of Vladimir to help clean what Jazz called *a mess of dirt and blood,* and again offered me a sip as a mental analgesic. That's when Jazz said something along the lines of "Booze? Olivia needs to reduce her inhibitions like I need another excuse to punch you in the face."

It didn't matter that I would've said no.

They started in on each other again, name-calling worse than ever, until the pressure building inside me threatened to rip the skin clear off my body.

"Go away!" I cried, covering my ears with my hands. "Both of you, just get away from me!"

I never yelled—not ever—but I guess I was pretty good at it when I put my mind to it, because they shut up.

"I mean it," I told them with a neon voice that warned, *I am seriously on the edge, don't push it or I will explode all over you.* "Take a time-out. You, that way." I pointed. "You, the other. Come back in five minutes."

And they left.

Huh.

Quiet all around me.

I was on my fourth shaky breath when I heard a familiar rush, off in the distance. I walked forward, over a small embankment, to find a snaking body of water spread out like a welcome mat.

The stream that coiled through Tramp was a thin trickle of a thing most of the year, but how it raged in springtime, filled my eyes with a fireworks show when I closed them to listen. Here there were no fireworks. Best I could tell, this was an easy stream. Not too loud or wide or rushing. Hobbs had mentioned that there was one nearby, that we'd need to run some of its water through his filter to refill our bottles. And though I wouldn't deny that a drink would taste good, what I needed then was something else.

I shucked my clothes down to my undies, then waded into the frigid water, into the heart of the stream, until it skimmed the flesh above my knees. I stood there with my eyes closed, my arms limp at my sides, and felt the drop of my pressure, steady and sure, and such a relief that I nearly wept with gratitude. Again, I was able to focus on things outside myself instead of everything crushing up against my insides and smothering my organs.

Silt and rocks cradled my feet.

Sunshine melted a cloak of heat over my arms.

Off in the far distance, a tumble of water, a small waterfall. I couldn't see it, but it shadow-danced along my eyelids in lemon and russet tones.

I walked against the current. Let the scent of moss take me back to me and Mama knee-deep in water just like this, fishing for lunch because we were sick of peanut butter and jelly. Of Mama and me collecting guppies to study. Of Mama taking a nap by the shore while I gathered pebbles, and Papa coming up on the both of us, seeing her there, kissing her eyelids until she woke and smiled up at him. *Prince Charming. I'd know you anywhere.*

I was still walking and thinking about that moment when someone grabbed my arm.

"Didn't you hear me?" he said over my gasp.

Hobbs. He turned away when I crossed my arms over my chest.

"I've been calling you, Livya."

It was the first time he'd used my name with that voice of his—a voice that smiled on its own even when he growled.

"You should've told someone you'd come out here," he continued. "What if something had happened?"

Should've tasted like unsent letters and unfinished stories. Like ghost breath on a mirror.

We should've thought about this kitchen, my father had said. *Should've made sure the door couldn't close all the way in case the gas was on and the light went out. Should've made sure the window was always cracked. Should've spent every cent we had to make the heat better so you could work at your desk all year round instead of in the kitchen, instead of always having to settle.* He opened the window and screamed my mother's name, cried right there over the sink. *Beth Moon! I should've told you I loved you more!*

It bruised my heart still to remember.

"Maybe I should've," I told Hobbs, as trickles of water made their way from my arms to my abdomen. "But sometimes I need to be by myself. Sometimes I need to get away."

"But you've said yourself that your eyes—"

"Don't do that," I said. "It's not like I'm going to forget about what's wrong with me, so I don't know why everyone keeps bringing it up like I will." My pressure started to rise all over again. "And it's not like I'm happy to need people. Trust me, there's nothing I'd like more right now than to not need anyone."

"Settle yourself, Wee Bit," he said. "I don't have to stick around."

I squeezed my eyes shut, and then I dropped my hands, cupped them in the water, and splashed my face. Droplets streamed down to the tip of my nose. "I'm sorry. I do want you to stick around." I wasn't upset with Hobbs. I was embarrassed because he'd found me stripped down in more ways than one. But I didn't need to be.

Ruby had said, *Be real*. This was real. No hiding.

"Should I—?" He glanced back in my direction, then away again. Still unsure whether to stay or go. Where the line might be. Where to put his eyes when in the presence of a strange girl in her underwear.

I'd make it easy for him. "Do me a favor?" I asked.

"What favor?

"Help me clean this mess?"

There was something about his awkwardness, as he removed what remained of my old bandages, that made me feel all the better. Strangely empowered, as he brushed over my wounds with careful fingers beneath the surface of the water, evicting dirt and blood. There was a trust pact here. And Hobbs was a nurturer. Who would've thought?

"What's that smile about?" he asked, which made me smile wider.

"I like you," I said.

"You don't know me to like me," he said.

I liked his habit of helping others—trapped dogs and stumbling

Californians and blind girls all. I liked the puzzle of him, wanted to understand things like why he found it so hard to hear a good word about himself without earning it in some clear way. I liked the way he emanated a scent all his own, the way it conjured up the image of a faraway place and of herbs I'd never tried before but might like simmered in a stew.

"I like what I know," I said, and he released my arm. I tried but couldn't read a single expression on his face.

"Maybe there's as much to *not* like as there is to like," he said. "Maybe you just can't see it."

"Your tattoos?"

"My cloven hooves."

"So that's what I heard on the trail back there."

"Very funny," he said, giving nothing away.

"I can be funny." I made my eyes round, realized I was flirting, and found that interesting.

I liked Hobbs. Maybe I *liked* Hobbs.

And why not? Had I ever met anyone so intriguing? Besides, it had been a long time since I'd had a fling—since Stan. He and I parted ways because death was the opposite of a fun time, which is all either of us had been in it for. It *had* been fun while it lasted, though. He hadn't minded that everyone in Tramp considered me a freak, and in return I hadn't minded that he was shorter than me by half an inch. Height didn't matter much in the backseat of a car, at any rate—not when the car was big enough.

"What are you up to?" asked Hobbs.

"Five foot two," I said, still trying to be funny. "How old are you?"

"Old enough for trouble, so you'd better be careful."

Maybe it was a warning I should heed. I thought again of Stan and that morning, and pushed it all back again. I wouldn't think about that when there was sun on my arms. Hobbs was not Stan. Stan's voice had looked like pieces of cheese falling from a grater. The curves of Hobbs's voice were smooth and perfect.

Voices could tell you things, if you listened, and I listened now more than ever.

"Nineteen," I guessed. "Twenty?" He shifted. Twenty, then. "What do your eyes look like?"

"Shards of glass."

"What color glass?"

He didn't answer. Neither did he move.

I stood as high as I could right there—extending my feet, finding a convenient and stable rock to climb upon—and brought my face right up alongside his. Hobbs was much taller than Stan, and thin as a shadow.

"What are you doing?" he said.

"Trying to climb a wall."

"What?"

"Just hush a second." I angled my head, tuned in as well as I could to the periphery. "Stay still."

A web of artful lines and arcs over his cheeks. Pale skin where there wasn't color. A wide mouth that formed a straight line. Big eyes. I couldn't be certain—it was harder to see color in the periphery than it was straight on, especially when that color was on a subject as small as an iris—but I could tell his eyes weren't dark as coal, so I made my prediction anyway: "Green."

He straightened right up, which is when I realized that he'd hunched, met me partway.

"Sounds like you can see just fine," he said, with a voice that said he wasn't happy to learn it.

I could've said it was a lucky guess on my part, but let it drop. He was funny, Hobbs, the way his moods turned.

I settled back onto the flats of my feet. "I can see well enough to hop a train, and walk a path without tripping too many times, and smell a chocolate morning."

"Chocolate?"

"Mmm," I said, and my mouth watered. "There's a lot you don't know about me, but I'll tell you everything, if you want. If you stick around."

"I'm here, right?" he said.

A small fish brushed by my leg in a flurry of life, dashed away.

Yes, he was there. And I was glad.

M y time with Hobbs in the stream would've made for a perfect memory if not for the way it ended. Two people stood in wait for us on the shore. My skin puckered when I realized it, and it wasn't just because I was cold and in my underwear.

"Red Grass." Hobbs's voice boomed across the water. He clutched my elbow as we waded forward, closer to land.

"Ho there," came a voice like gravel, a voice I recognized from the train. I felt better knowing it wasn't a pure stranger standing there, but I'd feel better still with my clothes on. I knew without anyone saying anything about it that the person with him was my sister; I felt her judging eyes all over me.

"How in hell did you find us?" Hobbs asked. "Where'd you go before? Did the bull get you?"

"Nah, call of nature," said Red Grass, setting down a pack that had to have been twice as large as Hobbs's, and his wasn't small. "But I knew I'd catch you again. Tracking's what I do, what I'm best at. And I got a new deal for you, Hobbs."

"Of course," Hobbs said under his breath.

"Where are those yuppie hoboes?" he asked.

"Surf and Jop took off," Hobbs said.

As soon as the water was shallow enough, I let go of him and made my way toward the clothes I'd left on the shore. Jazz came to stand beside me, a human shelter from the boys.

"Nice look." Her voice was a low hiss of noise. "What is wrong with you, Olivia?"

"I needed to cool off, so I did what I had to do," I said, not letting her ruin the calm inside me.

"Well, put your clothes on. I have something to tell you."

"Last I knew, I could hear with my clothes on or off," I said, though I slipped on the T-shirt. "Well?"

"In private," she said, hovering like the dark cloud she liked so well to emulate.

I wasn't in the mood for a private tongue-lashing, though, so I didn't rush. I tugged on my cutoffs, fighting the denim a little against my wet skin. I pulled on my socks, one at a time, and tied my sneakers.

"Livya?" Hobbs called.

I ignored the sharp words that tried to anchor me to my sister—"Olivia Moon, you come back here"—and walked right up to the guys.

"Give us a minute, Red," Hobbs said, and the older man moved away and started to sing.

Jazz swore behind me.

"If Red makes you uncomfortable, I can try to get him to piss off," Hobbs said, as Red Grass crooned on.

"*Catfish, catfish, going up a stream. Catfish, catfish, where you been?*"

"I can try," Hobbs repeated, "but I can't guarantee anything. I've known that guy for about a month, which is long enough to know he can be an annoying son of a bitch who tries to control things he shouldn't and is harder to shake than a dug-in tick."

"*I grabbed that catfish by the snout, Lord I pulled that catfish out!*"

"But he's got a tent you'd like," Hobbs said, "and you'll never go hungry with him around. Red, he knows how to fish."

"Olivia. Now," said Jazz, closing in on me.

There had to be some truth in it somewhere—a kind of rule or law of physics. Two control-freak types together would keep each other occupied, would need to define the alpha and the beta of it, and so would have something to say to each other. Probably a lot of somethings. Which meant a lot less of those somethings directed toward me.

"I'm fine with Red Grass," I said. "Really, I am."

Third Stage:

Bargaining

One must always hope when
one is desperate, and doubt
when one hopes.

—*Gustave Flaubert*

November 11, 1995

Dear Dad,

I thought you should know that you have another granddaughter! Olivia Francis Moon was born this past June, with a wisp of blond hair that turned black almost overnight and a look in her eye that said, "Hello, I'm trouble." She does not sleep, and would prefer to wear her dinner than eat it. Despite all of that, I've fallen madly in love with her.

Jazz is four now, and I can trust her to behave for short spans of time when I put Olivia down for a nap so that I can catch up on sleep or do some things for myself. This miracle can only be achieved because she's a good listener and as serious as a soldier when I ask her for help. My mother-in-law, Drahomira, says I'm lucky because most four-year-olds are the opposite of accommodating. (Was I difficult at that age? Do you remember?)

One day you'll meet them and see that I've made two healthy grandchildren for you, and become the

daughter you always wanted me to be. I'm calmer
now, Dad, and saner and more responsible. I
know that was always your greatest worry—that
my impulsivity would be my undoing, that I'd self-
destruct like Mom. But you'd be wrong to worry. I'll
bet you're calmer, too, and that soon you'll be ready
to put this behind us. Then you'll see that Branik,
despite a great lack of money, is a very good man.

Olivia's crying, so I'll close now.

Thinking of you,

Beth

CHAPTER NINE

A Fascination with Death

✳ JAZZ ✳

Babka replaced the biscuit bus with a modern van late last year. She had a friend who refurbished totaled vehicles, and that guy—Smitty—came into the store one day and told her he had a beaut he'd sell her "for cheap," because her creaky old bus was living on borrowed time. Smitty was a retired body-shop worker, so he knew a thing or two about fixing cars. The van had air-conditioning, he said, and fabric seats and a CD player and cassette slot both, so it didn't matter that the radio wouldn't work well. Smitty got his biscuits free after that, because of course she took him up on his offer.

Dad brought Olivia and me along on deliveries in that van for two solid weeks after our mother died. Maybe he was afraid for us, even though we could've stayed with Babka. Maybe he was afraid for himself. Maybe it was Babka's idea that we all stick together. I don't know, and can't recall if I ever did.

It was on the fifth day that I said I wanted to walk awhile on my own in Kennaton.

You all right? my father asked.

I had a flash then of my mother asking me that same question, countless times, trying to brush hair out of my eyes while I dodged her hand. Sometimes I'd walk past her without a word, just leave her there in the kitchen she'd die in one day, not realizing that I was giving up a moment I might've had or a conversation or a revelation or something. Never bothering to process that there were a finite number of possible moments, and I was skirting away from them as if they were a pile of dog heapings in the grass.

That first day alone in Kennaton, I walked until I ached, my head full of nothing. I watched a woman step into a grocery store laughing, smiling, and wondered *How?* The world had ended, didn't she know? My guts had been ripped out through my throat; couldn't she see? How could anyone feel . . . joy? Dad picked me up about two hours later, and we drove home.

The next day, I asked to be let out again, and walked until I found a shop. Didn't even have a sign, just a banner advertising coffee and a bagel for $1.25. I ate a plain bagel and drank three cups of coffee without tasting anything. And then I opened a newspaper on the countertop of a stained bar. No one else was there that day to see me flip to the death notices.

Marilyn Wilcox, age ninety, died in a nursing home.

Stuart Babcock, age eighty-one, died at home.

Alex Dimmock, age fifty-nine, died, who knew where.

Sandra Weber was only twenty-seven. No one said what happened to her or where she died. *A heart of gold stopped beating, two willing hands at rest*, went a poem. She was survived by her father as well as a sister, and a brother. She was predeceased by her mother.

At that point, I didn't have a copy of my mother's obituary. I hadn't seen or read it. Hadn't cut it out to keep or heard any discussion of it. Maybe she didn't have one at all, considering how she'd died, because what could it say?

Beth Moon killed herself. The end.

People didn't like to talk about that. Few had sent cards. Sometimes I caught sidelong, suspicious looks from people in town. *How horrible are you,* some of those looks asked, *that your mother committed suicide?* Others dripped pity, or wondered in loud silence, *Why did she do it?* I hated them all equally.

After that, I stole the obituary section every day we were in Kennaton. Later, in the privacy of my room, I removed the best essays, laid them across my bedspread, studied them, shuffled them around in search of something. A pattern, an answer.

When I was little, I used to play with marbles in the small room behind Babka's kitchen.

All the secrets of life are in that bag, she would tease.

What is it? I'd ask, and she'd say that she couldn't tell me, that I needed to figure it out for myself.

I believed her. I played, I watched. Red hits the blue, hits the green, hits the yellow. Red hits the blue, hits the yellow, hits the black. Red hits the blue, hits the white, hits the yellow. If there were answers in the marbles, I never found them, and whenever I put them away I felt disquieted.

That's how I felt after studying the obituaries as well, before I shoved them all inside my mother's old backpack. As if something significant had eluded me.

It happened while Olivia and Hobbs were in the stream. Everything changed after that.

I'd walked farther than I'd meant after my sister told me to leave her alone, past vines that scratched my arms, ankles, and calves, talking to myself the whole time: "You want me to go? Fine, I'll go all the way home, how's that? Leave you to figure it all out or die trying, which you seem set on doing with these ass-brained ideas. I will not be led around by the nose through the forest over bat-crazy bullshittery."

Eventually I reached the end of my invisible tether and stalled beside a huge dead tree, ancient and hunched as an old woman. A crow stared down at me from the branches.

"What are you looking at?"

It continued to stare.

Quiet minutes passed, as I thought through my meager options. Abandon her. Continue. There was no real choice. The anxiety I'd kept at bay by bitching and walking swelled like a bloated fish in my throat.

Why do I feel this way?

The sun had hitched itself across the sky, but I wasn't nervous over the approach of night, in and of itself. I wasn't afraid of the dark; it never promised anything, was never false. I wasn't afraid of the forest, or of sleeping without a bag or blanket or tent. I'd stay awake with one eye on Hobbs the whole time anyway, though I was not exactly afraid of him, either; we both knew I had a killer right hook.

What, then?

I dug my fingers into the tree's battered hide, full of dark grooves and bleached, flaking bark—its dead skin and hard-earned age spots. Some things were meant to fly, and others were bound by their roots.

This, I knew, I'd learned from my mother.

No matter how her life ticked on, she was always thinking about her roots—and her atonement. Raising us on a short leash. Our particular educations. Her transplanted dreams. The book she never finished, and its related trip to the glades. I had no doubt about what she prayed for, if she prayed at her altar. And all of it was sacred ground, not to be interfered with.

I shucked the pack from my back, remembering the last day my grandmother tried to help my mother with her story. I might've been ten or eleven years old. Babka had come over for Sunday dinner, as she always did, and was offering suggestions for my mother's story, as she always did, because my mother was always stuck. The heroine of the story—a sun fairy named Esme—had been kidnapped by a power-hungry warlock and made to forget herself via a curse of amnesia. There were plenty of twists and turns in store for Esme, but what was never clear was how she'd ever find her way back to her true self and the sky, which grew darker and darker without her presence. This was the crux of that night's debate.

The sun fairy's soul is in a teapot, Babka had said, drying dishes in our kitchen as my mother washed. Behind them, with my bare toes pressed against the refrigerator and the rest of me hunched over a piece of paper, I drew a teapot and decorated it with hearts. *If Esme finds the pot and removes the cover, her soul will be freed, and then she'll remember herself.*

There is no teapot, my mother said.

Then let the soul be hidden in a needle—everyone has a needle, said my grandmother, as I crossed out the teapot and drew a long needle with an oval eye. *The needle is in an egg, and the egg can be found in a rabbit, which lives in a chest that is buried under an oak—*

My mother pulled a wet cup out of the water and set it on the counter with a slosh. I pulled my toes off the refrigerator and swiveled around to find my mother's angry eyes.

I've already told you that I don't want to re-create Slavic fairy tales, Drahomira, she said. *Esme has lost her memory, not her soul. This is my story. Let me finish it my way.*

If my mother had listened to my grandmother, the story might've been finished years ago. Maybe then she wouldn't have been in the kitchen that morning with her work, wouldn't have—

The crow cawed when I swore.

"Oh, fly off!" I said, and, surprisingly, it flew away.

"Bird whisperer, are you?"

I jerked around so fast that I would've fallen if not for the tree. The fuzzy-haired, dough-faced man from the restaurant steps stood a few feet from me, wearing an oversized backpack and a holstered knife around his waist.

This is how bad things happen, I thought, as my anxiety found a real reason to surge inside me. *Knife out, in my side, across my throat, done.*

"You're the girl from the restaurant, right?" he asked. "The one with the watch?"

I covered my watch with my hand, sure he'd take it after killing me. Someone would find me someday, a hollowed-out shell, a few teeth and eye sockets. They would never know my name.

He whistled. "Hellooo, anybody home? What are you doing out here, a pretty young thing, all alone in the woods?"

When he leaned forward, I reached reflexively for my backpack, my fingers contracting around a strap. But I knew there was nothing inside the canvas that could help me. My defenses in this scenario would be basic and minimal; I could kick him in the groin, scratch him with my stub nails, scream.

"Put down your knife," I said.

Though my voice sounded far less commanding than I would've liked, he held both empty hands in the air like a duet of white flags. "Now, don't be scared. I'm not gonna hurt—"

"Throw it down," I said, my voice rising in pitch. "Do it, or I will claw your face off."

"Now, now, keep your shirt on," he said.

"I mean to."

His eyes widened. "Wait a minute, miss, you've got me all wrong. This here's a fishing knife."

"Well, since there aren't any fish here just now you shouldn't have a problem setting it down, right?" I said.

He lowered one hand slowly, unbuckled the knife—"For shit's sake"—then tossed the blade with a smooth motion so that it hit the ground between us in a puff of dirt, an earthy sigh.

"Why are you here?" I asked. His appearance could hardly be coincidental.

He shook his head. "I'm looking for somebody, tracking a boy with"—his fingers danced in the air—"skin colorings. Maybe you've seen him?"

I wasn't sure what to do. I didn't want to lead this stranger toward my sister and her unmissable guide until I understood what this was about. He reached for his pocket.

"Keep those hands where I can—"

"Calm yourself, missy. I'm thinking a picture's worth a thousand." With slow and careful fingers, he pulled a piece of paper out of his pocket, unfolded it, then held it up for me to see. There, on glossy paper and in living color, was the photo of a familiar inked-up male. Above his head, a single word blared in bold black type: WANTED.

"Is that official?"

"Official enough. These here are scattered all around the state, all the way to Kentucky."

"Hobbs is wanted?"

The man smiled, revealing a set of coffee-stained teeth. "You *have* seen him! Where's he gone, then? I got business with—Whoa, whoa," he said, moving his poster-holding hand behind him as I took a step forward with my fingers outstretched.

"What did he do?" I asked.

"Just a minute now."

"What did he do?" I repeated, my words as pointed as the knife I pinned under my foot.

The man refolded the paper with one hand, his eyes never leaving mine. "Nothing so bad as what you're thinking," he said. "It ain't a cop poster, is it?"

"Tell me, or I don't help you."

He laughed. "I'll find him with or without you, and that's the truth," he said, tucking the page back into his pocket. "But I don't want you afeard for your life, either."

"I'm not afraid."

Again, he laughed. "Sure you're not, but you can know he isn't a rapist or murderer or anything so unsavory as that. He's a thief, see? And it's me who'll bring him to justice if there's any justice to be had."

"If there's a reward to be had, you mean."

His smile faded. I looked him over again, took in the dirty ripped clothing, the grime—evidence of a hard life. Much harder than mine. At least we'd eaten three meals a day, had a roof over our heads. Clothes that were well-kept and well-fitted most of the time, too. Laces on our boots instead of ropes. Sure, he'd be hungry for a reward.

"Who's after him, if not the cops?" I asked. "What did he steal?"

"Nosy one, ain't you?"

"And you're evasive. What did he steal?"

His lips jutted out, like he was kissing the air and it tasted sour, but he remained quiet.

"Listen," I said. "I hate his guts, I want him gone, and I might be inclined to help you if you're honest with me now."

"*Hate*'s a mighty strong word," he said.

"Mighty true, though."

The corners of his eyes creased. "And how do I know you're not gonna turn around and tell him everything I might tell you, missy?" he said. "I've built a trust."

"Well, now you'll have to trust me, won't you?" I said, and crossed my arms over my chest. "What did he do?"

He regarded me. I regarded him back.

And then his features relaxed, and he flapped his lips like a horse. "Tough bird for a young thing," he said, shifting his backpack. "No wonder the crow listened to you."

"So?"

"It's over coins, if you have to know."

I leaned a little further into the conversation. "What sort of coins?"

"The sort you collect, what do you think?"

Quarters, dimes, or silver dollars, Hobbs didn't strike me as the kind of guy to collect coins. But did it matter? This stranger had just provided me with a powerful weapon. Being rid of Hobbs meant Olivia would rely on only me again. She'd have to listen to me, too, because I didn't have a clue how to get to the glades by foot. We'd go home. Today. Then the feeling inside me, the swelling, blistering cauldron of nameless anxiety, would fade into nothing.

"I'll show you where he is," I said, "but you have to take him straightaway."

"What do you mean, 'straightaway'? I can't drag him off by the hair now, can I?"

Why not? I wanted to ask. This man was bigger than Hobbs— just as tall maybe, but stockier.

"These things ain't so easy," he said. "Can't spook him. Gotta reel him in nice and slow-like. That's my way."

He nodded, seemed pleased with himself and his plan. I did not share this satisfaction.

"Your way sounds like it's going to take longer than I want it to take. I want this finished today. I don't want to go another step with him by my side." Or Olivia's.

He grunted. "You're like a hotshot."

"What?"

"A fast train. Too fast for this old man," he said. "I like things done a certain way, see? That's how I do business."

I wanted to grab at his doughy face, knead it until it suited. "This is important. He's manipulating my sister."

"Sister?" His voice sparked with interest. "The black-haired girl from the train, with the big eyes and lashes?"

"That's her," I said.

"Well, well. Yeah, I see some resemblances." He dragged a palm over his scruffy chin. "It's the sister that's the problem. I had things all squared up in Jewel, with a plan to get Hobbs where I wanted him to go. And then your sister showed up, and there went my plan. She's leading him way off course."

"You have that backward," I said. "Hobbs is the one throwing things off course."

He scratched his ear. "Well, don't matter much who's throwing who, does it? Point is, we have something in common here, don't we? A need to get them away from each other. Now, I can't make any promises that we'll find a town today, miss, though we might. I can't right predict what we'll find around a bend, because this ain't my part of the state, see?"

I could hear that in his voice, that he was from somewhere south of Tramp and by a long mile. But I needed something to cling to, if not a promise.

"I want the poster," I said.

"No way."

"Not to call him in but to show my sister. If she knows that he's—"

"No," he said. "The poster stays between us or there is no deal whatsoever, and that is right final. Right final."

I gritted my teeth. I would not be controlled by this new person. Neither could I afford to lose a golden opportunity just now. I'd have to play things just right.

"Then I'm keeping the knife," I said, covering the blade more completely with my foot.

He reared back as if I'd whopped him on the chin. "Now wait a minute, I—"

"Two strange men with two women out in the forest," I said. "I don't think it's too much to ask that I have a weapon on my side, if it turns out you're not as straight-up nice as you want me to think."

"I'd never, I'm not that kind of a—"

"I'm sure you're not," I said. "I still want the knife. Call it insurance."

His face turned whiter still before he grumbled, "Take it, then, but if I catch a fish you're cleaning it, missy."

"We'll see." I scooped up the knife.

His name, he said, was Red Grass, and his plan was simple. Get to civilization as soon as possible, then make the necessary call to turn in Hobbs. I'd take charge of a Hobbs-less Olivia after that.

This was Red Grass's Plan A.

This was not my Plan A.

My Plan A was to extract whatever common sense lay dormant in my sister, make it rise up, realize, and repent. Now. Today. This hour. And then we could go back, back, and I could stop berating myself over why I didn't know my own feelings, because what I'd feel then would be . . . relief.

Common sense. It had to be in there somewhere.

I led the way out of that nook in the forest, past tall weeds with purple flowers that scratched my ankles all over again. I felt a touch of dread when I didn't see Olivia right away, but then I heard voices and found the path that led down to a stream, and found my sister.

In the water. In her underwear. With Hobbs.

Red Grass saw, too, of course. "I'm thinking this isn't going to be easy," he said.

Loath as I was to admit it, I had a feeling he was right.

CHAPTER TEN

Another Way to Look at Things

✳ OLIVIA ✳

I never knew either of my grandfathers.

Papa's father died when he was just a baby. Dušan and Babka had come to America when they were barely out of their teens. Before that, her last name was Pekár, a word that means *baker*, which she said was a sign if ever there was one. (Dušan's last name was Moon, because his father was Scottish, but that's another story.) Babka might've gone back to her native country after Dušan died so young, raised Papa with the help of her own mother, but she decided to stick with the business and make it a success. She has a few pictures of Grandpa Dušan, and they're all dark and grainy. He had a beard. He wasn't thin, but he wasn't fat, either. Babka says he was her missing part, and made her laugh all the time.

Mama's father, Orin, was a different story. There was only one photo of him that I'd ever seen, and most days that stayed over-turned in my parents' bedroom. In the picture, he wore a dark sweater with a white shirt peeking out at the top, a little like a priest. I knew Mama never spoke to him, but she wrote to him in secret. It was eons ago that I made the discovery, after my knee smashed up against the loose floorboard under her desk while playing hide-and-seek with Jazz.

A stash of letters.

Those are private, Mama said when I asked her about them. *Please leave them alone.*

I listened, for the most part, even though I burned with curiosity and knew well enough how to steam open an envelope. (Boil some water in a pot. Hold the envelope, gummy side down, over the steam until you can wiggle a pinky under the sticky flap. Separate the edges real slow, so the paper doesn't rip. You're in.)

Finding the letters kick-started a sort of obsession with my grandfather when I was younger.

What's Grandpa Orin like? I'd ask my father.

A hard man, he'd say.

Strong?

Too strong.

Tall?

Over six feet.

Back then—I might've been seven—I thought Grandpa Orin was like Superman, and so I pictured him bending steel with his pinkie fingers and saving the world. Maybe that's why Mama couldn't see him again, I told myself, because he was so busy and important. Maybe that's why she slept with her bedroom window cracked most of the time, because she knew he'd fly to our house one night and take those letters himself.

My grandpa saves people, I told the kids at school. *No, he's not a policeman or a fireman or a priest. He can fly! He can make a burglar confess just by staring at him long enough, because his eyes can turn to lasers! He wears a bulletproof cape!*

Jazz gave me her blackest look in the lunchroom that day, because of course word got around. My father had to leave the bakery before all the work was done to come have a talk with me, too.

Your grandfather isn't a superhero, he said, as we sat together in the principal's office. *He disowned your mother. He doesn't want to speak with her, not ever again. It's his heart that's hard, not his muscles. He's a banker and an investment expert. A rich one at that. And a bastard*, he added under his breath.

This truth crushed me.

Later, I asked Mama about it, even though I'd been told not to. *Why won't Grandpa Orin talk to us? Why is his heart so hard? Is that why you keep his picture flipped over like a dead fly so much of the time?*

She said something abstract that I didn't understand and forgot straightaway, and left Papa to make dinner that night. She said she only needed a nap, but she slept until morning.

This was a lesson I'd never forget—the way my mind turned in a day, how what I'd *thought* was opposite of what truly *was*. It became my proof, of sorts, that there were at least two ways to look at things. Even when we didn't want to consider what those other ways might be.

My curiosity over Mama's letters never ended, though I didn't ask her about them or Grandpa Orin anymore after that. Every once in a secret while, I'd check to see if the quantity of envelopes in her room had turned yet from eleven to twelve, from twelve to thirteen. And sometimes I swore I felt their presence in our house. Maybe Mama felt them, too, each letter like grains of sand in her eyes, or a pair of leaden feet. Each letter like a wish.

After Mama died, when I was left with the last letter she'd never sent, I lifted the loose floorboard one final time. I wouldn't have added the letter I'd found to the others, but I felt it might be important to view them all together just the same, that maybe I'd learn something from their weight and the scent of their secrets.

But the letters were gone.

I couldn't even ask about them, because I shouldn't have known about them to begin with. So I kept the one letter in my possession, tucked it into a part of my coat where the lining had come unstitched to make a private pocket. I felt it whenever I wore that coat, through a winter that lasted into April, its edges as hard as Grandpa Orin's heart.

Red Grass was still singing his catfish song, and Hobbs had gathered our bottles to refill with filtered stream water, when Jazz pulled me away to stand near a thicket of trees. She'd said it was important, that she needed to talk, but I wouldn't believe she had anything to say that she hadn't already said or wasn't just trying a new tack to make me bend to her will.

As it turns out, I was right.

She used a low, serious voice that chafed like sandpaper. "I thought you'd like to know that your friend Hobbs is a criminal," she said.

Red Grass must've told her this. Maybe this was what Hobbs meant when he called him *an annoying son of a bitch.*

"I know. Hobbs told me himself," I said, and her voice turned to helium.

"And just what is it that he told you?"

I rested with care against the nearest tree, testing it. It was young; I could tell by its smooth bark and slender frame. But that didn't mean it wasn't stable, didn't mean it couldn't hold itself strong in a wind.

"He told me he stole something—"

"Coins," she interjected, but I talked over her.

"—because he wanted to be honest with me, because he wanted me to feel safe, because he's a good person."

"Oh, he's a prize all right. Probably has a blue ribbon tattooed to his ass," she said, and I straightened. "He's uglier than sin, you know, or maybe you're not particular about who you'll shuck your clothes for."

"Why do you hate him so much?" I asked. "You've never even had a regular conversation with him."

"Neither have I shown him my underwear, but there are some

things that aren't worth doing, Olivia. I don't need to talk with him to get what he's about. There's danger written all over his face. And his neck, and his arms, and probably his chest and back," she said. "Now explain this to me: How is it that you knew he was a criminal and left with him anyway? I've always known you had your own hard-to-picture take on life, but I never thought you might actually be stupid before today."

I winced. I'd known Jazz felt this way about me, but she'd never come right out and said she thought I was lacking in brains. I shouldn't have been so surprised to hear it now, should've had a ready response but didn't. I expected the familiar rise of my Jazz nerves—the ones that made me burble like a stream—but they were quiet. Too stunned, maybe, to make an appearance.

She found another sore spot to poke, said, "You're always talking about what Mama would've wanted, what would've made her happy. You think she would've approved of you running all over the state with the likes of Hobbs?"

"Yes," I said. "I think she would've liked him."

"That's bullshit," Jazz said. "She wouldn't have approved, and you know it. She wanted us safe, at home. That's why we never went anywhere."

"That's not why we never went anywhere," I said, full of confidence on this point at least. "We never went anywhere because Mama was afraid."

Brush rustled nearby, and I pictured an animal's search for food. Not all survival instincts were so clear.

"What do you mean, afraid?" Jazz asked, her voice different now, turned blue and thin like new ice.

I almost said, *Now who's blind?* but stopped myself.

Mama had mentioned her desire to see the glades often enough, though she'd never made any plans to visit. Two Septembers ago, after the biscuit bus was replaced with the new van, Papa asked Jazz if she'd be willing to take care of deliveries for a few days so he might surprise Mama with the trip she longed to take. The cranberries would be ripe—it was the perfect time to go. Jazz had agreed, and was already on her way with the biscuits when Papa—who radiated the scent of ripe summer grass even more than normal—gave my mother the news. I stood nearby listening, smiling, expecting elation. Expecting . . . not what happened.

Mama sat at the table and leaned against her hand, splayed fingers over her face like a flesh spider. *I can't, I can't,* she cried. *I don't know why, I—*

Beth? What's wrong, baby? Papa rubbed her back when her breathing turned ragged, his face a patchwork of concern and confusion.

I crouched beside Mama and took her hand, because I knew what to do when this happened, when her shallow sounds filled the house with diagonal sheets of rain.

She caught her breath after a time, but she was in a low mood for three and a half weeks after that. And while I never pressed her over why she couldn't bring herself to go—and she never again talked about going to the glades, for that matter—I thought about it a lot during my rambles, and came up with an idea that made sense enough to me.

Mama had a dream, a hope that if she went to the glades the end of her story would be inspired by one thing or another. She'd finish writing it, she'd send it to her father, and he'd come back to her. She believed, believed.

But not one hundred percent.

Because what if it didn't work? What if she wasn't able to imagine an end even after taking the trip? Or—worse—what if she was, and she finished the story, polished it, published it, made the *New York Times* bestsellers' list even, and Grandpa Orin still pretended that she didn't exist? Wouldn't it be better to stay at home and trust that things would work out when they were meant to, leave it to fate? Wouldn't it be safer to pray at the desk she called an altar, wedge those unsent letters under the floorboard, and keep hold of hope?

Hope was a powerful thing. Difficult to risk.

"Forget it," I said when Jazz nudged my shoulder, told me to wake up. I knew what she'd say about my theory. She'd call me stupid again, call me wrong, then try to derail me with her version of logic.

"Is there any part of you that's reasonable?" she snapped.

"I'm reasonable enough," I told her. "You don't even try to understand."

"You're right, I'll never understand. But, hey, don't let that bother you. You just go right ahead and take charge, Olivia Moon. That's fine with me!" She crossed her arms over her chest. "I'll follow wherever you lead, right off the edge of the fucking planet!"

"You swear too much," I said, right before she told me where I could stick my opinion of her vocabulary.

She thundered away like a black-icicle storm, pushed back at the trees, and made for the stream. Maybe she needed to take her clothes off, too, take a breath. But she wouldn't, that wasn't her way—even if she could use a good dunking.

Jazz may have been right about something, though. Mama might not have wanted us to go on this trip at all. She might even have been slam-on-the-brakes opposed. Because wasn't I risking her dreams by doing this? What if I didn't see a light? Would she have taken that as a sort of confirmation that she'd had the wrong dreams after all?

No. No, I wouldn't believe it. And I hated *what-ifs*; they tasted an awful lot like cheese from a can.

If I was going to do this, I had to believe, believe, one hundred percent from now on. No doubts allowed.

Though I expected something to click into place, for the air to vibrate with certainty, I felt nothing. But maybe it was too hard to notice clicks and vibrations when my sister yelled in the distance about getting to civilization and that we couldn't stop for the night yet. When Hobbs argued back that we were far from civilization and the sun was setting, that this was as good a place as any to sleep and she needed to pull the rod out of her ass. When Red Grass told her to clean the fish he'd caught, since she'd stolen his knife.

I'd listen for that click later, I resolved, when all was still and quiet.

*

The newborn fire that crackled beside the stream looked like a blur of dots after a toss of dice. I couldn't say why, but I felt unsettled by them, maybe because they made it harder to appreciate the red sky's promise of good weather for the next day. Whatever the reason, when an opportunity to step away from camp presented itself, I took it.

I followed Hobbs along the water's edge, stopping when brush snapped underfoot to collect twigs and slender branches already downed by nature.

"You don't have to help, you know." He stopped to assess a tree's black limb.

"I don't mind," I said, well aware that Hobbs didn't need help. It was hard to imagine him as anything other than self-sufficient. But someone had to have taught him along the way. Maybe that's why he took the time to pull folks up to the next rung on Darwin's ladder—to pay it forward, or pay it back. "How do you know to do all this stuff, anyhow?"

"Learned it." He pulled at the limb appraisingly. "Did what I had to do."

Your friend Hobbs is a criminal.

Maybe that was something he felt he'd had to do, too.

"Why did you take what you took from your father?" I asked him.

"The coins?" he said, as if I'd already known that detail. "Red put you up to this? He send you on a fishing expedition with me?"

"Red Grass didn't ask me anything about it." I crouched, added sticks to the growing pile in my arms. "Why would he?"

"I got stupid one night thanks to Vladimir, told Red I had some coins. Now he won't shut up about them—how he could sell them, how I could be rich and not even know it. Like I'd ever hand them over." He wrenched branches from the limb—one, then another. "You're the only one who knows the whole truth—that I took them and from who—so just keep it to yourself, hear?"

I rose again to my feet. "I will."

I might've told him he was wrong—that Jazz knew he'd stolen the coins, and probably Red Grass, because who else could've told her?—but I had a different goal then.

"What I asked, I asked just for me," I said. "I find you interesting, is all."

"Stop that."

"What?"

"Trying to get inside my head," he said, and continued crack-pop-cracking.

"Why? What's inside your head that isn't fit for company?"

He laughed, said, "Plenty. I'd offer to trade you one dark secret for another"—*crack*—"but my guess is you don't have any dark secrets to trade, little Livya."

"I blinded myself."

"What? How?" He turned toward me then, though I couldn't tell if his look conveyed interest, pity, or anything that might bear a label worth naming.

"Staring at the sun."

"Why would you do that?" he asked slowly. Interest.

I could've told him that the sun smelled like Mama. It might've been enough to hear, had been for my family. But even though it was true, I knew it wasn't the full truth. *Be real.*

"You tell me something first," I said.

Metallic mist came from his mouth when he made a sound like a deflating tire. "I hate my old man. Those coins are the one thing he cares about." A pause, and then, "Why did you do it?"

"I don't know why," I said. Truth.

"Don't you?" he asked. "People give a lot of fancy reasons for the things they do, but I've found it always comes down to one of two things." When I stared off to the side of him, I noticed a blur of art on his neck. "They're getting something for doing it, or they're avoiding something by doing it. Pleasure, or pain."

He made it sound so simple. As if the truth had to be a clear and accessible thing. As if it might never be as elusive as ghost breath.

I pushed myself, tried to find an answer. Why had I done it? How could a person not understand why she had done something like that? But there was little about that time—that repeated act— that I understood or wanted to remember.

March sunlight.

Dead grass under my legs.

My eyes watering for more than one reason.

A vague sense that I was doing a wrong thing. A bad, messed-up thing. A truly dysfunctional thing. Despite that, it seemed I had no choice but to do it, that my sacrifice would help in some way.

It had not helped. Why had I ever imagined that it would?

"There was no pleasure in it," I said, which was about the only thing I could say for sure.

"What were you thinking about when you did it?"

I hugged the small pile of brush in my arms, and a stick jabbed at the raw skin beneath my bandage. "Dreams."

"What sort of dreams?"

It wasn't comfortable having someone pick through your brain matter, I decided. Especially matter you hadn't already picked through yourself in a satisfactory way—that, frankly, you wanted to avoid.

"I don't want to talk about this anymore," I said, and walked away from him, farther from camp, catching stray beams of late-day sun between tree branches, losing them again in an erratic parade of shadow and light.

"Hey." He tossed branches onto the ground and followed behind me. "Nothing brings on pain like a dream. You don't need 'em."

"No?" I bent to gather more sticks. "I can't imagine life without 'em. Not any more than I can imagine living without the hills of West Virginia."

"I've lived without both just fine. Mountain after mountain out there to explore," he said, coming to stand beside me again, bringing that scent of his. "Plenty to life beyond what you see here."

I could picture this: Hobbs, walking for forever and a day. And despite my need to step away from a conversation that had become a little *too* real—or maybe because of that—I smiled.

"I like you," I said.

"You mentioned that once before."

"Some things are worth saying more than once."

"You don't know me to like me. That's worth repeating, too."

"I know enough, and I know what I like," I said. "I like your name. I like that you say what you think without caring too much how it comes out. I like that you help others, even if you don't like thanks for that help. I like your tattoos, even if I can't see them as well as I might. I like that you've traveled all over, that you move all the time to see new things and meet new people. It's probably why you smell so interesting."

"That's the nicest way anyone's ever told me that I stink."

"It's a good smell," I said with a laugh. "Like you've picked up layers from all the places you've visited. I like that, too." I just barely resisted the impulse to push my nose into his skin and sniff.

He settled his hands on his head. I couldn't tell what that meant—if he was hiding himself all of a sudden or feeling boastful that I'd named so many things to like. Another thing to figure out.

"How do you decide where you'll go next?" I asked, getting back to exploring his head instead of vice versa. "Do you trust fate to put you wherever you need to be?"

This had been one of Mama's primary philosophies, one that had always felt like a comfort. That all of life's twists and turns might be analyzed at some later date, shown to be necessary in order to arrive at some other point in the future—a point that would end up being important in a life.

If fate hadn't intervened, I might never have tripped on my heels, dug my teeth into your father's shoulder, and fallen in quick mad love, Mama had said more than once.

But Hobbs wasn't an enthusiast.

"I don't believe in fate," he said.

The dicelike imagery from the fire came to mind. While Papa had never been one to downplay fate, he'd been more vocal about the power of luck.

Lucky for me the side entrance to the store was locked when I arrived at the college the morning I met your mother, or I never would've had to take the back way or the stairs, Papa would say.

Maybe men preferred luck over fate, even if they were two sides of the same coin.

"Luck, then?" I asked.

"Knew a guy named Lucky once," Hobbs said. "He was a hopper, same as me, but one night he got drunk and fell asleep near the rails. Too near. Train went over his legs, took 'em both right off his body but left him living. Don't know where he is now, but I have a feeling he's not calling himself Lucky anymore."

I tried to shove the image of a man sliced like a pizza by a train out of my head. "Do you believe in anything at all?"

"My own two feet." He flicked his hands over his pants.

I stood to face him again. "And what if you didn't have those feet anymore? What would you do if you were like Lucky, and they were taken from you?"

"Probably wrap my mouth around the barrel of a gun."

My insides wrenched as a vision of him in our kitchen with an open oven door filled my head. I wanted to denounce what he'd said, convince him that he could survive without feet the way I'd survive without perfect vision and that life would still be worth living. Instead, I stood strong within my illusion of the not-quite-weakest-thing-in-the-forest and said, "Don't rely on anything but yourself." Luck or fate. Prayers or dreams. Another person. "That's your guide to life?"

"Living in the now and following instincts keeps me alive."

"I get that," I said, and felt a thread of steel in my spine again. "Instincts are what made me pack a bag with my mother's ashes, leave my family and all I've known to take this trip in the first place. They're what tell me even now that what I'm doing is the right thing, no matter who thinks I'm stupid for it."

"That's it," he said, coming closer. "That's freedom. Tastes good, doesn't it?"

I licked my lips, tasted sweetness in their dry cracks.

Hobbs laughed. "Maybe you'll live the life of a hopper yet, Wee Bit. All the best livin' happens on the edges."

My fingers flexed over the bark. "Does it?"

"It's like that saying: 'Beyond this place there be dragons.' Those dragons aren't out there for nothing," he said, and the curve of his voice gleamed like gold. "They have secrets hiding under all that loot of theirs, and they're worth finding. And the dragons at the edges of the map are friendlier than the ones at home, at any rate."

I wanted to ask him about that. Home. His parents. The loot he'd taken. But something inside—instinct—said not to probe any-more there now, that Hobbs would shut down on me just as he'd begun to open. Instead, I said, "So you think all of life's answers are out there for the taking. But where do the questions come from without dreams to pull you along?"

"I smell 'em on the wind."

"What do you smell on the wind, exactly?" I twisted my lips, enjoying myself more than I ever could've thought possible. "Wait, don't tell me. Dragons. Adventure."

"Ladies in need of saving."

And, just like that, I was over the slippery grip wall that was Hobbs. He wanted to matter, to be impactful. The scent of dragon was in truth the scent of human connection. He might not call it a dream, but it was *wanting* just the same, and semantics, to my way of thinking.

"Well, there is that, isn't there?" I said, giving him what he needed and what was true at the same time. "You *are* saving me—helping me, at any rate—and when I need you the most. Don't you think that's an argument in favor of things happening for a reason?

One for the folks who'd like to believe in the helpful hand of fate, or at least luck?"

"Maybe," he said, and then his tone darkened in a way I could only describe as plush. "But what makes you think I'm here to rescue you and not just devour?"

"I might still say it's luck," I said, my voice taking on a darkness all its own.

There were no snapping branches or movements between us then. Only a sense of seeing that went beyond what anyone might perceive with eyes.

He's uglier than sin, you know.

I doubted I would believe that even if I weren't living life on the periphery and bound for a further edge, if I could see Hobbs's dragon-camouflage skin with all its details. Liking him felt more honest than anything I'd experienced before, too, maybe because of its quick-form, raw-wound beginning and lack of clarity, its sheer instinct, and the fact that neither of us had turned yet to run in the other direction.

"You don't scare me, Hobbs."

"Said the girl who stared at the sun."

I imagined I could feel the gentle tug along the hairs of my arms as he breathed me in, assessing my need for saving, right before Jazz called out that she'd found a dead animal.

"We'd better check that out," I said, responding to the jittery pitch of my sister's voice, though I hated to move.

Hobbs gathered the wood he'd dropped to the forest floor before we made our way back to camp, as I wondered over the trails left by dragons, the remnants of their kills.

June 1, 1997

Dear Dad,

*I am having one of my up-and-downs. This is a
down, a black hole, worse than it's been in a long
time. Drahomíra moved out of the house a few weeks
ago, which has upset us all—most of all Branik, who
avoids conflict at all costs. It was because of me,
Dad—a fight she and I had over a piece of my past.
Our past.*

*Do you remember that old wooden chest I hauled
to the dorms at Kennaton? It must've been Mom's,
because when I first claimed it for my own I
discovered a few of her things. I think you must not
have known about it at all, or those things would've
made their way out of the house along with all the
rest of her "bling and glitz," as you called it. There
was a scarf in there, purple and breezy, with clear
beads on the fringe that might've chimed like bells but
(sadly) did not, because they were made of plastic.
There were some garter belts in there, too—black
with metal clips on the ends—and a bra that never*

would've fit me because I'd never be endowed like Mom. But none of those things attracted me as much as the coat.

The coat that hugged the bottom of the trunk took up too much room and weighed as much as a small child. It was a bell of a black fur coat, maybe more like a cape. Despite the omnipresent scent of mothballs, slipping it on made me feel like a diva extraordinaire. I kept it all, because there were so few parts of Mom to keep, and those things opened a window into her life—a life that I came to feel was nothing short of mysterious and, at times, scandalously appealing.

Now, imagine my six-year-old finding the trunk, and seeing it as the jackpot of all dress-up bins. I found her wearing the lot of it. The purple flounce of a scarf kissing up against her black hair. The obscenely pointed bra and matching garters sagging like elephant skin over her white panties and pink-bowed undershirt. And the black coat, floating despite its weight around her shoulders, sweeping the ground like the cape of a queen.

Drahomira laughed nearby as Jazz put on a show, dancing like a showgirl.

I hollered. Out of that stuff. Out of the trunk. Naughty girl.

I swatted my daughter's bottom once I'd pulled the clothes off her, and she ran to her room, crying.

Drahomira stared at me with an open mouth. What had Jazz done that was so horrible?

I couldn't say, "Jazz can't be like Suzanne Howell, the worst of all people on the planet. She shouldn't wear her clothes, dream her dreams, touch any part of her past or glorify her in any way. She shouldn't be tempted." I wanted the trunk to stay secret and mine. I wanted my daughter safe from an awareness that had rooted in me like a longing, despite my best efforts to keep those roots at bay.

Was that so wrong?

I'm sure there are gaps in my logic. I'm not myself right now, I know that. But however much sense

*I'm making now, I made much less with Drahomíra
then.*

*I can't recall how the conversation spun as it
did, into an argument about wasted lives and
opportunities. What became clear in those naked
moments, garters strewn all over the floor, was that
my mother-in-law disapproved of me. I was happy
to point out the things that should be different, she
said—the need for a town paper, a better sign at
the bakery, more money and a family vacation to
anywhere—yet I did nothing to create change. Why
didn't I work for what I wanted? There was no one
to stop me. Instead, I clung to my discontentment and
a moth-eaten coat, and acted the role of mercurial
queen whenever I wasn't indulging in a nap. Is
that what I wanted my children to learn from their
mother? she asked. How to live like a victim?*

*I think I told her to get out, though it's hazy to me,
like a faded nightmare. Get out. Of her own home.
The home she'd made in Tramp with her husband
before I was ever even born. The home she'd opened
to me when Branik and I married, when I carried*

her first grandchild. Get out. She left. She is staying with a friend down the road and says she'll remain there until she can find another place to live.

The next morning, Jazz decided to get out, too; she sneaked out of the house and down the road to see her grandmother. She knows I don't allow her out of the house without permission, and though this was the first time she's ever broken the rules, I was furious when I found her crawling back in through a window and learned what she'd done. I spanked her until we both cried. I know you believe a spank every now and then is okay, but I'd never laid an angry hand on her until the trunk incident, until I saw her glorying in Mom's old skeletons and awakened to the lure of their bones.

I will never hit her or anyone ever again. I swear this to you now, and, even more, I swear it to myself. Still, I feel . . . fractured, as if I've beaten my own bones and lost a piece of myself in the process. Branik says we can't change what's done, that he trusts me not to hit Jazz again, and that the well of despair I feel growing deeper is all in my head.

I know you always thought I let my emotions have too much control over my actions, Dad, that I needed to learn how to rule life with my brain. But I've never figured out how to suppress <u>feeling</u> when it surges in me like a tsunami, destroying all the sensible structures I've built up over time.

How do you suppress a tsunami?

I cannot control the shifts of land that cause them, or predict when those shifts will happen or even how they'll be triggered.

And Jazz . . . I don't know why I let it bother me so much that she's attached to Drahomira. I think she would move in with her grandmother if I let her, and then her future would be limited to running the bakery and making scratchy blankets out of squares of yarn. Is it so wrong to want more for her when she could do and be anything she set her mind to? If you knew her, you'd see what I mean. You'd find a way to hone her potential, because there's so much within her—a drive I never had, along with a brain and an ability to set her priorities in line and stick to them. She is so much like you.

I can't tell yet who Olivia resembles the most, though she is attached—wholly, thankfully, to me. And she is such a happy toddler. I can hardly bear to look at her sometimes, because the light of her brings tears to my eyes, like staring at the sun. Sometimes she's even able to pull me out of an up-and-down just by being herself. Sometimes not. Sometimes the tsunami takes me, and I can't even walk to the grocery store for milk or eggs, or stay awake. I suppose some wells of despair are too deep for even a light as bright as Olivia to fill.

Overly dramatic and self-pitying. That's me right now. Unfit company for even a paper father.

Beth

CHAPTER ELEVEN

A History of Oran

* JAZZ *

My mother's service was held at Rutherford & Son Funeral Home in Kennaton, with a handful of people in attendance—some I recognized and others I didn't know at all. Maybe the strangers were friends from some other life, from college. My eyes swept over them once, like dust under a rug.

My father was trying to hold it together, I could tell. Olivia and Babka cried openly. They had the same bone structure, the same heart-shaped face, the same arch to their eyebrows. They wore the same *how-did-this-happen, this-can't-be-happening* expression, as if they expected someone to wake them any second, pinch them into reality again, because this was not a thing that was possible.

Beth Moon could not be dead.

Beth Moon was a mother.

Beth Moon was a wife.

Beth Moon had been teacher to Olivia.

Beth Moon had a story to write.

Beth Moon could not be dead.

She could not have killed herself.

I watched it all from a strange position—beside my grandmother and my sister but somehow not there at all, like an arm out of joint, waiting for something to snap me back into place. I did not cry. I did not feel. I didn't want to, either.

Classical music played around us, soft and somber and low. I recognized piano. Violins. Three couches and eight chairs spanned the room. I noted their arrangement, the way each was decorated with pillows to be as aesthetically pleasing and as comfortable as possible. These were the things I thought as I tried not to look into my mother's open casket.

Dear friends, said someone—a priest, maybe—and I stood there and didn't listen.

Funerals were expensive; I wasn't sure how we would afford this. A random thought. I let it go.

The man stopped speaking.

The day ended, and we went home, and I crawled into bed but couldn't sleep.

Later, during that time when my father drove Olivia and me around with him in Kennaton, when my skin didn't feel like my own, when I walked the city and collected obituaries, I found my mother's death notice in the library.

BETH MOON
Beth Moon, 43, passed away the third Tuesday of
February at her home. She is survived by her husband,
Branik Moon; her two children, Jazz Marie, and Olivia
Francis; and her mother-in-law, Drahomíra Moon.
Funeral services will be held this coming Wednesday
at 1:00 P.M. at Rutherford & Son Funeral Home,
245 Main Street, Kennaton, with calling hours held
an hour before, from noon to 1:00.

Short and impersonal. Nothing about her parents, or any of that pain. Nothing about how she died. Nothing about her story or homeschooling my sister or the secrets she'd hidden under the floorboard—these things that filled the years and months and days of a now finished life. There was a person and now there was not a person. Now there was this piece of paper, and memories of a priest droning on in a smokescreen place about a woman he'd never known, and none of it made sense.

None of it made sense.

But when we got home that night and my father and sister went upstairs to sleep, it was I who stayed behind to check that all the lights were off, that the door was locked, that the gas was not running in the kitchen.

Finding an animal dead on the stream bank pushed me over the proverbial edge. A raccoon, Hobbs said, and probably rabid, considering how emaciated it looked, how dehydrated. So close to what it needed yet unable to take it in.

The anxiety I'd felt all day didn't care whether or not I understood it. It swelled inside me, consuming reason, leaving me with nothing but a bunch of irrational thoughts and skittery nerves. And so while Hobbs tended to the fire, while Olivia hummed a song, while Red Grass griped that I'd done a piss-poor job of preparing the fish, while somewhere my grandmother and father were at their homes, eating (or drinking), or taking a nap under familiar roofs and in familiar beds, I struggled to breathe.

It was almost as if my body had forgotten how to do it, my mind too busy racing from one thought to the next to remember: *in and out*. I'd wondered many times over the last few months what it might feel like to die. Now it crescendoed in me, a certainty that this was it, that I would die then and there.

Lost.
Homeless.
Wild.
Chaotic.
Emotional.

Reckless.

Mad.

Unbalanced.

Unreasonable.

Uncontrollable.

Unwilling.

Unthinking.

Unsafe.

Shaking.

Crushing.

Sweating.

Hot.

Freezing.

Tingling.

Floating.

Smothering.

Fading.

Failing.

Detaching.

Decaying.

Declining.

Turning to dust.

"Jazz?"

Olivia stood below me somehow; I felt outside of my own body, looking down on us both. And though I appeared alive there in the weeds beside her, I also seemed more beast than human. Panting, red in the face, so close to what I needed yet unable to take it in.

Hobbs and Red Grass closed in around us.

"The hell?" Hobbs said.

"Scared of bears or somethin'?" said Red Grass. "You see one, you stand up tall and pound your chest." He provided an example, growled.

I watched myself hold up my palm.

Go. Go away. If I was going to die, it would not be with two train hoppers hanging over me. I heard my heart pound double time in my chest, like I'd been running with a murderer on my tail.

"I'll take care of her," said Olivia. I watched her sit close to me, put her arms around me, put her palm against my head and rest it on her shoulder. "You guys go back to the fire."

"I'm dying," I heard myself say.

"You're not. I'm here. You're here."

"I'm not here."

"Feel this?" She rubbed her hand against my head. I felt it. "You're here, and you're going to be okay. Breathe slow breaths instead of quick ones and you'll feel better. Try."

"I think"—breathe—"my heart"—breathe—"is going"—breathe—"to explode."

"It won't," she said, and rubbed again. "Take a long breath this time, like this."

She breathed. I breathed.

It might've been fifteen minutes. It might've been seventeen hours. But we sat and breathed together until my heart slowed and I came back to myself, to weak muscles and heavy limbs and a dry mouth.

"You're exhausted," said Olivia. "Why don't you try to sleep? I'll take care of you."

I didn't have the will to argue.

The last thing I remember, before I closed my eyes and lay against a blanket I'd never seen before, was that I handed my sister the knife.

I dreamed of a city under siege. A pigeonless, treeless, gardenless city, forced into a state of quarantine after the rats came and the plague hit, its dying and scrambling citizens made to do without the railroad or contact with loved ones on the outside.

I stood inside the gate of this doomed place with my hands on the bars, begging for someone to let me out as blood-eyed vermin bit at my bare toes. Dozens of fellow citizens stood beside me, crashing against the bars as well. Their lips moved as if they, too, cried out, yet they made no noise. I continued to yell, they continued to hit. No one came.

Finally, another's cry—a real sound. I turned to find a closed casket behind me, which was not so strange in a city full of the dead, but saw no one.

"Help me, help!"

The plea came from inside the coffin.

My fingers curved around the lip of the wood, ready to lift the lid, when a shot rang out and the casket jolted.

"And stay dead!" said a man I couldn't see.

The silent people turned thin, then faded to ghost lights and disappeared like smoke. The casket became a bird cage, its bars narrower and narrower until I could see that inside it lay a mound of person with brown hair and freckles.

A hand landed on my shoulder, and I swung out at it.

"Jazz!"

I opened my eyes to find a night sky and a dim form over me.

"Are you all right?" Olivia asked.

Where was I? I felt like I'd been hit by a small biscuit bus. I pushed up on my elbows, reorienting myself. Oh, right. In the woods with my sister and two strangers; I'd left her alone with these men after my body forgot how to breathe. Left her, to dream about a place I'd read about in a book.

Again.

For whatever reason, my mind didn't seem able or willing to leave the city of Oran.

In the distance, a small tent sat beside a low-burning fire. Hobbs twirled a long stick in the flames. Someone snored. The only disaster, then, had been in my mind.

Olivia crouched beside me. "You were dreaming, I think. Do you remember what about?"

Oran, gun shots, and ghost lights. Our mother's face. I didn't want to talk about any of it, especially the feelings I'd had. These were not Olivia's realities or her nightmares.

"Nothing you'd understand." I wiped at my eyes, clearing away a rim of crust. "You've never felt trapped in your life."

"You have?"

There was genuine surprise in her voice. Which genuinely surprised me. Couldn't she see how different our lives had been growing up?

"Here's a wake-up call," I said. "We had different mothers. You had a buddy who let you wander through whatever subjects you felt like studying for your so-called school, and let you wander all over town, too, to have fun and do whatever the hell you wanted. I was made to take a different road. Stay in school and study everything like all the other kids, and stay at home instead of roaming around—unless it was to find you, of course. Learn to make some money if I could, or at least learn to make a good meal for the family." I slapped at my leg, sure that I'd been bitten by at least a hundred mosquitoes. "I was forced to do what was right and sane and sensible."

"Forced? Was what you would've done *not* right and sane and sensible?" When I didn't answer, her wide eyes went wider still. "Do you still feel trapped? Maybe working at the funeral home isn't—"

"Jesus Christ, here we go," I said. "Do me a favor and don't start with this right now." I took a breath—a long one—and let it out slowly.

After a minute, she said, "What happened to you earlier happened to Mama sometimes. She always said it was getting her breathing under control that was the key."

I stared at her. "I don't remember that happening. When did that happen?"

"At home," she said. "During the day most of the time, when it was just the two of us. It was always pretty quick. Has it ever happened to you before tonight?"

"No."

"Well, I'm glad you're all right now."

She told me that I'd been asleep for a few hours and missed a dinner of fish and beans, then brought me a handful of granola bars. Red Grass and Hobbs had made an inventory of the food we had between us earlier—biscuits and peanut butter, beef jerky and trail mix, tuna fish, more beans, oatmeal, Ramen noodles, and a block of cheese—before slinging the food bag over a tree limb to keep it from the bears. Olivia had kept a secret stash for me, but if I hadn't woken up before she went to sleep she would've eaten it herself and buried the wrappers until morning. She wouldn't risk bears.

Common sense. Foresight. What a surprise.

As I chewed on the last bite of the first granola bar, sitting across from my sister on that scratchy blanket, I struggled to find words to express what I needed to say. I wondered if Olivia sensed that, because she stayed rooted there, quiet, as if waiting. The first part, at least, was easy.

"Thank you for everything you did earlier," I said, brushing crumbs from my mouth. "You were there when I needed you, and I won't forget that anytime soon."

She nudged my foot with hers. "Sure."

I stumbled ahead. "There were a few seconds there, when all of that was happening, when I couldn't see anything." A handful of moments when everything went black, when fear peaked, when I thought for sure I'd die—or at least pass out. I knew it wasn't the same for Olivia, but it seemed the same enough. "I want you to know . . . I want to say that I'm sorry about your eyes."

I'd never said that before—that simple sentiment of regret for what was and couldn't be changed—but it seemed important, somehow, to say it now. And, regardless of how or why it had happened, I meant it.

"Thanks," she said. "That means a lot."

The fire popped. Red Grass continued to snore. I glanced at Hobbs, who sneered back at me.

"Do you still have that knife?" I asked Olivia, and she handed it over.

She lingered awhile longer, then joined Hobbs by the fire. I lay on my back, and while I traced the bumps on the knife's handle with my fingers, I traced the bars of Oran in the stars with my eyes. I didn't like thinking about it—my mother in a cage or a casket. *Just a dream*, part of me said, but another part said, *Maybe not*. She'd killed herself. And Olivia said she'd experienced the sort of anxiety I'd felt tonight, more than once.

Had our mother felt . . . trapped? Not just right before she turned on the oven gas but before? How often? What was going through her head when she felt that way? What had she done to make sense of it all? Or didn't she know herself any better than I knew myself?

Beth Moon, forty-three, passed away on the third Tuesday in February at her home after living a miserable life.

Unsatisfied.
Unhappy.
Smothered.
Fading.
Failing.
Detaching.
Decaying.
Declining.
Turning to dust.

Later, when I looked back up at the stars, I didn't imagine the bars of Oran. I saw the freckles that had covered my mother's face.

After I ate, and drank the rest of my water, I pulled the rough blanket I'd slept on toward what remained of the fire.

Olivia, at some point, had curled up beside the sleeping criminal. Just as I looked at him, his eyes opened, like I'd set off some sort of radar or something.

"Keep your hands off my sister," I said.

He smiled, said, "Can't help my draw with the ladies." So close to getting punched in the face for a second time.

A rattling snore came from inside the tent. I looked at it, then back at Hobbs.

He shrugged. "Red Grass wasn't about to let a good tent go to waste after you girls didn't seem to want it."

I kept my voice low. "How noble of you to step in and try to change his mind. You know we would've used it. I was just . . . indisposed."

"Call it whatever you want. I never said I was noble."

"I hate you more than I can express," I said.

"Oh, I don't know," he said, and closed his eyes. "I think you've expressed it pretty well."

"Fuck you," I whispered.

"Fuck you, too," he said, somehow hearing me. "And sweet dreams."

I stared after him, but he didn't open his eyes again. Minutes later, he was snoring lightly beside my sister.

That right there? Was something to watch.

Olivia and Hobbs were strangely alike, both wild as the wind. But whatever had started would end soon enough. Tomorrow we'd find civilization, Red Grass would implement his plan, and it would be over. Until then, I'd close my eyes for a few minutes. I'd breathe.

My hand was still wrapped around the knife when I awoke. The others were already up, had already stuffed the tent back into its pouch and reattached it to Red Grass's pack, pulled down the food bag, and refilled our water bottles. Olivia stood knee-deep in the stream wearing another of our mother's old T-shirts, her arms held out like she was the second coming, and whatever had happened between us in the night seemed a million miles away.

The anxiety I'd felt yesterday, that had crescendoed into a sort of personal hell the night before? That seemed better, for whatever reason. The men didn't ask about it, why I'd felt so terrified and lost and smothered by my own thoughts. This might've been an unanticipated show of politeness on their part or simple apathy, but regardless I was grateful. It might be a new day, but I didn't understand myself any more than I ever did. I could only hope I never experienced anything like that again, or had to endure another night in the woods. I scratched at my skin, counted twenty bug bites on my right arm alone.

I found a single biscuit beside an open jar of peanut butter on a nearby rock and ate it. Brought my bottle up to my lips and drank as a V of birds flew over us, heading who knew where. It didn't seem like the time of year for travel.

After we grabbed our packs and gathered the displaced bits of ourselves from the grasses and the bank, I asked Red Grass which way to civilization. I met his eyes and let mine ask, *We're still doing this, aren't we? Still on the same page?* He nodded, with his brows creased just enough to tell me what I needed to know, then pointed in a direction that seemed southerly based on the risen sun.

I took the lead. Maybe it was insensible, maybe I didn't know where we were going, exactly, but if someone had to lead the V, I'd rather be the one to do it. If anyone thought this was a bad idea, they wisely kept their opinion to themselves.

I still had the knife.

CHAPTER TWELVE

Crossroads

✳ OLIVIA ✳

A thin-fingered dawn touched the sky as I woke. The fire had died, and the air had chilled. Babka's words lingered in my mind like a fog.

You'll have to choose.

I'd dreamed again about my family, stuck in a hall. Papa was there, sitting with his legs crossed and spinning the blue jar that held Mama's ashes. When the jar stopped, he'd kiss it, then spin it again. Sometimes it spun itself into a bottle of Vladimir.

Babka stood before a wall that held the calendar in my mind. She warned me to be careful, then lifted a flaming *S* right off Saturday and stuck it in her pocket.

I didn't see Jazz, so I ran down the hall, following the sound of hissing ellipses and the fainter note of a drum—an animal-skin call of *wrongdreams, wrongdreams, wrongdreams.*

The hall split, each end bearing a bobbing ghost light. I stopped, unsure what to do, which way to go.

"I'm dying," someone said with a voice that washed itself of identity and direction.

Jazz?

"Dreams like feet better than knees," said Babka, her voice some-where above me. "What do your insides tell you to do?"

I didn't know.

"You'll have to choose."

I couldn't choose.

Beside me, Hobbs continued to sleep. I shifted until I could see my sister, and braided my hair until the sun rose.

J azz led the way that morning as we tramped through an espe-cially dry section of forest. The sound of sticks splintering crisply underfoot looked, in my mind, like shimmering Viking ships, with a swoop of features on either end—a curved tail, a crested head with teeth.

Maybe it was because I'd had a decent night's sleep, but I was get-ting better at this, tripping less. Avoiding more reliably the stumps and divots and rocks. It helped, too, that Hobbs had made my bag easier to deal with, attaching makeshift straps to the handle so that I could wear it on my back. It wasn't the most comfortable thing in the world, and it swished a broom-sweep of magenta alongside me with every step, but it was light enough and my hands liked their freedom.

"Hey, Hobbs!" my sister would call back on occasion.

"Bitch?" he'd say by way of address.

"This still the right way?"

He'd say we were fine or adjust us a bit, directing us through a patch of cattails or up a hill thick with the scent of warm pine. Once, I asked about the flowers we were passing—red and slight and dotting the land in abundance.

"I don't know, Olivia," Jazz said, assuming I was asking her. "I'm not equipped to be your tour guide."

Hobbs stopped and squatted near the plants. "They're a type of clover." He pulled something free. "And here's a find. You can eat these if you're hungry." He tucked half a dozen stems into my hand.

More than once, I felt his arm brush against mine in a way that might've been accidental or intentional but that always made me smile. There was a sort of comfort to having him nearby, this green-eyed boy with a voice that curved like a hammock, that made me want to crawl right into it and lie down. I kept him talking, asked him to tell a ghost story—because every West Virginian worth his salt knew at least a dozen. He didn't disappoint, told the tale of a man named Earl McGuffin who'd killed his three daughters and his wife by drowning them in a river before flinging himself off a bridge.

"Bridge used to be the color of stone," Hobbs said, his hand against my spine as we walked through a field, my calves pricked and tickled at once by tall growing things. "But now it's white with ghostly spirit. Buggers won't leave, neither."

I thought about spirits and their ways, and how water was a big mirror.

Afterward, he asked about the chocolate sky I'd mentioned the day before—the way I could see sound in voices, footfalls, even the suitcase bumping against my back—and I explained everything as best I could.

"One?" he asked, quizzing me on my numbers.

"One tastes like warm blueberries."

"Two?"

"Scrambled eggs, still hot."

"Three?"

"Raw hamburger."

"Four?"

"Undercooked spaghetti."

He groaned. "Torture. Is everything food?"

We were all ready for lunchtime, even though it was hours off yet. "Ask me about five."

"What is it?"

"Wet sand."

When I mentioned what music did to me, what it made me see, he stopped and unzipped his bag. Seconds later, I heard the reedy hum of a harmonica, and a bright zip of a song that painted the sky with dashes of cornfield blue and rich gold. Red Grass clapped and stomped, started to sing about creasy greens. I twirled a time or two myself, and kept to my feet despite a few rolling acorns beneath them.

The break was short-lived, but it was long enough to turn the course of things.

"Can we get going now, or do we want to just forget this whole hiking-to-the-glades thing and have us a concert?" said Jazz, who stood leaning against a tree. I heard the tap-tapping of her foot, out of time with everything else. "I'd like to get where we're going by nightfall."

"Hope you packed your broom," said Hobbs.

That's when it became clear that assumptions had been made and details lost in the shuffle of hot-and-dusty minutes the day before, and that Jazz hadn't been told exactly how long the trip would take by foot. She wasn't happy about the realities when I filled her in, either, her voice piercing the air like a dagger.

"Two more days?"

"Well, now, there's got to be something around here, Hobbs." I heard an eager note in Red Grass's voice, a tremble like a leaf clinging to its tree. "Someplace the little ladies can take a load off, have a burger, something? And you and me, we can do our business."

"We'd have to redirect to get to someplace like that now," Hobbs said, "and we shouldn't if—"

"Yes, we should," said Jazz.

"We got places to be, people to see," said Red Grass, patting his wrist as if he was wearing a watch, even though he wasn't. "Appointments."

I didn't know what Red Grass was talking about, what sort of appointments he might have with Hobbs, and it didn't seem like Hobbs knew what he was talking about, either.

"We don't have any plans, Red—not a single one. Now settle down," he said.

"Vittles are fading fast," said Red Grass, shaking his head. "Got some noodles for dinner, but we're gonna need something to stick to our ribs. Should I start hunting for rabbits?"

"You have a gun?" Jazz asked.

"Of course, I do," said Red Grass. "And no, I'm not gonna give it to you, missy, so don't bother asking."

Jazz continued to argue. She needed to call our grandmother, check on the bus, have a real meal, for God's sake—reminding me that she hadn't eaten more than granola bars and a biscuit with peanut butter over the last day. If there was a way to make it happen, to get us to a restaurant for food and a comfortable break, she wanted Hobbs to see it done.

"Olivia, tell him to do it. Be reasonable," she said, even though I'd stayed quiet, taking it all in.

"Your call, Wee Bit," said Hobbs. "But it means going off course."

I listened to Jazz's breathing, and thought maybe it was faster than it should've been. I didn't want her to feel again the way she'd felt last night. A chill skittered over my skin like a stone on water when I recalled how bad it had been for her.

I'm dying.

What if it happened again?

You'll have to choose.

We could go somewhere. Maybe that would be best. Find a restaurant, a phone. A new way to the glades that didn't involve trekking through the forest.

What do your insides tell you to do?

I still wasn't sure, but I said, "I guess it wouldn't hurt to get out of the woods for a while. You'll stay with us, won't you?" I asked Hobbs. "After we get there?"

When he answered, it was with a voice that lacked its usual curve. "We'll see," he said. "I still got both my feet."

He led the way after that, leaving my hands as empty as before, but chill and wanting.

✳

By late morning, it had become a boiling-oil day—so hot and murky it made the bird chatter turn to bursts of popcorn in the sky. My shirt stuck to my body. Everyone but Hobbs complained that their feet hurt and they wanted a nap. We stopped twice more for water. Kept going. Eventually we heard highway sounds.

"Civilization?" asked Jazz, her voice bright.

"It's life," said Hobbs. "But it's just a highway."

"Life," Red Grass echoed. "And death."

Beside the road stood a cross, tall and white. Beyond it, cars drove past in a scatter of eraser bits.

We found a long slab of rock sitting in the shade like a lazy dog and leaned against it as we pulled food from our bags. It was finally lunchtime. We ate cold beans and tuna with plastic forks, and used napkins for plates even though they bled through with juice. Maybe it was because that cross hovered nearby that death seemed to be on all our minds.

"Been a long time since I've been to see my wife, Elmira, at the cemetery," said Red Grass, who'd wedged himself between Hobbs and me. "She'd be right annoyed that I forgot to leave flowers for her birthday. It's easy enough to forget things like that when you're on a train most of the time, losing track of your days." His laugh was like a bark. "*Track*, heh. Get it?"

"Yes, Red. We get it," said Hobbs.

Red Grass talked about Elmira for a while. Told us how she used to dream of traveling, though not quite the way he was doing now. She never would've approved of the turn he'd taken, the way he'd chosen to live life on "a couple of inches of steel." She was what the train community called a *forty-miler*, he said—a homebody if ever there was one. She'd joked sometimes with their businessman son that she'd have to live vicariously through him, as he went winging off to Europe or Asia. She didn't like the idea of airplanes, thought they were dangerous contraptions, and had avoided them for sixty-two years.

"What happened to her?" Jazz asked.

Red Grass waited as two trucks passed on the highway, then said, "Had a heart attack on the way to my grandson's preschool class for grandparents' day. Left a pan of brownies all over the sidewalk. They were still warm."

"I'm sorry," I said, trying to envision Red Grass in a normal sort of life, attending a preschool function, full on family.

"It was hard, but nothing compared to losing my boy," he continued.

"What happened to him?" Jazz asked again.

"Someone set fire to his place." Red Grass's tumble-rock voice grew coarser still. "There ain't no mercy in fire, neither. Consumes everything. Leaves nothing but ash, and shattered glass, and busted dreams."

"Oh, Red." I found his hand, squeezed.

"Long time ago," he said. "Though sometimes it seems like just yesterday." He wiped his face against his sleeve. "But listen, death's no fit topic for lunch, and you kids are too young for tragedies like this at any rate."

"I wish," I said quietly. Our panes of glass might not have been shattered, but they were darkened just the same.

It was Hobbs who clarified the matter. "The girls lost their mother a few months ago, Red. They're taking this trip with her ashes, as a matter of fact. Looking for some closure."

"That true, now?" The older man grunted. "Well, that's a shame. I'm sorry for you girls."

"Thanks," I said.

Jazz stayed quiet. Maybe her thoughts, like mine, had drifted to the suitcase at my feet.

"I'll bet this boy Hobbs ain't never had any sort of loss," Red Grass continued.

"Yeah? Why's that?" said Hobbs, his voice as flat as a double yellow line.

"Statistics," said Red. "Someone here has to have a whole family. That leaves you."

Hobbs huffed. "Go on and call the Guinness people, then. There are six crosses behind my old man's house, not so different from this cross here. Sisters and brothers, born dead all. I saw one once, before it went into the ground. Tiny nose and a bow mouth. Bitty eyes shut like it was sleeping. That one was a boy."

I tried not to picture the dead baby, and failed.

"That's too bad for your mother," said Red Grass. "You, eh, got a father?"

"Guess so. That's how it happens, right? Man meets woman, they bang, make a kid."

"You sure know how to paint a romantic picture, boy," said Red Grass. "Sure your old man would appreciate that."

"Ain't nothing romantic about Bill. His wife, Alice, was the only mother I ever had," said Hobbs. "Those kids behind the house—they were hers. Hers with him. She never did have a kid of her own, and my old man reminded her every chance he got that I wasn't her blood. And then she left him, and that was that. Must've had a real mother at some point, but I don't know a thing about her. Maybe she left, too, or maybe she's under one of those crosses behind the house. If there's one thing Bill learned how to do well, it was build a cross."

We sat without words for a long time, listening to the highway noise.

"How old is your grandson, Red Grass?" I asked, trying to land on a lighter subject.

He pushed off the stone and walked away without a word.

The fire. Of course. It had taken the whole family. His son. A daughter-in-law, most likely. And a grandson.

"I don't like it here," I said. I wanted to walk, get away from this view and the conversation. "Can we leave?"

"Life sucks no matter where you go," said Jazz. "You can't escape it."

"Life doesn't suck," I said.

"Tell that to Red Grass," said Hobbs. "No wonder he's a hopper.

Wife and son and grandson, all gone. What else was left? That's how it happens, a lot of the time, how folks end up in this sort of life. They're just trying to replace something they've lost. They never succeed, but they keep on. Anything's better than facing the void left by all that absence."

A desperation I could not stop to dissect filled me, as I pushed myself off the rock and faced him.

"You talk like there's no hope at all, but it doesn't have to be that way," I said. "You're young and smart. Those two feet of yours could walk you to whatever life you want, onto a path that means you don't have to hop until you're old and gray like Red Grass."

"Not everyone can afford to dream as big as you, Wee Bit."

"Truth," said Jazz.

I ignored her, focused on Hobbs. "Isn't there anything out there you can imagine, at the edges or not? Try. Try now," I said with more force than I should've, considering Hobbs's life was not my life. But I couldn't quell the ferocity of my need just then—to have him acknowledge another way, make him see that there were two ways of looking at things.

He must've picked up on that, because he didn't brush me off or mock me, just stayed quiet for a while, then said, "I don't know. Maybe I could try for a new start somewhere. Sell some assets."

For half a second, a smile broke over my face. And then Jazz opened her mouth.

"The assets you stole, you mean?"

"Jazz!" I started, but Hobbs was already up and walking away with his bag in hand. "Hobbs, wait. I didn't say anything, I swear I didn't—"

He disappeared among the trees.

"That's brilliant," I told my sister, turning on her. "Now he's going to think *I* told you, when you and I both know I didn't. What if he keeps walking? What if we're left out here with no direction?"

"He won't leave," she said, pushing my hand away when I reached out to give her a pinch. "Not when he's staring after you the way he has been. Even if he did leave, it wouldn't be the end of all options. We're here, right beside a highway. We could hitchhike. I wouldn't love it, and we'd have to look for a woman to ride with, but we could—"

"It's not even the point, Jazz. Hobbs has gone out of his way to help me—to help our whole family—and you've gone out of your way to be as horrible as possible. You don't even know him at all as a person. You're judging him on his tattoos."

"I'm judging him on thievery," she said. "Real thievery."

"Thievery you learned about from who? Red Grass?" I asked her. "Because Hobbs never told Red Grass, and I, for one, believe Hobbs. Why would you trust Red Grass? Do you know something I don't know about him? Because if you do, now's the time to fill me in." She didn't answer. "Fine, keep your secrets. But I think I understand now why you want to work in a funeral home. You don't get on so well with folks who live and breathe."

"And you say *I'm* mean."

She walked away as well. Left me there with the cross and my charred thoughts—of fire and its uncaring ways, warm brownies capsized on the sidewalk, beautiful babies put into the ground, Mama in the kitchen breathing oven gas.

Of the void left by all that absence.

At first, I didn't set Hobbs straight on the truth due to pure pride on my part, because I didn't want to have to beg for anybody's trust when I hadn't done anything to betray it. Then he gave me another reason not to talk with him.

We found more crosses, a group of three, close to the highway and up a small hill. I'd heard of these clusters of crosses before, but it was Red Grass who explained about Mr. Coffindaffer—how he'd planted crosses all over America because he claimed God had told him to do it. Spent a fortune on his venture, too.

The heat such a thing provoked was beyond sense in my mind, but Hobbs and Red Grass really got into it—Hobbs yelling about the craziness of it all, Red Grass yelling back that one man's crazy is another man's salvation. Then Hobbs lost all semblance of cool.

"Salvation is for the fucking stupid, and the fucking lazy—people who think someone's gonna come and rescue them," he said with a voice full of nettles. "That's all bullshit, crutches for the weak. I believe in action, in taking care of myself."

"Your own two feet," I said.

"Yeah." I felt his eyes on me. "My own two feet. Can't trust no one or nothing but that."

Part of me wanted to leap on him right then, pinch him, tell him and tell him and tell him until he believed me that I hadn't shared what he'd told me in confidence. But this was about more than that. This was about him ripping my ideas up in my face and calling it done. He needed to chill and so did I, both of us under the effects of a boiling-oil day, so I said nothing. Instead, I pulled a smooth stone out of my pocket, one I'd found earlier, and turned it over in my hand, worrying it the way Babka sometimes did with her religious beads.

Again, I felt the haze of my dream. I might not be ready for it, might not understand it, but it was coming all the same. A cross-roads of one kind or another.

And I would have to choose.

February 1, 2000

Dear Dad,

It's the year 2000, and I keep wondering what
you thought of all the turn-of-the-century insanity!
Did you stock up on water and food, just in case?
Branik wasn't worried in the least, though I have to
admit to purchasing a ridiculous quantity of peanut
butter and bottled water. I had no doubt that if
worse came to worst my mother-in-law would still
somehow find a way to bake bread, and we would
all be well fed.

Things are quieter here at home, under better
control. Drahomira now lives in a house right next
door to her store, which she said was meant to be,
since it went on the market when she needed it.
Olivia has started school, though she doesn't seem
to like it yet. (She has attention issues, according to
her teachers.) Jazz keeps to herself a lot of the time,
but Branik says I was probably the same way when
I was nine years old.

The details of my life with you are fading from memory, and that saddens me sometimes. The other day, I thought about the rug we had in the living room. Random, I know, but I used to trace its pattern with my fingers, lying on my stomach while writing English papers and dreaming of my life as a future novelist. You'd think I would have committed it to memory, but now I'm unsure. Was it swirling, or were the shapes angular? Was it cream with green, or green with cream? It's not important, I know, but not being able to call up the visual still bothers me.

The nicest part of having a quieter house is having time to write. Yes, I am writing. Are you surprised? Though it's a far cry from the Macintosh in the study at home, I'm sidling up every day in my kitchen beside an ancient typewriter Branik's mother gave us. It's sort of fun to use, and I've already written a hundred pages. That's almost a quarter of a novel, at least according to one of my professors whose class I took so long ago.

You may think I'm crazy for it, but I feel in my gut that if I can do this—when I do this!—this book *will be evidence of the highest order that I'm okay. Not ruined at all. Whole and vital, the person you always knew I could be. Maybe this is the key to controlling those tsunamis. I feel better when I write, more centered. Maybe fiction can put life's unexplainables into perspective for me.*

Are you curious over what the story's about? I don't want to say much yet, because I don't want to jinx it, but I'll give you a hint. It involves a bog and ghost lights, and a lost girl determined to be found. I am quite certain that determined lost girls are the most powerful of all forces.

Well, as Sylvia Plath once said, "Nothing stinks like a pile of unpublished writing." Time to get to work.

Beth

CHAPTER THIRTEEN

Outlanders

* JAZZ *

C*an you try to find your sister?* my mother would ask me, all too
often, because Olivia had a way of landing in trouble. Like the time
she climbed the tallest tree in town during a rainstorm because she
said she liked the way it sounded when the drops hit the leaves. Or
liked the look of that sound, whatever that meant. I didn't ask for
details, only yelled at her until she got down, then dragged her body
home, both of us soaked to the marrow.

Like the time she walked alone clear out of town and into the
next just to see, in her words, "some old dogs." I found her at a tiny
house huddled beside a wire-haired white mutt, and talking to some
old man who had fewer teeth than fingers. My bark won.

Like the time she used a vacated ladder to reach the top of St.
Cyril's steepled roof and sat up there for hours, saying she was testing it out for our father because it seemed the best place in all the
world for a fiddle show. I threatened to tell Mama about her trip to
see the dogs all by herself if she breathed a word of that nonsense
to our father. I didn't think he'd dare climb a church roof in front
of God and all our neighbors to play his instrument, but I never

knew with my family and wouldn't risk him getting any ideas in his head—or breaking every bone in his body.

Then came the boys. Even the ones who'd long since labeled my sister the town weirdo were willing to ignore that for an afternoon once she turned thirteen, and developed breasts and long, flirtatious lashes. The town weirdo could still steam up a car. Though in truth I only caught her at that once, making out in a truck at the edge of town with Henry, that tall guy from my grade who, despite having a pretty good head for math, seemed destined to work his entire life at the liquor store his father owned. The Henry who'd asked me out once upon a time.

Asked *me*, Jazz Moon.

I'd said no.

Why didn't you go out with that nice boy? Babka asked.

Because he's too much like all the things I hate about Tramp. That's what I believed but could never say—not to my grandmother, who'd built a business and raised a son here, who'd chosen to stay. I told her I was picky.

Can you try to find your sister? my mother asked one day after a long nap, and off I went. But I couldn't find her. After searching the town as well as I could, I went home to report that I didn't have a clue where Olivia might be hiding.

I found my mother in her bedroom, on her hands and knees, and with her head under her desk. She flushed when she saw me. *Sorry for the wild-goose chase*, she said. *Your sister came home a few minutes ago. She's fine. But thanks for looking, Jazz. You're a good daughter, and a good sister, too.*

I strained to get a glimpse of what my mother had been doing, as she shifted the thin cloth that covered the plywood top back into place.

Curiosity warred with decency for the rest of the day, and later, when my mother left for Babka's with Olivia, I went straightaway to peer under her desk. The edge of one of the floorboards beneath it lacked nails and jutted up on one side. When I lifted it, I found the letters. Letters that weren't addressed, only dated beside my grand-father's name. The first: five months before I was born.

That's when curiosity beat decency to a pulp.

I opened that envelope with as much care as I could, tugging tenderly on the flap. I made one or two small tears, left behind a few flecks of glued paper. But overall it wasn't too hard to open; this was an old bond.

I read the letter, learned it just like that: My mother had married my father because she had to. Lost her father. Lost her comfort, her money, her education. She'd had bamboo in her house, and a cat named Fat Lizzy. She'd lost all of it, everything.

Because of me.

I'm sorry for getting into trouble out of wedlock. But I would never have quit college. I would never have chosen one over the other: you or Branik, college or motherhood. Those things were your doing. It's not too late to undo them. We can raise this baby between the three of us, can't we?

Under your influence, this child will strive for greatness. I will do better with your grandchild, Dad, than I did with myself. I promise. I promise I'll be a good daughter from now on, the perfect daughter. . . .

One letter for nearly every year since that time had been stuffed under the floorboard. I reached for the next one:

*Yes, she was born—pink, healthy, crying as she
should, and with a wickedly misshapen head.*

*Jazz is a good baby, I guess, in the way of babies.
She eats well; she is growing. She's a good baby, but
when I look at her I feel nothing.*

She has your eyes.

I dug my hand into the center of the pile this time, opened a
third envelope:

*You may think I'm crazy for it, but I feel in my gut
that if I can do this—when I do this!—this book will
fix us. It will be evidence of the highest order that I'm
okay. Not ruined at all.*

I'd read enough.

My mother lived her entire adult life thinking she'd have a
reunion someday with her father. That if she finished the book he'd
forgive her for sleeping with a man she'd loved and making a baby—
making *me*—and getting married without his express consent. She
believed it with everything in her.

It was just another fairy tale.

I found a bottle of glue in a kitchen drawer, so old I had to pry the hard seal off the cap with a butter knife. I smeared thick paste along the envelopes' open flaps, tried to reseal them even though my hands shook with a sort of fever, because I was standing—stupidly—right there in the kitchen, and my mother might've returned at any moment and found me there. Who knows, maybe I wanted to be caught. But I wasn't.

I went back upstairs, returned the letters to their place under the floorboard. And then I, Jazz Marie Moon, age seventeen, called Henry and asked if he wanted to hang out. He said yes. Henry was too much like all the things I hated about Tramp—he was happy enough to grow roots in the shit around him, never question the set course of his mediocre life. But that night I gave him my virginity beside a bougainvillea in deaf Mr. McDuffy's backyard.

It was the last time I can remember crying.

It didn't seem like a hard thing: Walk, just walk. We did it all the time without thinking about it. But when you did it all day, in an oppressive sort of heat and humidity, after an unknown amount of shallow sleep, with a bag that felt weightier by the second and sneakers that could've been a lot better quality, it wore a body down. My feet ached as if they'd been sandwiched in a vise, and I swear I felt every stone beneath them. My blistered heels were a constant source of misery, even though Red Grass offered two bandages when I mentioned it (a surprise) and I used them both. My face itched, and though I knew that it was probably from pollen, I wouldn't have ruled out an accidental roll in a patch of poison ivy at some point during the night, either. Not with my luck. I'd also developed an enormous bruise on my arm, and though it didn't hurt unless I poked at it, it looked like a plum had been buried under my skin.

Civilization. The one thought that kept me going.

Once we reached civilization, we'd be in good shape. We'd eat real food. Sit on a real seat instead of a rock or a log or the heaving mechanical parts of a train. Red Grass would make his move. Hobbs would disappear. I'd be free to carry on with Olivia. This was what Red Grass had assured me when I found him in the woods earlier, before we started walking again.

I'll take care of him, he said. *Trust me.*

I didn't trust him, of course I didn't—him with his knife and his hidden gun. But I had to rely on him.

The day wore on so long that the sky showed the first signs of dusk, and I thought it wouldn't happen at all—that we'd be out in the forest for another night, and another day, and who knew when this nightmare would end. Then, out of nowhere, it appeared before us: a square brick building, and a lot full of cars and trucks. We'd passed the occasional scattering of houses and trailers near the highway, seen the occasional homeowner out whacking weeds and such, but I was still surprised at the number of vehicles there when it seemed as though we'd been isolated from the rest of the world for the last two days.

Illuminated by a single cobweb-enshrined lightbulb was a sign that read OUTLANDERS. Boisterous laughter and the gritty beat of a song I didn't recognize poured out of open doors and windows along with the heady scent of tobacco. Inside was a regular bar, lined with customers staring at a game that played out on a huge television set overhead. Yankees, Red Sox. Smoke curled through the air, clinging thickly to the ceiling, and peanut shells covered the floor. I worried less about how I might look—and smell—after everything I'd been through since leaving Jim's.

Despite the crowd, there were plenty of seats available, probably because there was some sort of gambling going on in a corner, where a group had gathered in a huddle. Olivia and I walked off to use the bathroom, where I discovered with a single fleeting and regretted glance at the mirror that my hair had bloated to twice its normal volume thanks to the humidity. Afterward, we followed Hobbs to an open booth and made as neat a pile as we could of our bags on the floor. The plastic-covered bench wasn't special in the least, but when I slid in beside my sister it felt like I'd landed on a pile of down.

"Where's Red?" Hobbs stared at me with eyes like marbles, his face half buried in the hooded jacket he'd slipped on before we walked inside. It had to have been at least twenty degrees hotter in there than it was outdoors, which left only one good reason for him to hide his features: He knew people might recognize his colored mug from a wanted poster.

"Maybe he's still in the bathroom," I said, though I might've responded, *Removing you from our lives.*

A fortysomething woman with a confusion of highlights took our order of burgers and fries all around. A pitcher of water. A beer for Hobbs. The waitress didn't ask for ID, though I knew he had to be riding the twenty-one line. The three of us were quiet after that, which was awkward but would've been worse if the bar hadn't been loud anyway.

Time slurred. Olivia made a new braid in her hair, then poured three packets of sugar into her mouth. Hobbs ripped a napkin into tiny pieces, then tried to build something with them—a napkin structure that failed in all ways. The group in the corner bellowed: a big win or loss for someone. While I watched the door, I traced my thumbnail down irregular grooves covering our table, imagined someone had taken a steak knife to the wood at some point. The heedless act of a child, maybe, or the rebellious act of someone who knew better, who'd forgotten how to be good.

Twenty minutes later, our burgers arrived—enormous things on sesame-seed-speckled buns. I dug in without bothering over ketchup. And though I felt my body's gratitude for the meal, I also felt entirely distracted.

There was still no sign of Red Grass.

I went over my simple plan again. Wait until it all went down and Hobbs was out the door, then convince Olivia—who should realize we wouldn't be able to manage alone—that it was time to give up and call family. Though I hadn't yet seen a pay phone, there had to be one around somewhere. Whatever, if I had to ask every stranger at the bar if I could borrow a cell, I'd do it. I oversalted my fries, ate two at a time.

As I swallowed the last bite of my burger, Red Grass resurfaced. Beside him was a short, thin man wearing a shirt and tie, a pair of black pants; he looked distinctly out of place.

"What's this?" Hobbs asked when they stood right beside us.

"Meetings," said Red Grass, his voice full of satisfaction.

Hobbs cursed. I tried not to smile as I dragged my body out of the booth. "Let's go, Olivia," I said.

She kept her seat. "What?"

"They have business," I said, "and this is a booth for four, not five. C'mon."

When Hobbs didn't say anything to stop her, she slugged out after me. We settled into a booth that kissed up against the other one, as the men sat.

" 'They have business, and this is a booth for four?' " Olivia said, leaning close to me. "Why are you being considerate over Hobbs all of a sudden?"

"Shh." I turned my head, focused on the conversation from the booth at my back. Listened as this new man—Beckett, Red Grass had called him—tried to convince Hobbs that showing him the coins was the right thing to do. Didn't he want to know how much they were worth? Didn't he want to make a new life for himself if he could—a life off the rails? Hobbs might make a whole lot of money by selling, Beckett teased. But first he'd need to see them for appraisal. He wouldn't buy them, he clarified, or arrange for a sale—though he could put Hobbs in contact with someone later if he needed a referral. His job was purely to make sure Hobbs had an accurate idea of value to avoid being swindled down the road, in order for him to make the most of this opportunity and his life.

Beckett was a master persuader; he must've been an undercover police investigator or something. Even I'd have fallen into his net.

"What's going on, Jazz?" Olivia hissed. Likely she couldn't hear much from her side of the table.

Behind me, the familiar clink of coins sounded to my ears like the toll of freedom bells. The wheels were in motion, nothing she could do now to stop them. It was as good a time as any to prepare her for what was to come.

"Hobbs is about to be brought to justice," I told her. "Red Grass turned him in for the reward money over those coins." She started to rise. I grabbed her hand, said, "You'll stay in your seat, Olivia Moon. Justice is a good thing. Whoever owns those coins for real should have them back, and we're not going to interfere with the law."

Her blue eyes misted over as she sat back down. "How could you have known this was coming and not say anything? You hate him that much? He trusted us, and he trusted me, and trust doesn't come easy to him."

I said, "That's interesting, considering he's a thief."

"You always do that!" She hit her palms against the table. "You see just a part of people—the bit you want to see, or the bit you can. Why can't you admit that Hobbs has done nothing but help us?"

"Help us? The scope of your delusion amazes me," I said.

A swell of noise came from the gamblers in the corner. From Hobbs's table I picked a few words from the ongoing conversation, heard "scam," "one week." Adrenaline coursed through me. What would happen in one week? A trial? Would he be in jail until then, held on bail?

"He has helped *me*," Olivia said, starting in again. "He's helped me see things I didn't see before. More than that, he doesn't make me feel like an inconvenience for having a mind of my own, or call me stupid or delusional for—"

I shushed her again when Red Grass stood, sure Hobbs would stand next, maybe even be led out in handcuffs. Tonight we'd sleep in our own beds. Tomorrow I'd deal with the bus, and—

"I'll go get us a round of shots to celebrate," said Red Grass.

I blinked. Celebrate?

I'd missed something somewhere—an important piece of the puzzle. I shifted my entire body around to stare up at him, make him aware of my presence, waited for him to throw me a reassuring nod or wink, some indication that we were still on track, about to drop a net. But he was too busy glowing at the table he'd vacated to look my way.

Beckett stood as well. "My wife smells liquor on me before dinner and I'll be on the couch for a week. But it was nice to meet you, Hobbs. I guarantee you won't be sorry."

"I'll be in touch," Red Grass told Beckett. "For negotiations of fees and things."

Fees?

Beckett nodded. "One step at a time," he said, then walked away, weaving through the crowd and back toward the main entrance.

I waited for something more to happen. Anything. Held to hope that this was part of an elaborate setup, that a league of cops would come crashing in at any moment and make sense of all this. I looked from Red Grass to the door and back again. But Red Grass only laughed, said he was buying those drinks anyway. He pivoted toward the bar.

Whatever had just happened wasn't about turning Hobbs in or collecting a reward. I'd been lied to. Duped. Left in exactly the same position I'd been in for the last two days—at the mercy of everyone else's whims. This was the way life would continue, too, unless I did something about it.

With slow and deliberate movements, I rose to my feet, stepped in front of Hobbs's table, and locked eyes with my nemesis. Words flowed like ivy as Olivia scrambled to my side.

"There's a pretty picture with your face on it out there, a reward poster for finding you," I said, over my sister's protests. "I thought you might like to know that I'm going to call you in myself. Not tomorrow, not in an hour, but right now. Consider this fair warning."

His eyes flashed with his own special brand of fury and all the edges came out in his face like razor blades. I wasn't afraid of that look, or of him.

I turned to the bar. No Red Grass. Walked right up to the men's room and pushed open the door. Red Grass stood in front of the corner urinal, doing the shake.

"God Almighty," he said when he saw me, fumbling with his pants. "Couldn't you wait an ever-loving second?"

"That's it, huh?" I said as the door swung shut behind me. The room smelled like a neglected horse stall. "That's you turning him in? Laughing, buying drinks? Collecting fees for your services? What are you, his broker or something?"

"Now, now," he said, red-faced, his palms up. A fly buzzed behind him. "Be patient, missy, all in good—"

"Tell the truth for once in your life," I said. "Did you ever call that number on the poster?"

Water dripped into the room's lone sink—two, three, four times—before he stumbled nervously through a series of vague excuses. "Need to take it to the next level . . . better authentication . . . can't rush these—"

"Oh, fuck you and the train you rode in on," I said. "You played me."

I lunged for the poster that I spied jutting from his pocket like my last hope. Pulled it loose even though he surged away from me, tried and failed to evade me, cursed a blue streak. Held it away from him when he made to take it back, and kept it away from him.

"You're not going to make that call?" I said. "I will. This ends now."

I stormed out like I'd stormed in, and right away spied a phone lurking in the deep shadow at the end of the hall—an old-fashioned booth with a long crack down the glass. A dim light flickered overhead when I stepped in and shut the door behind me. I inserted quarters, flicked open the poster, punched numbers with trembling hands.

It rang three times. And then, an answer.

"Hello, Jazz," came a familiar voice.

Not possible. I opened the glass door to find Red Grass standing on the other side, a cell phone pressed against his ear. A cell phone! But, before I could ask any of the hundred questions swelling in my mind over this latest sucker punch, he said something that changed everything.

Hobbs and Olivia were gone.

CHAPTER FOURTEEN

The Edge of the Periphery

✳ OLIVIA ✳

I knew how my sister saw me—like a child, weak. But that wasn't how I saw myself, and it wasn't how it was.

My father's favorite sandwich was peanut butter and jelly, loaded with so much peanut butter that it was as thick as the bread. Sour-cherry jelly was his favorite, the kind Babka made every year herself, but he liked other kinds, too—blackberry, strawberry, raspberry, blueberry, orange marmalade, even store-bought grape sometimes. He stopped eating sandwiches after Mama died, though. Started losing weight. Reaching for the liquor cabinet instead of food, and reaching at any time of day.

Jazz liked being alone; she always had. But things changed after Mama died. She was always on the move. Moving away from Papa and me as soon as we appeared. Rifling through closets and boxes in the basement, and then leaving home to take a drive. Staying away.

It took strength to notice things, sometimes, when those things were hidden away in dark places, stuck on the edges of the periphery. Strength to point to them and say *that matters enough that I need to do something about it*, especially when no one else blinked over them or everyone else forgot they were important.

Mama broke her arm once about a year ago. She'd been getting something down from the attic, on the ladder, and she missed a step and landed in a heap on the floor. The bone in her arm pierced straight through her skin. The doctors prescribed narcotics for her, which made her sleep hard. Too hard. She said that drugged sort of sleep was like death, and she said she hated it. I remember that; I'm sure that's what she said. She took a few pills to get her over the hump, then left the rest in the cupboard. She called them her *just-in-case pills*—just in case she ever felt that much pain again and needed relief. They were there, in the house, but she never used them again.

She never used them.

Hobbs didn't run when he left Outlanders. Instead, he stood and walked away with his pack on his back. I walked, too, shadowed him across the room, out the door, across the parking lot, to its edge and beyond, into the woods.

The forest at night smelled like secrets, and the violet pinpricks of bug chatter seemed brighter than the evening before. I didn't say anything, just followed him and the beam of his flashlight as we walked along a path of quiet things—moss and pine needles and dead leaves ground into soft flakes. Strangely, I felt better able to navigate the woods at night than during the day, as my blind spot blurred into the surrounding darkness and my peripheral vision rose to a new level of attention, honing in on Hobbs's movement.

Minutes passed before I stepped on a branch, loud and revealing. Hobbs's reaction was immediate. He made sounds that were pieces of words but nothing that made any sense—like *Geeffgahbbuh*, as if he'd whacked his funny bone so hard that his arm went numb but he couldn't swear because he was standing next to a nun.

"What the hell are you doing?" was the first thing I puzzled out. He marched right up to me, let his bag slide off his shoulder and onto the forest floor.

"Following you," I said, even though this was obvious.

"Well, don't," he said, and pulled down his hood. "Go back."

"I can't."

"Why?"

"I need to tell you something," I said, realizing it was true as the words sprang from my mouth.

There was unfinished business between us, though I wasn't sure I could pin it down to name it or figure out what to do with it. The only thing that had become clear was that Hobbs was more than a way down to the glades for me, and I wouldn't let him walk away without knowing it.

"I need to thank you," I said. A start.

"You don't."

"It's important, what you've done for me. I need to thank you."

"All right," he said. "You've thanked me. Now turn yourself around and go back to Outlanders. If you need me to take you, I will, because I know you're supposed to be blind, but I have to tell you I'm starting not to believe that story. Blind but following me around in the dark doesn't add up."

"You know I'm not all the way blind. And you have a flashlight to go along with a moon that seems full enough in the sky tonight." I gestured upward. "It's not so hard to follow."

He grunted, which I took for reluctant concession.

"And I'm not ready to go back," I told him. "This, between us, isn't finished."

"Livya—"

"It isn't. We've been good for each other, and—"

"Good? See what happened because I let you get to me?"

"I got to you?"

"I told you nothing ever worth a damn comes from dreaming, but you made me think about it." He raised his hands to his head as he'd done once before—yesterday, while we gathered wood. "You waved those ideas of yours around like a pretty package—how much better life could be if I imagined something different—and look what happened."

A breeze cut through, slapped leaves on trees, rattled branches in a quick swirl of cinnamon heat, then was gone. Left was the scent of my own desperation.

"I'm sorry about Jazz and Red Grass, and whatever else is going on with those coins, even if I didn't know about any of it," I said. "But I'm not sorry that you started to think about more for yourself. If it makes you feel any better, you've done the same for me."

"Stop."

The word tasted like bricks, like I was right back where I'd started with Hobbs, with a wall that touched clouds standing between us. When I reached for his arm, he took a step away.

"People aren't dragons, Hobbs," I said, my voice leaking a sadness that I couldn't quite contain. "Who made you think that way? Not everyone is out to hurt you. Not everyone would. I wouldn't."

He cracked a knuckle, but his voice lacked toughness when he answered; in fact, he sounded abashed.

"None of that can matter right now. Right now I've got some serious baggage chasing after me, and others need to be where I am not. You." He shifted. "You, Livya Moon, need to be where I am not," he said, which is when I decided that dragon slayers might make loyal mates after working through their trust issues.

"You can handle Red Grass," I said.

"I'm sure I can, but it's not him I'm worried about."

"Aren't you?" I had questions—lots of them—but first I had to tell Hobbs what I knew. "Red Grass was going to turn you in for some sort of reward money. That's what Jazz told me just before she went off on you."

He swore under his breath. "Guess I shouldn't be surprised Red would throw me over for a chunk of change. I wonder how much my old man is paying for a lump of my flesh?"

"Your dad?"

"It's him behind the posters, I'm sure of it. He wants his coins back, wants me gone."

It was Hobbs's father who'd made him so fearful, so angry sometimes, so eager to kick back at friends and shut doors.

Those coins are the one thing he cares about.

Pride made a poor friend, I decided. Time to set things straight.

"You didn't think much of me earlier," I said, fingering a new-found hole in the hem of my shirt. "You seemed almost glad to believe I'd stabbed you in the back. Maybe you don't know me well enough yet to know I don't do things like that, but here's the truth for you to believe or not. I didn't tell Jazz about you taking those coins. I didn't tell her or anyone what you told me. She knew it, somehow, after meeting Red Grass. My guess is he's known for a long time, since before we came along anyhow."

"All right." He crossed his arms over his chest. "I believe you. But it doesn't change anything. You have to go back, and I have to go on. That's the simple truth of it."

"It's not simple, and it's not a set truth. It's a choice." A cross-roads. "And a different choice could change everything if you let it. You need a friend you can trust. I need a friend I can trust, too, someone to help me get to the glades. We can help each other. And I don't want to go back. I won't go back," I added, and my voice grew bristles. "I want to stay with you. And I want you to take me to that bog like we planned."

"That wasn't the plan, if you remember," he said.

I did, of course. He was going to take us only so far, then go his own way. But things had changed.

"I started to say this earlier, and I'd like to finish now. I'm not the same person I was when I first met you," I told him.

"I'm sorry."

"Don't be stupid, you know I don't mean it like that," I said, and felt the threat of ellipses that went on forever, like a line of stammering people who didn't take chances or make choices or say what they meant. So I'd say what I meant, before it all erupted out of me like the stuffings in an overfilled closet. "Talking to you about the importance of dreams made me realize that I was struggling, too, not trusting one hundred percent even after I told myself I had to. You helped me see that maybe that's okay, and that people can't count on fate or luck, even if they do want to believe things happen for a reason. You reminded me that we hold a lot of power in our own two feet, and that we have to use those feet to face the edges sometimes, and take risks. And dream a dream bigger than sauce— even if you might not exactly like the word *dream*."

"Sauce?"

I tipped my head, wondered if Hobbs liked pizza. He would. Of course he would. Especially with my sauce all over it.

"Forget the sauce for now," I said. "The point is you made me think I needed more in my life, for myself. And I know we haven't known each other for long in hours, and maybe you don't like me that way, but you made me dream of walking to the edge. With you."

The crickets sounded louder when Hobbs went quiet, and for long seconds I stopped breathing altogether.

"Listen, Wee Bit," he said. "You can't do this. I can't do this."

"Why?" I dug in my heels. "Why are you afraid of this when I've never been so sure of anything in my life, when you take more risks in a week than most folks do in a lifetime?"

"Because I'm ruined, Livya," he said.

Something in his voice nudged my memory toward an ancient misery. I veered sharply away from that, even as my fingers curled around the smooth stone I'd pocketed earlier.

"Well, I've been ruined, too, several times over, so we're even," I told him, trying for funny.

His voice ruffled like peacock feathers. "Is that so?"

I took a chance and stepped close again. This time he didn't move away.

"I think you want me around even if you won't admit it," I said. "Because under all your tough talk you want to believe, too, and you know you can count on me. We need to stick together, Hobbs."

He gave a silvery huff of air, like a laugh but not. "You're either the bravest girl I've ever met or the stupidest."

"Can I pick which?" I smiled. "There's one other thing."

"What?"

"This." I held my free hand out to him, and when he took it I pulled the stone I'd been worrying from my pocket, let it go. It hit the forest floor in a dull ink-like splat.

And, just like that, the choice was made. Yes, Jazz would be upset with me again, even furious. But this wasn't about Jazz; it was about me and what I needed to do. I felt it in my bones, trusted it; this was right, this would work.

"You're impossible," he said.

"You're not the first to mention that."

I pulled him close. He tugged at one of my braids. We kissed for the first time, with the moon looking down on us, but I knew right away that it wouldn't be our last.

He tasted like tomorrow.

We walked awhile longer until we left the forest and found a road. Not the highway. Not anywhere I'd been before, I don't think. Walking a few miles at night wasn't appealing to either of us, and Hobbs said there was some rough terrain up ahead. The good news was that we were a few miles from the home of a friend of his, he said, reminding me that he had reasons of his own for making the trip and hadn't just been wandering in my general direction. It was because we were so close that he was willing to break his usual rule and hitch, trust something other than his own two feet for a few minutes.

We got lucky. After a short time, a pickup came down the road. I stuck out my thumb as Hobbs advised—"A pretty girl always stops traffic"—with him by my side. The truck stopped.

"Where you kids headed?" asked a man with a voice to match his engine.

Hobbs shouted above the sound. "You know the bridge at Miner's Barren?"

"What do you want to go there for? Bridge is condemned, butts up against nothing but forest."

"There's a cottage out there," Hobbs answered. "And the bridge is safe enough to walk over if you know the right spots."

"Isn't there another path to that land? That might be a sounder way to go," said the man.

"There is," said Hobbs. "But it's miles off and more effort than we need if you're heading in this direction."

The man hesitated a second. "All right, then. Come on."

Inside, his truck smelled of cigarettes and a pine that was stronger than anything I'd noticed in the forest. He made a few more inquiries about the cottage. He'd lived twenty miles from the bridge all his life and never knew there was anything still back there. Once, there had been, before homes and families were wiped out overnight. He didn't name the tragedy that had swept over the land—a fire, a flood, a famine, illness, or even a curse—but now the land was haunted by some of the fiercest ghosts in all West Virginia, he said. So fierce no one wanted to live there. No one but Hobbs's friend, at any rate.

I'd grown up around stories like these, and because of that I'd grown pretty immune to fear. But this story made my skin skitter. Maybe because ghostly talk reminded me of the story Hobbs had told earlier—the tale of Earl McGuffin and the white bridge haunted by his whole family. Maybe because I was with Hobbs, and my nerves were already bunched as tight as my braids. To calm myself, I started to undo them, one at a time—the braid over my left ear, the one on my right that always flew up and knocked me in the eye.

We were there real fast, which made me think we should've tried hitching a long time ago, even if Hobbs wasn't a fan of wheels over feet.

"You kids watch yourselves," the man said as we slid out of the seat and onto pavement.

"You bet," said Hobbs, and the truck drove off in a spray of red eraser bits, left us to the dark. He turned on his flashlight, reached for my hand, which was trembling a little. "Those stories scare you?" he asked me.

"Maybe," I said.

"Nothing to be afraid of, Wee Bit." I heard a smile in his voice. "I'll take care of you."

He led us down an overgrown path until the sound of running water grew louder. This stream sounded small, but angry, and I could barely make out the bridge even with Hobbs's flashlight. We ducked under a barrier and began to walk over the old structure, staying close to the side Hobbs said was best.

"Tiny steps, Livya," he said as I followed behind him.

There was one moment when there might've been trouble, when my left foot slid through a gap in the bridge that Hobbs hadn't noticed to warn me about. But he caught me up, and I caught myself up.

"Careful," he said, breathless.

"Maybe the ghosts want me."

"Maybe they can't have you," he said, and I grabbed the back of his shirt.

We kissed once we'd made it across to the other side. It was a different sort of kiss from the first kiss. This kiss, the low noise Hobbs made, burst on my tongue like sprinkled sugar. Said *hunger*, said *I know what I want: you*, said *now*. When I touched his face with my hands, he pulled them away, encouraged them lower, and the heat and humidity still held in the air by the boiling-oil day felt exactly right.

"Who needs a bed?" Hobbs said, and I agreed as we sank to our knees. Just two more animals on the forest floor.

September 12, 2001

Dear Dad,

The most horrific thing happened yesterday, as I'm sure you've heard. Everyone has heard. The Twin Towers are gone. I couldn't sleep last night thinking of everything that happened, all the lives that were lost, all the people left behind. I thought especially of the people who jumped—how they made a choice to escape fire and smoke and the destruction of stairs and elevators and sprinkler systems, like a last moment of freedom. And because there was nothing better to hope for. Nothing at all.

I will write more when I am feeling less.

Beth

CHAPTER FIFTEEN

The Long Memory of Old Dreams

∗ JAZZ ∗

The last time my mother mentioned college to me was the day a catalog for Kennaton State arrived in the mail with my name on it. I hadn't asked for it, and the sight of it brought me to within a degree of furious. I'd finished my junior year of high school the week before and was looking forward to a summer free of my peers, most of whom I disliked. I couldn't wait to be out of school altogether and working with Babka in the one environment that had ever made me feel at ease. The only expectation at the bakery was to make dough, roll it out and shape it, watch it brown, then see it sold. This was not an expectation I minded, and, in fact, was one I enjoyed. Here was a beginning, middle, and end—a complete process. I felt a keen appreciation for the crisp of a well-made crust, and the resilience of a well-made dough—the way it bounced back when poked with a finger, as if to say, "I'm perfect the way I am; don't try to change me." A lesson my mother could learn.

I found her slouched, asleep in a hard plastic chair alongside the house, her hair pulled back with a white-and-red striped scarf, her bare knees dirty, and a trowel stuck in the ground at her side. Her freckled nose looked sunburned. Behind her were four scraggly tomato plants, each with one or two yellow buds, and an herb bush I could not identify. Heaped beside them lay a pile of wilting weeds. A line of delineation marked where her efforts had stalled, between the second and third plants, after which the weeds were thick and hearty and positively in control.

I tapped the catalog against my leg and stared at her. Surely she had to feel me there, my anger. Still, she slept. My mother is lazy, I thought. She is so lazy, sleeping while her plants choke, asking them to grow and produce even when they're smothered in weeds.

I glanced up for a few seconds when a plane flew overhead, and when I looked back at my mother her eyes opened. She noticed me and what I held, and had the audacity to smile.

The catalog came, she said after a yawn. *Good. We can go through it—*

I told you I won't go to college, I said.

You don't mean that, Jazz. You're so bright, you—

I won't go, no matter how good my chances might be of getting in, I said. *I don't want to go.*

She nudged her body upright, rubbed the back of her neck with one hand. *But you don't mean that. Of course you want to go. Who wouldn't? It's a wonderful opportunity, and you should—*

You're so high on it, why don't you go back? I said. *You're one semester short of your English degree, right?*

She looked down at her dirty fingers. *That was a long time ago.*

Who cares how long ago it was? I said. *Why don't you just go back and finish, be a teacher, or whatever it was you wanted to be? Is it because of money?*

Money doesn't have to stand in your way, if that's what you're worried about, she said, her eyes on me again. *You can get a scholarship, and loans. You're a smart girl.*

So I go to college, and then what? Come back to work as the most overqualified baker in Tramp?

She sat straighter. *No. You can do better.*

Why would I want to?

Why wouldn't you?

I shook my head, angry because my grandmother had built some-thing our whole family relied upon, and it seemed like my mother was almost ashamed of it. Angry, too, because I could not forget the letters I'd read, what my mother had written about Tramp, about me, about her father.

Is the reason you won't finish your degree because you're trapped here with Dad and us anyway? I said. *And you'd never be able to use it because there isn't anything to use it for around here and you can't drive to get to anything away from here, so why bother—*

Jazz. Her warning voice.

But I can, can't I? I said. *I can try to do what you couldn't bring yourself to do. Finish the degree. Have at least the slimmest possibility of making something of myself.*

This was the meanest thing I'd ever said to my mother, and left no doubt that I'd crossed a line into no-rules-here territory. My muscles tautened, and I half expected the air between us to rumble with tension, for words that would be worse, that would roll out like cannons, for all-out war. Instead, my mother slid back down in her chair, a visible sign of defeat.

My mother is weak, I thought. She is the weakest person I know.

Resentment flourished in me like wild weeds, and I used it, sure that I'd never find a more ideal moment to end all this.

Stop shoving your dreams on me, I said. *I'm not going to do what you want just because you want it. I'm not going to live my life so some-one else can live theirs through me. I'm not going to be molded into the family savior, or the feather in the family cap, or whatever it is you want me to be. This is my life. Mine alone.*

I turned and walked away from her, refusing to be shaped like dough according to another person's appetite.

I prowled the crushed stone lot outside, my eyes stumbling around in the dark.

No Olivia.

I couldn't comprehend this. I'd been gone for less than five minutes. She and Hobbs couldn't have gone far, but I had no idea which direction they'd taken. If I chose wrong, I could lose her, maybe forever. Raging streams, wild animals, cliffs, cars, even Hobbs himself. I tried not to think of the many ways Olivia might fall into a bad situation out there in the wild. Even die.

What would I do? What could I do?

Overwhelmed, I leaned against the doorjamb at Outlanders. Moths flew near the bulb beside me, some already caught in the rangy spiderwebs decorating the exterior, the others sure to meet the same end.

Red Grass came through the door and stopped when he saw me there. " 'One moment of carelessness can cause a lifetime of sorrow.' You know who said that?" When I didn't reply, he answered himself. "Duffy Littlejohn, a train hopper. That man saved my life, and I mean that literally."

He reached behind him, and a moment later dragged all our bags outside. Including my sister's.

The bag with our mother's ashes inside it.

This was worse. This was far worse than I'd imagined.

I took the bag, too overcome with dread even to chew him a new one for his duplicity, his role in this mess. Besides, my role was bigger. I'd told Hobbs I was about to turn him in. I'd birthed this new chaos; I was its creator. Red Grass hadn't once stuck my nose in that truth, which is more than I would've done if it had been my foot in that particular shoe. I'd been stupid. So, so stupid.

"I know what it's like to lose family," he said, "and I won't let it happen here if I can help it. We'll find them." He pulled a thin black flashlight out of his bag of tricks. It was the sort of flashlight cops used, he explained, and would help us travel in the dark as we searched.

Questions toppled out of me.

Where did you get that flashlight? Are you a cop?

Why did you let me believe you were after a reward when that wasn't the case? What is the case?

Did you really make that poster yourself? Scatter it across the state and all the way to Kentucky, even though you knew where Hobbs was well enough? Why?

What do you want with him?

What's the big deal with those coins?

It seemed obvious that the coins were at the root of everything, as Red Grass was always fixated on them. But it had also seemed obvious that Red Grass was nothing more than a dirt-poor, train-hopping scamp looking to make a quick buck, and not someone who would have a fancy cell phone in his pocket, or a state-of-the-art flashlight, so I wasn't sure what to believe anymore.

He didn't answer any of my questions, though, and what he did say failed to ease my nerves.

"I told you I needed more time to verify some things. My friend tonight, he took some of those coins and he plans to do some research. The next phase happens after that."

"Phase? You're not seriously asking me to believe this is still on? That you're still planning to take care of Hobbs?"

"Yes. Yes, I am asking you to believe it." He looked from the dark sky, back to me, pierced me through with the sort of look I'd usually attribute to Hobbs. "You can't always read a thing on the surface and understand it all the way through, missy, and you're driving everyone away because you think you can, with your snap judgments and all that heat."

Hadn't Olivia said this same thing to me minutes ago? And now she was gone. Gone like my mother was gone. Had I done something to drive my mother away, too? Could I have prevented . . . everything somehow? I hugged the suitcase to my chest, couldn't help a slight tremble.

Red Grass must've read the pain on my face, because he patted my shoulder. "I'll tell you this so you don't worry overmuch about finding them again." He glanced away as a truck in the lot pulled out, beams flashing in his eyes, and then he looked straight at me. "I've got a tracking device on that boy."

I followed Red Grass, as he walked back into the thick of trees and weeds and dark and quiet, and away from Outlanders and all its smoke and light and noise. I would never have left at all, would've sat in the lot hoping Olivia would come to her senses and return. But when he showed me the tracking device—about the size of a cell phone but with a map schematic and red flashing light—and how far Hobbs already was from us, I understood the safer bet. He wouldn't, of course, tell me why he had the device, and was as evasive as ever.

"You want me to bring you to them or not?" he asked—a choice that was no choice at all.

"Of course I do."

"Then stop pummeling me with questions I'm not about to answer and let's go."

> I wish you a night
> full of leg cramps and flea bites,
> you pushy old man.

And so we went, marching through the woods with a single spotlight beam to guide us, which isn't anything I'd recommend if you're not the one carrying the flashlight, even if it is Quality. I cursed Hobbs when I tripped over something that felt like a vine; it didn't matter that he wasn't around to hear me.

"Doesn't take much to get on your bad side, does it?" Red Grass said.

"Oh, right, because stealing my sister away from me twice isn't reason enough to be pissed at Hobbs. I'm just a hotheaded, overreacting—"

"I told you already, you can't always trust your eyes."

"No? Well, I can't replace the ones I have." To our left, something scurried in the brush. With my free hand, I found the knife in my pocket and held tight.

"That's where you're wrong. You can replace them, in a fashion. See that there?" He stopped so fast that I nearly ran into him.

"What?"

He flashed his light into the brush.

"Bushes?" I asked, not bothering to hide my annoyance.

"There are berries on them bushes," he said, and I honed in on them, red and round.

"I don't think now's the time for berry picking."

"You can't eat them, girly," he said. "Those are smilax berries. Horrid things to eat, nothing at all to smile about—unless you're a deer or bird or what have you. Seems one thing, is another—you get me?"

"Smilax berries?" I brushed a hand across my cheek. "Smilax berries are real?"

"Of course they're real. Open your eyes."

I'd assumed that my mother had invented smilax. Certainly, I'd never heard of it outside of her story. In her story, a particular patch of berries marked a gateway of sorts—a keyhole into the land of the will-o'-the-wisps. The land of hope.

"Wait," I said, shifting Olivia's bag to my other hand when Red Grass continued on the path. "Hold up, old man."

"Hmmph?"

He turned the light on me, and enough of it bled over so that I could see the fruit again. I pushed a branch out of the way, stepped far enough into a thicket that I could reach the bush, then plucked off a berry with my free hand. Rolled it—chill and firm—between my fingers. Real.

"I'm not going to eat it. Never mind," I said, when he wanted to know why I'd taken one. "I didn't harangue you over your devices, did I?"

"As a matter of fact, you did."

He shined the light in my eyes, and I slammed my lids shut, raised my arm to block my face. "Watch where you're pointing that thing!"

"You're a negative Nellie, is what you are," he said. "You don't do something with all that anger it'll eat you up, and don't think I don't know what I'm talking about. You didn't see me after that fire killed my boy, after the cops said they couldn't find the one who set it. I let anger take me like slack action. You know what that is?"

"No, and I don't care."

"Slack action," he said, ignoring me, "is the give between cars and can bring a hell ton of trouble when a train's in crisis. *Give* means no real support, no way to stop one car from crashing into its neighbor. That was how I lived for a while, crashing around, every part of me off the rails. It's not the way, I'm telling you. But when you push away from that anger, stretch yourself like train cars set to rights, you can see things you might not notice otherwise."

"I'm not going to see anything at all unless you get that damned light out of my face." He didn't respond. I moved my arm, saw the light had moved to target my midriff.

"You have to fling all that anger away," he said.

"Fling?"

"Fling it away." Red Grass jerked his hand to the right, and the flashlight he'd been holding somersaulted through the air and landed beside a tree. "I'm just saying."

And, for the first time since the disaster began, I smiled.

I pushed Red Grass a few times more about Hobbs, about why he was following him, about what he knew. He gave little, next to nothing.

"Sometimes," he said, "you just have to follow your gut, even if you don't understand it all the way through. That's why I'm doing it, and that's all you need to know, young thing miss."

"Stretching with those nicknames, Red."

"Young missy," he grumbled.

My thoughts jumped to the job at the funeral home—how I'd wanted it, taken it even though it didn't make much sense to my family or even to me, how I felt almost desperate to start work. When would I begin? Was it in three days now, or four? I'd lost my sense of time.

"Well, shiiit," Red Grass said, and stopped just ahead of me. "They must've hitched a ride."

"What?" I skirted around him to peer down at the tracking device in his hands, though I had no idea what I was looking at. "How can you tell?"

"Because here's where we are"—he pointed at a red light—"and here's where they are"—and another—"and there ain't no way they walked to where they are now in the time they've had. Good news is—"

"There's good news?"

"Good news is the dot's not moving anymore. They're somewhere, at least for now, and three or so miles out. We'll be able to walk it in an hour or so. But, oh, shiiit," he said again. "This is bad."

"Why? What?" How could things become worse?

"Can't track a car by foot," he said. "Not even Aragorn could've tracked a damned car driving on a damned road at night in the rain."

"Rain?"

The sky rumbled with thunder.

"Perfect."

"You aren't a talent at noticing things around you, are you?" he said, then barreled on before I could voice offense. "And this is the opposite of perfect. Hobbs is gonna know something's wrong. He's gonna know I've been tracking him, and not without technology."

"So what?" I said. "We have to keep going. We can't give up now."

"What a leaker you are. I didn't say anything about giving up, did I? But we find them the way I say we find them, because this ain't your neck on the line."

"It's my sister on the line."

"Just hush. Let me think a minute." He pulled off his bulky pack and sat right there on the ground.

Sat, while time ticked on. While the sky lit with the storm and the beam from his jostled flashlight.

"We need to keep moving," I said when my patience wore out. "We need to do something, right now."

"All right," he said, sliding me a complicated look. "But you've got to say and do what I tell you to, you got me?"

"Why should I—"

"Because you want her back, that's why. I have an idea—a crazy fool's idea." His face was half in shadow, the dark dancing over his stubbled chin, and I wondered if I should be afraid.

CHAPTER SIXTEEN

A Hollow Heart

✳ OLIVIA ✳

Mama wasn't the best cook in the world, but she sure did try. One of my earliest memories was of her taking me and Jazz to a big store in Kennaton to look for "kitchen gear," as she called it, when I was about four or so. Mama still had her license at that point, and drove a small orange car that was nearly as loud as the biscuit bus. She'd been working in Honeybee Hill, which was a bigger town than Tramp but not as far off as Kennaton, in a plant shop called Begonia's, and had saved up some of her money. It was a good job for her to have at the time, because there was a room in the back that the owner let us sit in for play during Mama's shift.

We're going to buy some kitchen knives today, she told us, as we arrived at the store. *Your father deserves a proper dinner now and then, and I'll have better luck at that if I have a proper set of knives.*

It was my first time in Kennaton. Later, I'd be big enough to see out the windows and realize how different that city was from Tramp, but even then walking into the store felt like entering another world altogether. Four floors of stuff in one building—two of them just for clothes, and appliances and kitchen gear on a floor of their own. We walked past mannequins garbed in swingy dresses, jackets with ties, and polka-dot bikinis. And when we stepped inside an elevator and started to rise, the lavender- and yellow-circle shapes I'd seen from the music all around us began to spin like a tunnel, a pastel tornado I felt in the pit of my stomach.

The appliances and kitchen-gadgets floor seemed boring, filled with tall things I couldn't see well, even though my interest spiked when Mama stopped to open a refrigerator door or admire the stoves—but only because I wanted to crawl inside. (*Another few years at the flower shop, and we'll buy a whole new kitchen,* she said.) Ladles, whisks, funnels, toasters, kettles, cutting boards, gravy boats, blenders, and coffeemakers; there were rows and rows of kitchen things. To combat my boredom, I picked a red colander off a reachable shelf and stuck it on my head. Playing with kitchen stuff was one of my favorite things to do at home—taking pots and pans and plastic bowls out of the two low cupboards, pretending to make sauce with a wooden spoon. But at the store I wasn't able to play. Mama took the bowl off my head, asked Jazz to take me out of the gadgets section for a while until she'd finished looking for her knives. If we were quiet and polite, we might play a game of hide-and-seek, she suggested.

In those days, Jazz took the job of big sister to heart, and so she laced her fingers with mine and we walked back the way we'd come. But I wasn't good at playing hide-and-seek with my sister. She found me every time. I was halfway inside a refrigerator, with one leg left to pull in behind me, when a woman with a badge opened the door all the way and scowled.

I couldn't do things like that, she told me, just before Jazz grabbed my hand and walked me to the end of the row, where we leaned against a washing machine. She wore a printed dress with multicolored stripes that my mother had made. The stripes didn't line up well, and one of the black buttons hung by a thread. I reached for the thread, but Jazz said I couldn't play with her dress, either.

There was too much I couldn't do. I couldn't wear the colander and I couldn't hide in the refrigerator and I couldn't touch a black shiny button that didn't want to be on that dress anyhow. But I could win at hide-and-seek; I was determined. So the next time Jazz started to count to twenty, I went to the elevator and waited. And when an older couple stepped into it once the doors opened, I followed. They didn't bother looking at me, didn't even seem to notice, which made me glad. I had a big smile on my face as I watched the lavender and yellow circles turn into a tornado from the music again, and we went down and down, and then the doors opened.

I stepped out onto a clothing floor, which was good, because I wanted to see the polka-dot bathing suits again. But all I could see were jeans and T-shirts and shoes and purses. I was polite, just how Mama would want me to be, for the first five minutes or so of looking, and then I got worried, because it occurred to me that Mama wouldn't think I was polite at all for getting on the elevator and leaving my sister alone with the refrigerators. I ran back the way I'd come, tried to find the elevator again using the music as a guide, but the music was everywhere and I couldn't see it clearly anymore. After a few futile minutes, I started to cry. People stared at me. I didn't like that, so I found a shelf full of scarves and squatted beside it, making myself as small as possible. I might not have been able to label it *regret* back then, but I remember this: My heart felt hollow. I missed my family.

A man with a shaggy voice found me—*You lost, little one?*—and offered his hand, which I took even though Mama said never to go off with strangers, because I didn't know what else to do. He led me to a service counter, where they stopped the music to announce that I'd been found and let Mama know where she could pick me up.

I thought she'd be mad, but when she came with Jazz she knelt right down and hugged me, her body shaking like she was real cold. I remember wanting to curl up inside Mama, crawl right into the gap between her buttons and burrow under her shirt. My heart felt normal again, not hollow, as we all said sorry to one another for our part in what had gone wrong.

Mama took a hard look at Jazz's dress and my scuffed shoes, then decided that she only needed one knife—a big chef's knife she had tucked under her arm in a plastic case—and that the others could wait. Instead, we bought new shoes for me and for Jazz, and a bunch of shirts on sale.

We never did go back for those other knives, though. Begonia's closed five days later, and Mama slept more after that. But we kept the chef's knife, and used it for cutting meat and vegetables, and mincing herbs, and smashing garlic. While I wouldn't say it made Mama a great chef, I think it made her glad to hold it in her hand and use it every day, knowing she'd bought it with money she'd earned herself.

A few months after that, I saw her with her hands pressed together at her desk, using it just then like an altar. I asked if she was praying for those other knives. She said no, that wasn't what she hoped for, and then she hugged me, drew me nearer to the beat of her hollow heart.

The house might've been invisible. I couldn't see it at all until we were inches away from the dark-wood door. Hobbs said it wasn't just me, wasn't just the night, either. The cabin had been built into a hill long ago, and its log roof was covered in thick moss. Music filtered out from the inside, full of round color, like airy bubbles of blue and orange and yellow, drifting together, floating apart again. It reminded me of the love sounds my parents used to make, the door to their bedroom closed, their minds turned off to the possibility that their two daughters might be near, ears pressed against the thin wall.

Hobbs knocked—"J.D., man, it's Hobbs"—and seconds later the music cut, and the door swung open to reveal a thin man with dark hair, dressed all in blue.

"There's a face I know," this man—J.D.—said, and the two embraced.

"I hope you don't mind us showing up at your door like this," said Hobbs. "I would've given you a heads-up that I was coming to visit, but things have happened, and now . . . We need a place to crash."

We stepped inside as the sky cracked with thunder, and all that I saw was coated for an instant with mustard-gold fog. Fresh guilt pinched at me when I thought of Jazz, wondered where she was and what she was doing. There was something else, too. Something that asked for my attention, even as I asked for it to wait so that I might focus on the here and now.

The area beside the door was bright thanks to a solitary oil lamp, but everything beyond lay in shadow. I could make out a rose-colored chair and an instrument leaning against it—a fiddle, maybe, though it hadn't sounded like a fiddle on the other side of the wood.

"J.D., this is Livya," Hobbs said. He pulled something out of my hair—a leaf, I think.

"It's nice to meet you," I said, and held out my hand. J.D. took it.

"Your girl?" he asked. Hobbs didn't say anything or nod that I could tell, but maybe he smiled, because J.D. squeezed my hand. "Good for you. Be happy." His voice yielded like bread straight from the oven or the ground after a hard rain. He wasn't from West Virginia, but I couldn't say where he *was* from. He spoke in a way that was different from anything I'd heard before. Maybe he'd lived awhile in a foreign land. Maybe he was someone Hobbs had met at the edges.

I pointed at the instrument. "Is that a violin?"

"It is," he said. "Please, sit. I'll light more lamps."

Within a minute, the room filled with a brighter glow, revealing another chair, and—farther on—what looked like two beds and a woodstove. Other parts of the room remained dark.

"It's not much, I know," J.D. said.

"We've been in the woods for days, man, and on the rails before that." Hobbs led me to one of the beds. The mattress creaked under us, and my body wanted to puddle down, become one with the soft comforter. "This is like the plushest suite at the Holiday Inn. Besides, electricity's overrated."

"You must be hungry," said J.D. "Let's see what I can do about that." He disappeared from the ring of light, into the shadows of the room.

"It's not right to be hungry so soon after we ate, is it?" I asked Hobbs.

"Oh, I don't know. I'm hungry again." He made the mattress bounce, bumped his arm up against mine. "Next time, it'll be a bed," he whispered, and I hummed.

We talked as we ate herbed eggs over greens, welcoming food even though we'd hardly digested our burgers. Hobbs spoke of things he'd done since the last time he'd been to visit J.D. He'd gone to Maryland, he said, and seen the sea—all by taking trains and walking. He'd had a bad experience with a hitch, driving around with a guy high on something who wouldn't let him out when he asked, and decided after that to give it up. (That explained that.) In the end, he said, he'd missed the mountains.

Can't live with 'em, can't imagine living life without 'em.

I indulged myself then, a moment of imagining life without 'em. A life of waves and sand. Standing on a shore and looking beyond this place and clear across to the other side. Lying on a beach with Hobbs, kissing his tomorrow mouth, tasting all the colors of his body as he surged inside me like a wave.

Hobbs, unaware that I'd disrobed and was having my way with him in my mind, seemed to feel a rare ease with J.D. And so I wasn't surprised when he brought up the coins he'd taken from his father, or the situation he found himself in because of them. What surprised me was how easy he was with *me* being in the same room when he talked about everything, as stripped down and honest as could be.

He trusted me. The wall? Gone. Not because I'd scaled it but because he'd removed it himself.

He explained to J.D. how he'd need to get to Red Grass—"that two-faced ass flea"—long enough to learn how to connect again with Beckett, who'd taken some of his coins and made him believe they might be worth something, a new future. He avoided the word *dream.*

"This Beckett must have a business somewhere," J.D. said. "I'll drive you into town tomorrow if you want, and we'll find a phone book, try to track him down. If that doesn't work, I'm sure someone in Porktown knows about him and his reputation. Appraisals, and buying and selling art and all of that, are part of their world."

J.D. worked as a builder on some of the rich houses in Porktown—which wasn't really the town's name, he said, just what the locals called it because every rich person in West Virginia seemed to own a home there.

"It's good that you're doing this," J.D. said. "About time you all were rid of those coins."

There was a long pause.

"What's that look about?" Hobbs asked, and I tilted my head, tried to get a sense of the expression on J.D.'s face but came away with nothing.

J.D. said, "Your father was here last week."

"Bill, here? There's only one reason he'd drag his sorry sack down here. Looking for me, wasn't he?"

"He was looking for you," said J.D. "I didn't know you'd taken the coins, and he didn't say, but now it all makes sense. Madder than I've seen him in ages. You should avoid him, if you can."

Another clap of thunder echoed through the house, and the door rattled with wind. I reached for Hobbs's hand. He squeezed it.

"Maybe we shouldn't be here. I don't want to put you out or bring trouble your way," he said, but J.D. shushed him.

The coins, I learned, were thought to be valuable, with names like Double Eagle and Flowing Hair. Some were minted during wartime. But the coin they talked about the most was a silver dollar from the 1800s. That coin might've been worth a true fortune, J.D. said, but Bill never wanted it touched or seen, and never would've allowed it to be cashed in. Instead, Hobbs and his family lived a life defined by hunger, ill-fitting clothes, and broken things. Instead, Bill started to lose his mind. Instead, Bill's second wife, Alice—who, it turned out, was J.D.'s sister—had left them both.

I didn't ask where the coins had been kept, and it didn't matter, but I was sure they'd been hidden away somewhere. Hiding was what you did when you were afraid, and Hobbs's father was afraid; I was sure of that, too. Maybe he'd buried them under a cross in his backyard, beside one of his dead babies. Maybe he'd put them under a loose floorboard, or under an altar. Or maybe he'd stashed them in the secret pocket of an old coat.

They continued to speak of the coins, but carefully—like they were a sort of sickness. A plague.

We hadn't been with J.D. for long before it hit me—the realization of what I'd done, what I'd forgotten, what I'd felt tugging at me like a wanting child. I'd left behind my suitcase and my mother's ashes. Shame swept through me like a fast-growing cancer, and a dull ache radiated in my chest.

"We'll go back tomorrow," said Hobbs, perched on the arm of the chair I dropped myself into. "Maybe your bag's right where you left it, or maybe someone stuck it behind the bar."

I nodded but couldn't dredge up any optimism. It wasn't Hobbs's fault, but just then the air tasted strongly of regret.

In an effort to cheer me up, J.D. picked up his violin and Hobbs pulled out his harmonica. Music had a way of sanding the lumps off a mood, and their bluesy violin-and-harmonica duet did its best. Even distracted, I was able to appreciate the blend of two instruments I never would've thought to put together. And though the multicolored whirlwinds they made were worthy of a dance, I couldn't bring myself to stand. Watching J.D. bow his violin reminded me of Papa and his fiddle, reminded me of Jazz, who might've been out there somewhere in the rain.

Wet, cold, and alone.

Afraid. Lost. In danger.

Having trouble breathing.

Why hadn't I considered any of that before?

Yes, Jazz had made mistakes. Yes, Jazz had made me angry. But she was still family. Mama would've been ashamed of me, and I felt ashamed of myself. How could I have done it?

People give a lot of fancy reasons for what they do, but it usually comes down to one of two things, Hobbs had said. *They're getting something or they're avoiding something.*

I had gotten something: a stronger connection to the man I wanted to be with. But I was avoiding something, too. Running from it, even. I'd allowed myself to become distracted, drawn into another world, because the world I'd inhabited since Mama died was hard, and it felt good to leave it for a while. It was as straightforward as that, not that there was any solace to be had from understanding it.

I felt a strong need for fresh air, and was about to step outside and risk offending Hobbs and J.D., when that whirlwind of color was interrupted by a quick splat of indigo—a knock at the door.

The music stopped. We all froze.

"Shit," said Hobbs, and I knew he was thinking of his father.

The rain sputtered on. Wind thrashed against the wood. Hobbs came up beside me, seemed to close up and around me like a house.

"Who is it?" J.D. asked through the door.

"I'm looking for my sister," said someone with a voice that looked at first like a familiar straight line. And then like a cardiac monitor from a medical TV show when the patient comes to life again— "Olivia, are you in there? Please." A voice full of peaks and valleys, like home, like West Virginia.

I bolted forward and opened the door to find my sister and Red Grass. "Jazz!" Before I could reach for her, Hobbs thrust his arm in front of me.

"What the hell are you doing?" he said. "Put down the gun, right now."

Gun? I tipped my head, sure that I couldn't be processing things right. But though it was dark and my blind spot made it impossible to see details, it looked for all the world to be true: an object the size of a pistol was tucked into Red Grass's side. And held by my sister's hand.

September 22, 2006

Dear Dad,

After countless arguments with the school about Olivia's unique needs, I decided to take her out altogether and teach her from home. That's right. Me, a teacher. Remember how you once told me I'd make a good teacher? Look, you are a prophet! I joke, but I'm petrified that I won't be able to do it, that she'll fail because I won't be good enough. But I will try my best, and the truth is I love having her at home with me.

It's possible I've made a breakthrough with my tsunamis, too. I've had a lot of high-tide feelings of late—anger at the school, frustration and fascination over Olivia's undiagnosed (until now) synesthesia—and I've managed most of my emotions. But tsunami-fighting takes a toll, which might account for my exhaustion and the fact that I sometimes fall asleep at the worst possible time. I've lost my driver's license and

two jobs in the last year. I wasn't even able to
help out at the school. We won't talk about that,
though, or I'll land myself in the up-and-downs.
The "glass half full" perspective is that now I
wouldn't be able to accept an outside job even if
I wanted to, because Olivia _is_ my job and my
worthier purpose.

She's so good for me, Dad. She reminds me of me,
but in a different time, when I was still your best
girl. She makes me remember what it means to have
fun again. And her descriptions of life wrapped in
surrealism prove that the gray I sometimes feel is all
in my head. I can just close my eyes and imagine
things are however I want them to be, a thousand
shades of happy—even though this sometimes makes
it hard to breathe.

Things with my firstborn are more challenging, but
I'll find a way to overcome. Jazz is her own person.
My charge as her mother is to help her become all
she can be, not settle.

Well, I'll close now. I have math to teach, and science to remember, and I never did well with geography. Time to get to work.

Beth

p.s. Funny, but I seem to be writing more despite all this busyness.

CHAPTER SEVENTEEN

Scars

✳ JAZZ ✳

When I was a child, I dreamed of being a writer one day like my mother, and there was no one more excited over her book. The end of the story loomed like a mysterious doorway—the portal to Narnia or the passageway to the world of the will-o'-the-wisps that my mother wrote about.

The fairy-tale nature of her writings made it easy to dream big back then. My mother would be an author, and we'd take grand trips, buy a fancy house, and drive the best cars built. We'd hire a maid, and a cook. We'd wear designer clothes and shoes, and everyone in school would be envious of me for once. As I grew, the idea of her finishing appealed on a more philosophical level. Finishing one story would mean being able to start another. It would mark both the completion of a cycle and an evolution. Be a proof, of sorts, that you could overcome difficulties and that perseverance paid off.

The End. What would happen when we reached The End?

But every time my mother faced the final chapters she'd grow sleepy, need to take another nap. Finding her bent over the typewriter, her eyelids drooping and with a blank page before her, was not an uncommon sight at any time of day.

As the years passed, I hated more and more that I felt any disappointment over this, that I was still capable of caring. Hated, too, that every once in a while my mind still tried to write—sometimes when I was at the shop, kneading bread, or when I was at home, boiling water for pasta, or about to drift off to sleep. I'd think up a new premise for a play, or have a thought and not realize I'd formulated it as a haiku.

> Knead it, let it rise.
> Roll it, fold, and roll again:
> Journey of the dough.

In this small way, I understood her, though. Not the specifics, like how she thought finishing her book might initiate a reunion with her father. How he would enter, stage left, and present her former life to her like a prize. How the puzzle pieces would fit together with gratifying perfection. How, then, everything would be forgiven. What I understood was the bigger picture.

Old habits died hard.

Old dreams died harder.

We walked in the rain and dark for two miles. My Band-Aids fell off, and the fatigue I'd felt throughout the day hit me full force. Red Grass said more than once that his idea was crazy, but I hadn't realized how crazy it would seem until I had to press a gun into his side.

Everyone stared at me—my sister in her half-cocked sort of way, Hobbs right behind her, a stranger beside him, and Red Grass—as rain dripped off my nose. My back burned with the need to be rid of my pack, but I couldn't do it. Not yet. It was time for my line. I had to say this right, or I'd ruin everything.

"You have a lot of nerve showing up here," said Hobbs. I glanced at him, the anger in his eyes as clear as the array of tattoos on his skin, and everything I'd threatened him with earlier came back to me with all the comfort of wet socks. "How the hell did you even find us?"

The perfect segue.

"He was tracking you." I cleared my throat, repeated myself with more assuredness, and didn't squirm as I looked into eyes that labeled me *detestable*. "He has a fancy device; I can show it to you. He planted the tracker somewhere on your water filter, I guess, put it there one day when you—"

I had more lines—a whole Oscar-worthy story of how a smallish woman might snatch a gun from a biggish man—but it didn't matter just then. Hobbs and J.D. pushed by, took Red Grass by the arms.

"Don't hurt him," I whispered, which wasn't one of my lines, as the men walked off together into the night.

"Come in," Olivia said like a hostess, and I retrieved her suitcase from beside the door. She gasped, pulled it into her hands and to her chest, and thanked me half a dozen times before leading me inside.

Archaic oil lamps cast a flickering radiance on the wooden walls. Around the room lay a random assortment of odd furniture, including a table and chairs made of leather-lashed tree parts, a solitary canoe paddle in a corner, and two mattresses covered with patchwork comforters. At the line where the room was lost to darkness sat a woodstove with a flat top for cooking; I half expected Ma Ingalls to appear with a spoon in her hand.

The door closed behind us, and I spun around, looked past my sister. It was beyond sense to be worried for Red Grass, of all people. If anyone could take care of himself . . . And it was his turn to say the right lines now. I'd done my part.

"They won't hurt him," Olivia said, as if sensing my thoughts, tasting them on her tongue. "They just want answers."

Shadows bobbed around her, made her fierce, a giantess. Her braids were untangled. Her skin glowed. And maybe it was because of what Red Grass had said to me about how I chased people away that I couldn't even summon a proper scold for what she'd put me through. What I asked, I asked without anger, because I needed to know.

"Why do you keep running away like this? Are you testing me? Do you hate me?"

"No, Jazz. I love you," she said. "And I'm sorry. It was wrong, what I did, and my heart felt hollow for it."

I cried for the first time in years, a warm berry still cradled in my hand.

An hour later, Olivia and Hobbs sat together like Siamese twins in a frayed mauve chair, with her head nestled into his shoulder and his arm slung around her in a show of couplery. Whatever tension had existed between them earlier? Gone. Which left me and my desire to go home at a distinct disadvantage.

I needed to be with him, Olivia told me earlier when I pressed her about why she'd left. For once I didn't question her dangerous attraction, was grateful in that moment simply to have found her and too welled up with emotion to say much anyway.

It was a different story altogether when Hobbs and his friend J.D. returned without Red Grass. So after Hobbs found the disk on the bottom of his water filter and J.D. left to flush that disk down the toilet—which worked somehow, though there didn't seem to be any electricity in the house—I asked plenty of questions.

Where's Red Grass? What have you done with him?

Red Grass was locked up somewhere for the night.

Where?

In an outbuilding on J.D.'s land. Somewhere he wouldn't cause more trouble while everyone got a good night's sleep, Hobbs explained, as J.D. reappeared with a blanket and water in hand, then went out the front door once again.

I relaxed a little. It seemed, at least, that Red was being treated humanely.

Hobbs sat in the worn chair, said it was time to figure me out because I was just full of surprises, and I was reminded, strangely, of my interview with Emilia Bryce. Olivia climbed into the chair beside him as the lines came back to me, the story Red Grass had asked me to tell. How I'd seen him with the tracking device at the restaurant and recognized it for what it was. How I knew that following him was the only way I'd see Olivia again. How I'd trailed him in secret for a while before realizing that handing him over would be the only way to prove myself trustworthy again. How a golden opportunity presented itself when he tripped hard, and I was able to snatch his bag—and the gun inside it. How he'd been a surprisingly good listener with a pistol pressed into his side.

Two ways to look at things.

I held my breath. Waited to see if they'd buy it.

Hobbs held out his hand. "I'll take that gun," he said.

I closed in like the hills of West Virginia over the Kennaton U pack resting against my legs—home now to Red Grass's knife, gun, and phone, which lost reception somewhere in the woods. How opportune it would've been to call home if it had worked, *insist* that my father come to get us, *make* him remove us from these people who were turning us into stranger-selves. I should've done that in the first place—insist my father step up and take charge of my sister. This never should've been my responsibility. Would the world crash down around us if he let go of his grief—and his booze—for one day? He was the damned dad.

He was the damned dad.

And I'd tell him that now if I could, if the damned phone worked.

"I'm keeping the gun," I said. "Call it insurance. Two men and—"

"—two women together," Hobbs finished. "Isn't that how you got Red Grass to give you his knife? But a gun and a knife aren't the same thing by a long shot, are they? No pun intended."

Maybe not, but he wasn't getting it—or the opportunity to realize that the Smith & Wesson was bullet-free, that Red Grass had taken the ammunition out himself.

"You'll just have to trust me," I said.

"Will I?" His eyes sharpened. "And what's my insurance? How do I know you didn't call me in and that my father's not already halfway here?"

Father? I didn't show my surprise or tell him that he was wrong—that it was Red Grass's phone number on the poster, that there wasn't anyone to call but him. As I watched my sister's hand land on Hobbs's chest, I decided to respect Red's request and say nothing about those truths. The poster had made Hobbs run and hide, therefore the poster was power. Besides, this was interesting. Why had Hobbs stolen from his father?

"I didn't call you in. I won't do that now, either, as a goodwill gesture for you taking care of Olivia," I said. "I just wanted to be back with my family."

He brushed a hand over my sleepy sister's hair, and she burrowed closer to him. This had turned into more than something to watch; this had become something to worry over. And, from the look in his eyes, he knew that I knew it, which gave him a sort of power, too.

"So you'll play the good girl now?" His eyes dared me to reveal myself, as rain battered the cabin's solitary window. "That's what you want me to believe?"

I knew that nothing more would happen tonight, as long as I agreed. Tomorrow I'd have to deal somehow with the man locked in an outbuilding. Tomorrow I'd have to tear Olivia away from all this, and it wouldn't be easy. *I'd* be the blind one not to see how this life suited her—the wild adventure of it all, even the bad boy she'd latched on to. But tonight? All I had to do was agree. Easy. Still, every part of me felt like a clenched fist when I did it.

I'd be a good girl.

For now.

Anyone would examine the devil if presented with a safe opportunity, which is why I studied Hobbs once he'd climbed into bed beside my sister, left me with the empty mattress. I wasn't stupid. I waited until I knew he was asleep—his breath sounds deep and even, his features smoothed over like stained glass. He lay across from me, and the light from J.D.'s reading lamp, cast from the other side of the room where he would sleep, hit him just so.

The devil had a bump toward the bridge of his nose; no surprise that I hadn't been the first to punch him. Too-long brown hair flung over his face like dirty mop strands. He had a cleft in his chin. I wasn't sure how I felt about those, but it worked with his tough-guy image, and was one of the few tattoo-free parts of his face. There were other tattoos, I knew, along his arms: faces that disintegrated, shapes that were half-man and half-beast, boats and birds and mountains. He wasn't horribly ugly, I guess.

I closed my eyes, felt the sting of salt and dirt and exhaustion behind my lids. Tried to tally the amount of sleep I'd had since leaving home. Couldn't honestly recall. Breathed. Counted to a hundred. Shifted my legs. Opened my eyes. This, at least, was normal. I rarely had an easy time falling asleep, even when I was dog-tired. Olivia, on the other hand, could sleep anywhere, at any time, as if she'd dipped into the genetic pond that was our mother's tendency for constant sleepiness enough never to be troubled by insomnia.

I got up, walked past Hobbs on light feet. J.D. sat in his shabby chair, reading a book. Lonely or content, I couldn't tell.

"J.D., I'm sorry to bug you," I said as quietly as I could, "but can I get a glass of water?" Sometimes it helped bring sleep, sometimes it didn't.

He set the book aside—"Of course"—and returned in short order with a tall glass, which I drank in a way that would best be described as hungry. My throat opened, and I gulped, eager for the water. He refilled the glass.

"You're dehydrated. Sometimes it sneaks up on you. You're cold, too," he said when I shivered.

"A little damp." I patted my denim shorts.

He reached into the shadows and opened a wooden chest behind the chair. J.D. at least was no devil, with his ready smile and sociable manner. He wasn't conventionally attractive—his dark hair threaded through with gray, his nose filling too much of his face, and his brown eyes both close-set and wide—but he was easy enough to look at.

"My sister left the country years ago and asked me to keep a few of her things," he said, still bent over, rifling through the container. "I'm sure she wouldn't mind if . . . Ah, here we go."

He produced a pair of sweatpants, which I gratefully traded for my wet shorts in his bathroom—a small room with a toilet and a yellow tub that felt too modern by a mile for the cabin, and a mirror that I avoided. When I returned to the main room, I found J.D. in one of the wooden chairs, holding a child's coat and with a wistful expression on his face.

He motioned me toward the cushioned seat. "Better?" he asked, as I parked myself.

"A million times." I nodded toward the coat. "Is that your sister's too?"

"Alice tried to have children of her own, but . . ." He grimaced, and I recalled the story Hobbs told about the crosses occupying the land behind his house. "It's Hobbs's jacket," J.D. continued. "Alice married his father and became his sort-of mother for a good part of his life. I guess that makes me his sort-of uncle."

I raised a brow. "Well, you're nothing alike."

"No?"

The question hung in the air as I took another sip of water. "He's reckless, dangerous, a drifter, and a thief," I said. "You, on the other hand, seem like a nice person. Sorry, I know you like him, and that he's sort-of family."

His expression never changed. He really did have the strangest eyes. Open-diary eyes.

"I wouldn't say Hobbs is dangerous," J.D. said. "Reckless?"

My fingers tapped the glass. "You don't think it's dangerous to live the life of a train hopper, or reckless to cover your whole body with tattoos? He's going to regret the hell out of that when he's eighty-four." *If he lives that long*, I added silently.

"It wasn't always tattoos," said J.D.

"You mean he looked normal once?"

"It used to be pen markings." J.D. held my gaze. "He'd draw all over his arms and face. Red pen, blue pen, green. He liked green."

"See now, that's weird, you have to admit," I said with a quirk of my lips. "What's wrong with plain old skin?"

"Nothing, but his wasn't plain. It was scarred with cigarette burns and worse. The drawings covered the scars for a while. I'd draw them myself sometimes. Eventually he made them permanent with tattoos. I think they make him feel . . . normal."

Shame wasn't something I'd often felt. A few times, but not often. I felt it now, though. Remembered the thought I'd had a few minutes before while looking at Hobbs's dented nose: *No surprise that I hadn't been the first to punch him.*

"Who did that to him? His father?"

"He's not a good man. Hobbs has always said his time with my sister was the happiest in his life. Your sister seems to make him happy, too."

Now I understood better why the poster had made Hobbs run, what it was that he feared. I could tell J.D. the truth—that it wasn't Bill's phone number on the poster, that there wasn't anything to fear over that at all. I could do that. I could tell Hobbs, too, in the morning. But the poster might've been the last power I had left. I'd have to think about it.

My quiet didn't go unnoticed by J.D.

"I'm sorry. I've made you uncomfortable."

"No, I'm glad you told me," I said, but didn't loosen my grip on the glass.

"At least you know the truth. If Hobbs were all bad, would he have asked that I drive you and your sister to the glades tomorrow *before* trying to find Beckett—this man who has some of his coins?"

"Wait—" I leaned forward. "You have a *car?*"

"Truck."

"Oh, my God"—I stood, all but leaped out of my skin—"you can take us home!" I lowered my voice. "Please take us home."

"I'll help you, but first he wants to make good on his promise to your sister. He wants me to get her to the glades in his stead, because he can't do it himself anymore. Isn't that what you want, too?" J.D. watched me with a curious light in his eyes, his fingers steepled near his chin.

I nodded woodenly, reminded myself that this was progress. This was Olivia at her destination. This was a vehicle, taking us to a place where there would be a working phone. This was the promise of a ride home.

I returned to bed after saying good night to J.D. Turned on my side. Looked again at Hobbs, those tattoos.

Train hopper, thief, devil. Victim.

Every time I thought I knew how to categorize him, something changed; he wouldn't sit neatly in his box. I reminded myself that I couldn't afford to care. Tomorrow, control would shift back to me. And maybe it made me a bad person, but I wasn't above using Hobbs's fear to end my personal nightmare.

The nightmare didn't end that night, though. Once I finally slept, I dreamed again of the caged city of Oran, but this time Hobbs was outside the gates, dodging hands that meant to drag him through the bars, one set of them mine. And I had a feeling that maybe Olivia, who'd always been the freest bird I knew, was right there beside me.

Fourth Stage:

DEPRESSION

Depression is something that
makes you lose your sight.

—*Michael Schenker*

CHAPTER EIGHTEEN

Wishes

* OLIVIA *

Playing games after Christmas Eve dinner at Babka's was one of our traditions. Some of the games were carried over from her childhood in Slovakia, like throwing walnuts into the corner of the room, then opening them with hope that the nut wasn't fractured or rotten. Other games were invented.

My favorite invented game was called Wishes.

Here's how it worked: Think of something you'd wish for someone else. Write it on a slip of paper. (While writing, you could not get pen marks on Babka's white tablecloth or the wish would be void and you would have to wait a whole year before you could wish it again.) Fold the paper in half, exactly. Sleep with the wish under your pillow for seven nights, and dream every night about the wish. If the wish was pure enough, if it was worthy, it would come true.

There was no rule that said you couldn't share wishes—it didn't make them void or anything—but, for the most part, Babka was the only person who shared her wish. Every year, she wished that Grandpa Dušan was at peace, and then she'd look at the empty chair she'd put at the table for him in case his spirit came for the meal.

I'd shared my wishes when I was little, but back then they might not have been called worthy. I wished a Hollywood star would drive through Tramp and try some of Babka's biscuits, then tell all of her friends so we could become famous. I wished everyone could see voices and colored letters, and taste words. (*That's impossible*, Jazz said.) I wished Jazz would get married to someone with a big house, and we could all live with her and their twelve dogs. I wished my sauce could win a million-dollar prize in a sauce contest. (I wished I could find a sauce contest.) My wishes turned more serious as time went on, though, and they turned private, too.

Sometimes I wish I could forget him, Mama said to me once about her father. *I don't want to miss him anymore*. She fell into a long up-and-down after that. That was the first Christmas I made a wish for her:

I wish Mama would forget about Grandpa Orin, because it's what she wants, too.

Every year after that, I made a wish for Mama. I'd put the paper under my pillow—folded exactly in half—and leave it there for seven nights starting on Christmas Eve.

I wish Baby Jesus or Santa Claus would come to our house and take the letters and put them in Grandpa Orin's mailbox.

I wish Grandpa Orin would forgive Mama and un-disown her.

I wish Mama would finish her story and send it to Grandpa Orin, and that it makes him love her again.

I wish Mama and Grandpa Orin could be reunited.

It never occurred to me until after Mama died that there might be a danger in the way we went about wishing, by asking a force outside ourselves—be it fate or luck, Santa Claus or Baby Jesus—to make something come true. Maybe wishing made it less likely that we'd try to make things come true on our own. Maybe wishing made something inside us go lax.

The house was empty of people but full of the scent of pancakes when I woke, making me nostalgic right from the start. Papa used to make pancakes every Tuesday, because it was a day that needed something special, he always said. Huckleberry corn cakes were his specialty, which he said was more about the process than anything else: Heat an inch of oil on the stove, then spoon in the cornmeal-and-berry batter, turn the heat down right away, and wait for the edges to crisp before the flip. There was nothing quite like the first bite of one of those cakes—the crunch as satisfying as the look on my father's face.

He hadn't touched the cornmeal tin since Mama died. As much as I hurt over losing her, Papa had to hurt all the worse. How would it feel to lose your lover of twenty-odd years, know you'd never touch that person's skin again or kiss their lips, share a hug or even a conversation?

I pulled my suitcase up beside me on the bed and opened it. Inside were a few of Mama's shirts—old favorites that still held her smell. But today felt like an orange-tank day, so I reached for the top that had only ever been my own and did a quick change in the open because no one was around to care.

Before closing the case, I grazed my fingers over the bag of Mama's ashes. "I'm sorry. I won't leave you behind again."

I sat there awhile longer, until the quiet of the house felt too loud, then walked barefoot to the front door of J.D.'s cabin and pushed it open.

"Hello?" I called.

The sun's rays felt long and welcoming on my arms as I stepped outside and made my way up the dandelion-dotted hill under which sat J.D.'s home. Soft blades of grass and mounds of furry moss cushioned the undersides of my feet as I marked the curve of the land with careful steps. When I sensed that the slope had started to turn down again, I stopped and sat, believing I was just above the front door—unmissable by the masses once they returned from wherever they were.

I spread my palms out on the ground, turned my face up to the sky, and closed my eyes. There was no evil on this land, no matter what folks might believe. I smelled the scent of rich soil, kneaded by yesterday's rain, and a hint of worms. Felt the heaviness of the still air, the humidity curling my hair at the ends. Heard the buzz of bees searching for pollen around me—and then my sister's voice calling my name.

I answered, then heard her approaching footsteps.

"Olivia, good grief." She cast me in shade as she hovered over me. "I'm in the bathroom for a few minutes and next thing I know you're gone again."

"Not gone," I said. "Here I am."

She'd changed into sweatpants and a T-shirt that was either pink or light orange, and that I hoped meant she'd shed her storm-cloud mood.

"We need to talk," she said. "There are things you need to know about Hobbs."

I stiffened. There was something in the look of her voice that reminded me of yesterday, of Hobbs when he'd said, *I'm ruined, Livya.* Then I'd been able to escape what I'd sensed, force him away from his thoughts, too, with a diversion. Now it came fully into my consciousness. The affect in Jazz's voice was something I'd observed with voices once before, long ago, whenever anyone spoke about a particular person.

Jane. A neighbor who'd left. She'd been my age, skinny as a line, with eyes like violets and long blond hair all the girls had envied.

And she was bright. Bright and bold and beaten.

And worse.

Voices decayed when people talked about her, but only in ways I could see. Tiny black holes poked through them, like an echo of people's thoughts. No one wanted to imagine the full picture; the truth was too dire to process completely.

"I'm sorry again about yesterday," I said.

"That's not what I came to talk about."

Maybe it wasn't, but I needed to get away from the subject of Hobbs and things I couldn't process completely.

"Well, I was too tired before to talk much about why I did what I did," I said. "I want to talk now, if you'll listen."

"Fine." She sat beside me, and sunlight kissed my flesh again. "I'm listening."

What to say? How to explain running away from what you wanted most to a person like Jazz?

I said, "I think I left everything so important behind me—you and the suitcase with Mama's ashes—because I'm worried that what we're doing may not matter in the way I need, even though it's still what I want. Does that make any sense?"

"Nope," she said, "which makes this like every other talk we've had in our lives."

A thin red-coil crow of a rooster sounded off from a distance, and I sighed.

"Let's try this, then," I said. "As much as I want and need to go to the glades, I think there's a part of me that *doesn't* want to go."

"Is that so? Can I talk to that part for a minute?"

I smiled, even though I didn't mean it.

Sometimes you *had* to go places, but that didn't mean you weren't afraid of what might be waiting for you there.

Violet-eyed Jane hadn't wanted to leave Tramp, or her friends. She'd wanted to leave her abusers. But they—her parents or her older brother, we never knew—were leaving, too, making her go. She couldn't escape them any more than she could escape her own skin.

What had Hobbs been trying to escape?

What was I trying to escape?

"So what are you worried about?" Jazz asked.

"The easiest answer?" I dug a finger deep into the moss beside me. "That I may not see a will-o'-the-wisp."

"Well, you'd better prepare yourself for that eventuality," Jazz said. "Not to rain acid all over your parade, but wanting to see one of those is not going to magically equate with seeing one. And it's Friday, in case you didn't realize, which means it's a day later than

I said I'd give over to this insanity. After today's trip, we're done. Unlike this will-o'-the-wisp business, I know a job is out there waiting for me, and I need to spend some time getting ready for it."

I remembered the dream I'd had—Babka pointing toward Saturday—but didn't say anything. And I couldn't get Hobbs's voice out of my head.

I'm ruined, Livya.

"Do you believe in dreams? That some are wrong and some are right?" I asked, my thoughts wandering recklessly, away and away from *ruined*.

"I don't know," she said. "Does it matter?"

I wiggled my finger deeper into the moss, until dirt wedged under my nail. "Mama thought her dreams were flawed. Almost the last thing I said to her was about dreams—that there was nothing wrong with her dreams. It was me, you know, who was the last to talk to her. I was the last one to see her alive."

Jazz's voice turned soft as a dog's belly. "I know, and that's rough. I'm sorry."

I took a chance and reached for her hand. It had been such a long time since we'd locked fingers. When she didn't push me away, when she squeezed back, I let loose words I'd never have said if my mind hadn't been a fracture of thoughts.

"There was a letter by her side when she died. I have it."

"What?" Her voice wilted along with her grip. "What did it say?"

"I never opened the envelope."

"You didn't—You found her with a letter and still argue that she didn't kill herself?"

Jazz tried to pull away, but I clung to her hand, her flesh and blood and bone, as adrenaline spiked in me. What had I done? But I could not take back the words.

"We don't know what it says," I told her.

"Olivia!"

"It's not meant for us."

"Of course it's meant for us! Who else would it be meant for?

You should've shared it to begin with! Now we have to open it after all this time, and all the wounds that might've crusted over the tiniest bit are going to split open along with it. What do you think this will do to Dad, or didn't you ever consider that?"

"The letter's not for us," I repeated desperately, "because she wouldn't do it, she didn't." *Suicide, suicide.* "It's for Grandpa Orin, just like the others. Why don't we try to find his address, and then we can send them all? You have them, don't you? The other letters?"

Leaves slapped at one another on a sudden gust of wind. My hands shook.

"Listen up, Olivia Francis Moon. You're going to give that letter to Dad as soon as we get back. It's *his* to have. *His* to decide what to do with, and that's the end of it."

"That's not what she would've wanted."

"Of course it's what she would've wanted," she hissed, and I dropped her hand as if it had bitten me, turned into a snake. "It's a letter. Letters are meant to be read."

"Not her letters."

"You're crazy," she said. "And you're making me dizzy, talking in circles."

I felt crazy. "I was the last one with her." Me. "I heard what she said." Me. "I know what she was thinking." Me. "I was the last." Me. "I'll never believe that she did it, that she could've. Her life meant something. Dreams and hopes are worth something." My dark spot throbbed, felt twice its normal size. "It'll taste like hope."

"Taste like hope? What are you talking about, the letter? Jesus Christ, tell me you didn't eat it."

"The will-o'-the-wisp," I said, before a rumbling motor cut through the morning quiet.

"We're about to have company, so we'll have to finish talking about this later. And don't think we won't," Jazz said, her voice edged with teeth. "J.D. has a truck, and he's going to take us to the glades. We can go as soon as we're ready."

"Go?" I couldn't comprehend this, as my mind churned with

new arguments to try with my sister. Then something snagged my focus. "J.D.?" I blinked. "You mean Hobbs."

"Hobbs can't go to a public park, Olivia, you must realize that," she said, as the noise grew. "There are posters out there showing his face, and it's not like the guy fades into the woodwork. Besides, I'm pretty sure he's taking off today, getting out of here while he still can."

Getting out. Going. Gone.

I had never seen Jane again.

I scrambled to my feet, started to run back the way I'd come, but a sudden sharp pain pierced my right foot, and I crumpled to the ground.

"And that's what you get for not wearing shoes on a hill full of bees." Jazz reappeared by my side and pulled my throbbing bare foot out of my hands. "Stingers. Two of them. You never can do things simply, can you? Let's hope J.D. has some tweezers, because I don't have nails enough to get those out. Oh, come on, it's not so bad, is it?" she asked with forced cheer when I didn't move or speak. "We're going to the glades, after all. It's what you wanted, right?"

"Stop talking to me like I'm a child."

"Stop acting like one," she snapped.

Somewhere in the distance, the engine cut and a door slammed shut.

"We're not going this minute, are we?" My heart raced. Everything was moving too fast. "I can't lose another person. I can't lose Hobbs."

"Olivia, you've known him for three days."

"I love him!" I said, and knew it was true the moment the words left my lips.

I loved Hobbs.

No matter what had happened to him.

No matter what or who it was he was running from.

How he'd been ruined.

I loved him.

I'd have to tell him. And hope that it mattered.

A s it turned out, I'd stepped on three bees, not two, and J.D. didn't have any tweezers. I knew that if my skin got soft enough we'd get at the stingers, though, so I stationed myself on the edge of his tub and soaked my foot. Beside me, light from the oil lamp played off the water. I wished my mother would appear in its reflection or come through the uncovered mirror on the wall and tell me what to do about Hobbs. I couldn't lose him to the edges, to the trains or the sea. If I never saw him again, none of this would ever make sense, and I couldn't believe my feelings were for nothing.

And what would I do about the letter? Why, why, why had I opened my big mouth and told Jazz about that?

"Where's Livya?"

My stomach twisted with a fresh wave of nausea when I heard Hobbs's voice in the other room. Hobbs, come to say goodbye. Seconds later, footsteps. And then he was there, beside me, and the words I'd wanted to say locked up as if my throat had been bee-stung, too.

"Hey."

"Hey."

Boots hit the floor, and then he swiveled around and added his bare feet to the water beside mine. "You all right?"

"Bee stings aren't the worst news of my day," I said, and noticed the pull of his mouth.

"We both knew this would happen at some point," he said. "I'd go my way, you'd go yours. And now, with everything going on with my old man, well. . . ." Dark pinpricks marred the curve of his voice again. "We can't keep Red Grass locked up forever," he finished.

I should ask about that—how things were with Red Grass, if he'd admitted to anything or if they'd learned any more about Beckett. But I didn't care much then.

"Whatever happened in your past won't change how I feel about you," I said. "It doesn't change anything."

He laughed, but there was no humor in it. "It changes everything, all the time. But I want you to know that I'd go, Wee Bit, if I could. I'd go to the glades with you."

My eyes pricked. "What if I said I wanted to stay with you? You said once that I might be cut out for life on the rails."

He rolled his foot in the water. "I shouldn't have said that. A girl like you doesn't belong in this sort of life for keeps. It's not the way of it. It's not the way of me, either. I like to go it alone, and that's the truth."

"But that's because you've had to," I argued. "You don't have to anymore."

"I do have to," he said. "Doesn't mean we haven't had fun, though, right?"

It's been fun. It was such a Stan thing to say.

When his foot grazed mine, I pulled away, reached up into my hair and separated a handful into pieces.

"Come on, Livya." He bumped my shoulder with his. "This might be our last time alone. Don't be mad."

"I'm not mad." What I felt was more complicated than *mad* or *sad*. What I felt was disillusioned. Robbed. "You were supposed to be all of my next days."

"What?"

"You tasted like tomorrow."

Awkward seconds passed as he said nothing. And then the light distorted in the water as he pulled out of the tub, left me there with a swollen foot, and words of love wilted like a dying bud on my tongue.

April 4, 2008

Dear Dad,

I just finished watching a television show on reunions. One after another, people were invited onto a stage, and settled onto a comfortable couch. They wore their best clothes, and had their hair fixed up. And then they were introduced— reintroduced—to someone they'd lost. A mother went concave around the daughter she'd given up for adoption as a fourteen-year-old. Twins separated at birth, who'd maintained a startling number of identical behaviors throughout their lives, met their mirror selves for the first time. A brother and sister in their eighties, who'd had a fight about one thing or another more than fifty years ago, decided to bury the hatchet. Most touching, a prisoner of war was reunited with his wife. She'd already been told that he was alive, but she thought she'd been invited to the show to discuss her feelings. When he walked onto the stage, she stood, and I swear it seemed her legs would give out. He ran up to her and hugged her, and they had to cut to a commercial, because everyone was too busy sobbing after that to talk.

They were saying all these things that resonated so deeply with me that I scrambled to find a pen and wrote them down on a napkin:

"You can tell yourself to let it go, berate yourself every time your thoughts swing in that direction, but some people are as essential as skin and bone."

"He is all parts of my past. He's the hope of my best self and the fear of my worst. That's why I couldn't face him for such a long time. I didn't know what I'd see."

"I know I hurt her when I chose another life over her. But I think it also hurt her, because it seemed I was choosing one version of myself over another."

"I felt him like a missing limb all those years. Now I'm whole again."

I turned off the television after that and thought about us—how you are, as others before me have said, like a missing limb. How you are both there and not there, all the time, and how I feel your presence even when I don't want to.

But here's the part that might surprise you: I also thought about Mom.

"She doesn't exist anymore, Bethie. We won't give her that power over us, will we?"

Do you remember saying that? I remember. Those words imprinted on me after she left, the way you imprinted on me as the everlasting root in my life, the only foundation I had left. I wonder now if that's what you told yourself after I married Branik, when—like it or not—I chose one version of myself over the other: that I didn't exist anymore, and you wouldn't let me have power over you.

I wonder what Mom is doing now. If she's alive. If she ever thinks of us. If you ever think of her.

I wonder if she ever reached out to you to have you cut her off.

I wonder if she ever tried to contact me.

And I wonder, Dad, if you ever think of me, even if you don't want to—if I'm like your missing limb, or even your tsunami. What would you do if I sent you a card today, right now, filled with pictures of your granddaughters? Would I be able to face you after all this time if you suddenly reached out, or would I feel like that woman on the show—afraid of what version of myself I might see?

Beth

CHAPTER NINETEEN

The Plague

∗ JAZZ ∗

A few days before my mother died I began reading *The Plague*, by Albert Camus. The book had been in her college trunk, which I'd found one snowy day in the small space under the stairs. The orange scythe on the cover intrigued me, and the first line of the second paragraph hooked me:

The town itself, let us admit, is ugly.

The town's name was Oran.

I read half of the book that first night, and thought about it all the next day as I sifted together flour, baking powder, and salt, cut in shortening, and added milk to make biscuits for Susie's. I arrived home late that afternoon, eager to consume the last half. My mother stood in the kitchen, still in the robe I'd seen her in that morning, her arms locked against the table, and her eyes focused on something beside her clunky typewriter. This was not an unusual sight, finding her staring at papers or off into space.

I set a bag of biscuits on the counter for dinner, and was ready to slip by my mother and head to my room, when I realized that what she stared at was a newspaper clipping. We didn't get the paper at our house, because Tramp didn't have a paper. Kennaton was the closest city that put out the daily news, but we'd decided the money my father brought home would be better spent on food and clothes than on information about a city that didn't involve us. So it was strange to see a clipping. A note lay beside her, too, and I recognized the bold teal stripe at the top of the stationery used by my mother's sometimes-friend Bonnie, who lived in Kennaton.

I peered over her shoulder and read:

ORIN HOWELL
Orinthal "Orin" Howell, 73, passed away on February 12, 2013, at Kennaton Hospital. He was predeceased by his parents, John and Victoria Howell; his first wife, Suzanne Howell; and his daughter, Beth Howell. He is survived by his second wife, Helena Howell, and five stepchildren: Stuart Marshall, Liza Monahue, Treena Marshall, Joseph Marshall, and Gretchen Schultz. Orin Howell founded and managed Future Bright Bank during the 1980s. A special thanks to the staff at Kennaton Hospital for the exemplary care provided to Orin in his final days. Funeral Services will be held on Friday, at 2:00 P.M., at the Rutherford & Son Funeral Home, 245 Main Street, Kennaton, with calling hours held an hour before, from 1:00 to 2:00 P.M. Burial will be in Kennaton Hills Memorial Park.

Orin Howell. My grandfather.
Beth Howell. My mother.
I'd known for years that my mother had been disowned by her father, but seeing it in black and white—that she'd been listed in his obituary as a deceased child—made the room chill by degrees even for me. I couldn't imagine how she felt. And, of course, her father was dead. Her father, who must've seemed like a stranger then. She'd missed his funeral by a day, too.

"I'm sorry," I said, and touched her arm. "Do you need anything?"

She didn't respond.

"Mom? Want me to go back to the store and get Dad?"

She shook her head and began to fold the paper. In half. Into quarters. Into eighths. She folded that piece of paper until it no longer resembled squares; it looked like a tiny ball. And then she stuffed it into the pocket of her robe.

"Don't say anything to anyone about this," she said. "I don't want to talk about it."

I tried to give her a hug, but she rolled her shoulders, wouldn't be touched. Rebuffed me, as I'd rebuffed her so many times. So I left her there, went up to my room and opened *The Plague*.

The world's a bitch, and then you die, said Camus, throughout the course of two hundred and seventy-eight pages. It's a world that's unsympathetic to people's individual plights. It's a world without meaning, even though people tried, all the time, to find significance in everything. You may or may not agree, but here's the truth: Rats die. Diseases spread. Criminals thrive. My mother's father disowned her, and his second wife had her officially killed in his obituary. One week later, my mother died in our kitchen with the gas on, contained there as neatly, as utterly, as a citizen of Oran.

I removed the horrific, concentrated ball of meanness that was my grandfather's obituary from the pocket of my mother's robe long before my father got rid of it, and said nothing about it—to honor my word and because there was no point.

No crumpled piece of paper had ever felt so heavy.

When I felt the familiar tug to retreat after my talk with Olivia— and knowing that it would be a while before we could leave, thanks to those bee stings—I didn't bother trying to repress it. I grabbed my backpack and left for a walk on J.D.'s land, a forest dense with young trees that showed off too much sky. I wandered over hills and thin streams, my head overfilled with everything my sister had said.

I was the last one to see her alive.

I'd known this, of course, but hadn't spent time thinking about what that might've been like for Olivia.

There was a letter by her side when she died.

A letter that Olivia had kept secret for months. Because she preferred to hang on to her delusions rather than hear the truth? How could she still insist that our mother's death had been an accident?

I'll never believe that she did it, that she could've. It can't be true!

Will-o'-the-wisps taste like hope.

Was that what this whole trip was about, chasing after some form of hope that only Olivia understood? What the hell was I supposed to do with that?

An overturned boat propped against a tree in the distance caught my eye, and I headed for it, kicking the heads off a dozen mushrooms along the way. My feet were still firmly on the ground when I leaned against its warm metal body, raised my crossed arms to my face, and squeezed my eyes shut.

That letter. What were we supposed to do about that letter?

It's for Grandpa Orin, just like the others!

What would Olivia do if she knew our grandfather died a week before our mother turned on the oven and closed the kitchen door? In my mind, there was no doubt that she'd killed herself. She'd wagered everything on some potential future reconciliation, wagered her family. All my life she'd polished me to be the trophy child, hoped I'd be enough to show off to the Great Orin, that he'd forgive her, then, for having me in the first place.

And now he was dead.

Cause. Effect.

Even though part of me wanted to tell Olivia right then to set the record straight, another part warned that she wasn't in the right headspace to hear the truth. The wild-eyed look of my sister when I'd pushed about the letter lingered behind my lids. That look screamed, *Stop now, I've reached the edge.*

I wasn't good at figuring things out even on my best days, and today was far from my best day. Today everything felt as wrong-sided, as upside-down, as the boat. I rocked its weight beneath me, back and forth, forth and back, trying to understand the way Olivia's mind worked. Though I'd long believed that she had a different and sometimes infuriating perception of things, I'd never considered she might be in some ways fragile because of that.

Will-o'-the-wisps taste like hope?

Was I supposed to divine some sort of significance from that? Was that supposed to be as clear to me as how sending letters to a man, even if he were alive, could matter to any of us—least of all to a woman who'd decided that life wasn't worth sticking around for anyway?

What could this letter—this final letter—possibly say?

Dear Family,

It is over. Please carry on without me, and do your best to figure things out.

p.s. Jazz, take care of your sister.

"I hate this shit," I said to no one, my chest once more filled with anger at my mother for leaving us. Leaving so many things unfinished. Leaving me to figure it all out for myself.

What would hope taste like, anyway? Would I walk a week for a chance to savor it, if I could, if I needed it?

What would I hope for?

A thought crossed my mind. What might my mother's life have

been without judgment and condemnation from her father? What might it have been with acceptance?

Could I do that for Olivia? Try harder not just to endure her point of view but to respect it, even though I could never share it? The last time I tried to put myself in her figurative shoes, I'd been a child. Once upon a time, I went through an entire storybook and colored all the letters to match what Olivia said she saw. *A* was red, I remembered. Tuesday tasted like pancakes. The sun smelled like Mama.

I tried to remember what my mother smelled like.

Fabric softener. Cherry lip balm. Coffee.

Sometimes she'd smelled like rose water or garden soil or oniony ramps. Sometimes like the inside of a book.

Dear Family,

It hurts too much to carry on. I'm sorry if this hurts you, too, but know I will miss and love you for forever.

"I hate this shit," I said again, rubbing at my eyes with the palms of my hands.

When I dropped my arms, I spied a slender trail between tall evergreens in the distance, the hint of a blue building obscured by brush. I walked toward the winding path, glad to escape my thoughts.

The building itself was neat, with what appeared to be a fresh coat of blue paint over its pine exterior and a tar-patched roof. A set of wide double doors was secured with a padlock.

I put my hand against the warm sun-streaked door and set my

bag near my feet. Though I didn't think anyone was around to hear me but him, I spoke his name quietly. "Red Grass?"

"Girly?" he said from inside, not so quiet. "It's about time you came to spring me."

"I don't have a key," I said, and rattled the lock with my hand. "But I have some questions."

He grumbled something indecipherable from the other side of the wood, complaining no doubt about my need for answers.

"You're a bounty hunter, aren't you?"

The idea didn't seem outrageous, and fit what I'd come to know about him: He was tenacious, sneaky, and owned professional equipment. And payment could come directly from the coins. In fact, maybe the coins that had been taken from Hobbs at the restaurant *were* payment for hunting him. Maybe that's why Red Grass had been so obsessed with getting them into his hands. For that matter, maybe that's why he'd been so keen on buying drinks for everyone at the bar that night; instant wealth had a way of making a person generous.

It was no surprise to me when he didn't respond. Red Grass being forthcoming all of a sudden would be too great a change.

"Are you working for Hobbs's father?" I pressed my ear against the wood, squinted as if this might improve my hearing. Still, nothing. "All right, then, stay quiet. But I'm not sticking around. See ya."

"Wait a gosh dang minute," he bellowed. "You can't just leave me here!"

"See now, you can talk just fine when it suits you, but you don't give a thing. That's not how it works, old man."

"You'll ruin it all," he grumbled.

"What will I ruin, exactly?"

He turned the subject. "You got my knife?"

"Why? You don't think I'm actually going to hand it over, do you?"

"Oh, come on, missy. Have a care for an old man. They tied my ropes too tight and cut off circulation to my feet," he said, and I felt a double pinch of guilt. But I also knew that Red could fabricate a truth when it served, and I had a hard time believing that J.D. would tie anyone's ropes too tight.

"Are you working for Hobbs's father?" I asked, and this time he responded without a threat or bargaining chip slid across our mental table.

"No," he said. "I'm not."

His tone was all poker, though, too even to give anything away. Without being able to see his face, I couldn't scrutinize his expression for dishonesty.

"You'd better hope not," I told him. "Otherwise you're no better than one of the devil's minions. From what I learned about that man last night, he's about as bad as a person can get."

"What do you mean?" he asked, and this time his voice cracked.

I repeated what J.D. had told me about the way Hobbs was raised, the abuse he'd suffered. There was more to Hobbs than anyone could know from a glancing look at him and his life, I said, recognizing and giving voice to the stark shift in my feelings.

I wasn't so sure I wanted to be a part of Hobbs's downfall anymore.

And though I might not approve of him as a partner for my sister, neither did I want to play Orin in this scenario—trying to keep two people apart who liked each other. Burning bridges and birthing dysfunction by forcing Olivia to make a choice that wouldn't be necessary with a little more tolerance thrown into the mix.

"You've hardly shut up a second as long as I've known you, and now you have nothing to say?" I asked, when silence loomed after I told the story.

"Just one thing." He raised his voice. "I can't feel my fecking feet!"

"Here's my best advice: Wiggle your toes."

He howled when he realized I wouldn't give him the knife, but that's how it would be, even if I did still feel a double pinch of guilt.

"I'm sorry, Red," I said. "I just can't help without understanding the truth of what's going on."

He didn't respond. And then I walked away.

*

The realization that I'd spent two hours in the woods hit when I saw that J.D.'s house was empty of life—and checked my watch. Maybe the others were out looking for me. Wherever they were, I felt sure they'd be back. I didn't believe Olivia would run off again, not after the last time.

In the bathroom, I traded my borrowed sweatpants for shorts, then stalled when my eyes met themselves in J.D.'s mirror. Physical and mental exhaustion reflected back at me, along with the swirl of questions I still had to answer.

Time for some choices.

I would not tell my sister about our grandfather's obituary, not until I had a better sense of her mind-set and could have a rational conversation with her about the letter she'd found.

I would stop questioning Olivia's trek to see—and *taste*—a will-o'-the-wisp. It seemed important to her, wrapped up in her processing of our mother's death. I'd try to respect that, even though I felt as incapable of understanding it as of how she'd fallen for the likes of Hobbs.

I'd try to control just two things today: our trip to the glades, and our trip back home.

A stranger's face appeared in the mirror beside mine, and I swiveled around, my heart like a battering ram against my ribs. Then I realized . . .

"Hobbs?" His skin was free of color and, despite a few bumps that I recognized as scars, appeared utterly normal. "How did—? You removed your tattoos?"

He smiled, revealing a dimple. "Not exactly."

As it turned out, he'd had the art on his face covered with makeup by a local tattoo artist. "Less painful, and I didn't have a month to lose," he joked, though I couldn't find my voice to respond. He hadn't covered his arms, but those, he explained, were easy enough to conceal with a shirt.

"Chances of running into my old man down there are slim to none," he said, "but if there's one poster, there could be more, and I'm not stupid. Posters show a guy with color, though. No one'll blink at this guy. This guy"—he gestured to himself—"is clean and smooth, lived a good life. This guy's figured out how to wear an invisibility cloak." He dipped his eyes, then locked them on mine. "And it means a lot to her, right?"

A swell of emotion I'd never be able to dissect flooded over me, made my nose tingle. I spun around, turned on the faucet, and splashed water over my face, hoping he hadn't seen it.

After soaking her foot, Olivia had gone to sit alone in a shaded slingback chair near J.D.'s cabin, unaware of all that Hobbs had done. He was the first to close in on her, as J.D. and I watched from a few feet away. Disbelief morphed into joy on my sister's face as Hobbs filled her in on his new appearance, and his intentions.

"Come on, Wee Bit, and look. I know you want to," he said, then bent his head until his face was all but on her shoulder.

"You're beautiful," she said. "But you always were."

He smiled. "I'd let you kiss me, but you'd ruin my makeup."

She kissed him anyway.

"It's like Christmas," said J.D. beside me, and somehow I knew what he meant.

The afternoon passed in a haze of waiting. We ate sandwiches—ham on hearty rye, drizzled with mustard—and J.D. and I played cards in the grass. The plan was simple enough: Olivia, Hobbs, and I would go to the Visitors Center at the end of the workday, when everyone else would be filing out but we could still grab maps. We'd trek out to the glades, then resume waiting. I pocketed the cards for later; I was a master at solitaire.

When it was time to leave, we made our way to the rough drive beside the cabin. I didn't notice Hobbs hauling Red Grass's tent until we were at the pickup, loading our bags.

"Why do we need that?" I asked.

"Because wisps come out at night," Olivia said, opening the passenger-side door.

"And Red wasn't about to mind that we borrowed it," Hobbs added. "I took his bag into custody, you might say, last night."

"We're not—" I started, but Olivia cut me off.

"Come on, Jazz," she said with exasperation. "What do you think we did all this for? You can't see wisps during the day."

I had to count to ten, remind myself of my newborn decisions.

Her own perspective.

Respect it even if you can't understand it.

Wisps taste like hope.

"Fine." I shoved my bag beside my sister's in the truck. "But this is it. This is the end of me doing whatever the hell you say. And I want the tent."

"Okay by me," she said. "I don't plan on sleeping."

It wasn't until we were on the road that I looked down at my sister's suitcase, which had been bumping against my leg for the last few miles, and realized it. The letter our mother had written, her last words, might be inside. If Olivia was anything like me, she would've kept that close.

Dear Family, I have a message for each of you . . .

I knew then that I'd do whatever I had to do to get my hands on that letter.

CHAPTER TWENTY

Cranberry Glades

∗ OLIVIA ∗

Tramp's cemetery was small, but Papa wanted Mama buried there and not in some fancy cemetery out in Kennaton where none of us would hardly ever visit. Mama died in February, when the ground was rock solid, but once spring came some men went out in the cemetery beyond St. Cyril's Church and dug a fresh hole next to a gravestone that was so old the letters weren't visible anymore. They put the box of Mama's ashes in the ground—minus the small amount we'd kept in a jar—then covered it with a fresh mound of dirt. I left her favorite houseplant there, a big thing with wide green leaves that bloomed sometimes with white flowers, which was a stupid thing to do, because it was dead two days later. Afterward, I left things that couldn't be hurt by weather. I sprinkled tea leaves over her, because she liked tea. I left a heart-shaped rock, a biscuit, and a handful of dandelions.

People grieved in different ways. Jazz wanted to be left alone. Papa got rid of Mama's things and started drinking. Babka went to Mass twice a week and then again on Sunday. I looked at the sun. And when I couldn't see it anymore I still went to the cemetery and put my face against Mama's gravestone, and traced the engraved letters of her name over and over. These letters would never fade and flatten. No one would ever wonder whose stone this was, with letters that weren't visible anymore.

The trip was a short one, with Hobbs, Jazz, and me seated side by side in J.D.'s pickup, Hobbs driving with his own two feet on the pedals. I pulled my knees up to my chest and hummed, like a teakettle with too much going on inside to stay quiet, as we drove up and down switchback hills, and past fields full of hay rolls and horses. I kept trying to catch a better look at Hobbs, still not believing what he'd done for me. I wished I could've focused, seen every part of him when he walked into the sunlight and under a chocolate-coffee sky with flesh-toned skin. I'd never wished for my glasses before then.

Soon we hit the highway and Hobbs announced the first signs for Cranberry Glades Visitors Center. Fifteen minutes with four wheels or an entire day on two feet—there was no comparison, and even Jazz, who'd been quiet, agreed. (I hadn't mentioned the letter again. Neither had she. And for now I was glad enough to let that particular sleeping dog lie.)

We found an end-of-the-day scattering of cars in the Visitors Center parking lot when we arrived. While Jazz went inside to grab maps, Hobbs covered himself with a baseball cap, a hoodie, and a pair of sunglasses. And when Jazz returned we had to make our first decision. There was a short boardwalk tour, she reported, that we could take ourselves, set up to display different sorts of plants along the bog. There was also a seven-mile walk along something called the Cowpasture Trail, which circled the glades.

"What do you want to do, Olivia?" she said, and I felt them both staring at me.

What *did* I want to do? I had no rules, no idea what Mama would've done if she'd been there herself, other than make her way to the bog and hope to see a wisp. I guess I didn't think we'd see one of those on a common boardwalk tour. Good thing my foot wasn't bothering me after the long soak I had earlier, and the removal of those stingers.

"It has to be the trail," I said, feigning confidence.

The Cowpasture Trail was hard-packed, and cut through a forest of trees and rhododendron bushes before opening into a wide-open field. There we found the ruins of an old prison, bird boxes, and the overgrown remains of a roadway. We passed a defunct well and a purposeless chunk of old stairs, then followed a stream for a while before crossing a bridge.

"We're going off trail up here. Best way to avoid any campers," Hobbs said.

We did it right where he said we should—left the trail and walked into the fieldlike boglands, where the ground sucked at our feet like wet blankets.

"This is illegal, you know, leaving the trail," Jazz said, and Hobbs laughed.

"We're not going to hurt anything," he said. "Just relax."

Jazz gasped. "Olivia!"

"What?"

She crouched, and when she stood again she held something beside my face. "They're cranberries, see?"

"What happened to 'This is illegal'?" Hobbs asked.

"Oh, shut up," said Jazz.

With care, I took the berries from her and brought them so close that my eyelashes brushed over them. "They're green."

"And?"

"Nothing," I said, and tried not to think of this as a sign that our timing was somehow off.

We walked until Jazz's heels started to bother her again, and then Hobbs pulled out his tarp and settled it on the ground, said right there was as good a place as any to stop. When Jazz took off her shoes and socks, I followed suit, and then the three of us sat together, me in the middle.

"Hawk," Hobbs said, and I followed the flight of the bird as best I could.

Minutes ticked by as water lulled beneath us and the sun sagged in the sky. I stretched my toes, breathed in the pine-scented air.

"Did you bring any snacks, Olivia?" Jazz asked. "I'm hungry again."

"No," I said, but she still leaned close when I opened my suitcase. I shifted it away from her.

"What did you bring anyway?" she asked.

"Only one thing that matters," I said, and settled Mama's ashes on the tarp between us before closing the latches.

"You going to scatter those?" Hobbs asked, handing each of us a sandwich. Soft bread gave under my fingers, beneath a thin layer of plastic.

"No," I said. "But she always wanted to come here. She's here now, so she should be out with us and not stuck in a bag."

"She's still stuck in a bag," Jazz muttered, and whatever had existed of my appetite vanished altogether. Mama's ashes were in a bag like the one holding my dinner. I rested my sandwich on the tarp and tucked my knees against my chest.

My mind wandered as they ate. Leapfrogged from one topic to another. How my father was doing, and Babka. The letter my sister and I had argued about. Hobbs. The green cranberries.

Mama. How she might've been sitting beside me in the flesh, instead of as dust, if things had been different.

We made it, Olivia.

A breeze kicked up, turned my skin to gooseflesh.

"Not hungry, Wee Bit?" Hobbs asked, then lifted his water bottle for a drink.

I listened to his gulps as I rubbed my hands over the prickle of new hair on my legs. "Not yet."

"I keep thinking about Mom's story," Jazz said, surprising me. "She always thought if she got down here she'd be inspired, but I don't know that I'd call this an inspirational setting."

I lay back and flipped onto my stomach. Stretched my arms beyond the edge of the tarp until they grazed long grasses, pushed my fingertips down into wet earth. Wondered over bodies that might be held captive in the acidic bogland beneath us. If that didn't inspire a story or two, I wasn't sure what would.

Hobbs leaned back on his elbows beside me. "Tell me about this tale. Is it a worthy West Virginia ghost story?"

"It's worthy," I said, turning onto my back again. "But it's not a ghost story. And it isn't finished. You sure you want to hear?"

It was Jazz who told it—or an abbreviated version of it anyway—whether he wanted to hear or not.

"Once upon a time," she said, "there was a sun fairy who fell asleep in the forest. A power-hungry warlock found and took her and her gold-saturated cloak, then cast a spell on her so she'd forget her actual identity. He wanted the gold cloak, at least at first. That's all he cared about."

"That warlock's name Bill, by any chance?" asked Hobbs, and I took his hand and squeezed it.

"Cillian," said Jazz. "He holed her up in his tree house, and—"

"Tree house?" asked Hobbs.

"It was a fancy tree house, all right?" she said, and I smiled when I caught a hint of defensiveness in her voice over our mother's creative choices. "As I was saying," she continued, "he holed her up in his tree house, then proceeded to take over her life. He ate pieces of her."

"That's nice," said Hobbs.

"It's what a warlock had to do to transmogrify into another living thing," she said. "That's a mouthful, isn't it? Transmogrify. But that was that greedy warlock's plan—to become a god, in truth."

The wisps played a central role, Jazz explained. They knew the fairy's true identity—their land was where Cillian had found her to begin with—but most of them had been captured and immobilized in a box. Maybe they'd be able to somehow reveal the truth if they were set free, but it wasn't clear how, or if, that would happen.

"So there isn't an ending?" asked Hobbs.

"Nope," Jazz said. "Grates, doesn't it?"

I laughed. "I thought you hated this story."

"I do," she said. "Completely."

"Hmm."

"You know what I think?" Jazz said. "I think that whole peanut-butter-and-jelly ending thing threw her off."

Hobbs made a noise of justifiable confusion.

"Mama promised Papa one Valentine's Day that she'd find a way to work his favorite sandwich into the end of her book," I told him. "She said she'd find a way to do it if it was the last thing she did."

Jazz snorted. "That's what happens when you don't make your husband a card or even a decent meal on Valentine's Day. I think she forgot, I really do, so she made up that ridiculous promise on the spot. Stupidest thing ever. I could've written a hundred ends to that story."

"I still don't get it," Hobbs said, and I patted his arm.

"It's complicated."

"All right, then." He stood. "I should get that tent set up before it gets full dark, anyway. Be back."

I listened to his retreating steps, my thoughts still on the story. Though I couldn't say for certain why the sun smelled like my mother, my brain with its crossed wires probably made the connection a long time ago, with Mama writing about a sun fairy and all. It's too bad the story was never finished. I'd always liked it—its roundness, the way it rolled over my imagination like a warm peach. Maybe Jazz was right and there were a hundred ways it could've been ended, but I remembered too well the panic in Mama's eyes when Papa wanted to take her to the glades.

I can't, I can't. I don't know why, I . . .

Hope was a powerful thing. Difficult to risk.

"So what will you do?" Jazz asked. "Sit out here with Hobbs until morning?"

I focused on the thin hum of mosquitoes. Twilight was upon us. "Hobbs and the bugs," I told her.

She muttered something about being prepared, then unzipped her backpack; in my mind, a black ladder sprouted from the bag like a fast-growing weed. Seconds later, she handed me a bottle of spray. I sat and pumped repellent into my hands, rubbed it over my arms and legs.

"You'll be all right?" she asked.

"I'll be fine."

"Will you be tomorrow?"

I grimaced and handed the spray back to her as the wind kicked up again. "When I fail, you mean?"

"Cut me some slack, will you, Olivia? I'm trying here."

I wasn't sure what to say to that, wasn't used to my sister *trying*.

"You have something extra to wear in case it gets cold later?" she asked. "What *did* you pack in that bag of yours?"

"Stop worrying about what I packed all of a sudden. I'll be fine."

She pulled on her socks. "I'm going to the tent as soon as Hobbs puts it up," she said. "The two of you make me feel like an extra part, and I'm tired anyway. I didn't sleep well last night."

It had been my journey all along, but I still felt a stab of disappointment that Jazz wasn't more invested or even a little curious about what the night might bring.

"You don't want to stick around and look for inspirations?" I said. "I think you're a liar, you know. You don't hate Mama's story at all."

"I do hate it," she said, but her voice turned to cotton.

We sat without speaking for a while, as small noises echoed from the edges, where Hobbs worked to set up the tent.

"What do you hope for that you want to taste it so much anyway?" Jazz asked, and I jerked around to face her. "Why are you doing this, for real?"

"You know why," I said. "I'm doing it for her. For Mama."

"But she's gone, Olivia. The dead don't need hope."

I shifted the bag of ashes closer to my side. "Sometimes it's like you have no emotions at all," I told her. "You're untouchable."

"I'm not—" She sighed, and silver dust glinted against the darkening sky. "I'm not trying to be mean, all right? All I'm trying to say is that it might be dangerous to give another person—or anything—too much power over your actions."

It wasn't a surprising thing to hear coming from Jazz's mouth. She preferred to control everything herself.

"I just want to talk a minute—don't start freaking out," she said, and I realized that my hand was in my hair again. "I'm not untouchable. But I've thought about it some since Mom died, and I think it's wrong to take on or inherit another person's life goals. Sometimes I felt that was all Mom wanted for me—to be a better version of her. I hated that."

Jazz had never talked like this with me before—like a confidante, a friend. But, as much as I appreciated the turn things had taken, I wished she'd chosen a different topic. I didn't want to criticize Mama, not in any way, ever. At the same time, I remembered the conversation I had with her so many years ago about Jazz and college, and knew that what Jazz said held at least some truth.

"I'm not trying to live another person's dreams," I said, putting the spotlight back on me, even though I didn't want it there, either. Calling a dream a *dream*, too, and not *life goals* or—Hobbs's version—*wanting*.

She wedged her feet back into her sneakers. "What does hope taste like, anyway?"

Despite not being able to see the fine details of her face, I could tell by her voice that she was serious.

"God, your eyes get huge when you're surprised at something," she said. "I'm just curious, all right?"

"All right, but it's not easy to describe."

Truth was, hope didn't taste like anything at all in real life. But that particular perception had been in a dream, beginning with a layered scent that had wound its way to my tongue. Familiar and unknown, cold and dark, tart and rich and creamy. And that was just the start of it. How would I ever encapsulate all of that for Jazz? I cleared my throat.

"If I had to say, it might've been like a mix of berries, just a hair shy of ripe, with a drizzle of honey and another drizzle of lemon, and coffee with cream, and ice water when you hold it in your mouth until the ice melts. With a dash of salt. And maybe some mint. Yes,"—I nodded—"mint."

She was still and silent for a few moments, and then she began to laugh. Really laugh. Laugh like I hadn't heard her laugh since our childhood. Laugh so hard that I started to laugh, too, just because.

"Oh, Olivia." She wiped at her eyes. "Sometimes I wish I could be you for half a minute."

"Sounds like I'm missing some fun," Hobbs said, walking toward us as Jazz got to her feet.

"The fun is all yours now." She slung her bag across her back. "I'm going to turn in, before the bugs come to feast on my flesh again. But I hope you find what you're looking for, Olivia. I really do." Then she bent and said in a low voice, "Don't let that boy into your knickers," before turning on her heel.

"Did she just tell you not to let me into your knickers?" When Hobbs sat beside me, the ground gave like a bedspring.

"You have good ears."

"One of my many talents. *Are* you going to let me into your knickers?" He nudged my arm, and I laughed.

"After I see that wisp. You'll have to help me, with your good eyes."

"At the whim of ghost lights. This could take a while."

He lay down and pulled back his knees. After a minute or so, he began a song on his harmonica. It sounded like something ghosts would enjoy—low and long-lined and round at the end, like bones.

After a time, I said, "What if nothing happens tonight?"

He stopped. "What if nothing does? It won't take away from what you're trying to do by coming out here."

Part of me wanted to argue, *But I dreamed about this. I need this. I can't fail.*

Instead I said, "I know, you're right," and tried to sound as if I meant it. "But I'm going to hope anyway."

He lifted the harmonica to his mouth, set it down again. "Alice kept a hope chest all those years she lived with us, full to the top with baby clothes so small they looked like they were for dolls. Stuffed bears, too, and rattles and blankets. Even spoons. Some people have a harder time letting go than others. Those people do what they have to do to get through it. I don't think there's anything wrong with that."

"You know something, too, about getting through it, don't you?"

He paused, said, "Yeah, I do."

"I admire you for that."

"Well" was all he said, but there were fewer pinpricks marring the curve of his voice.

He played a tune I'd never heard before—a quiet song that felt full of thought.

"What if I forget her?" I said, once he'd finished.

Not just the way she moved or the sound of her voice but the way it felt to hug her or laugh with her. What if I forgot her sun-drenched scent, the way the smell of a person fades on clothing over time?

"You won't forget her," Hobbs said. "You'll keep parts of her— maybe not blankets and spoons, like Alice, but memories—and those things will be what keep you going."

I twined my arm around his denim-covered knee and squeezed, my heart so heavy that it hurt. Hobbs sat up and looped his arms around me, kissed the side of my head.

"I'm sorry, Livya," he said. "What do I know? Maybe hoping is too close to dreaming anyway, and you know how I feel about that."

Through long hours, I sat and watched for lights, and hoped. But the night reeked of doubt. And the lights never came.

The sun rose over fog-coated mountains as morning bird chatter swelled around us. Behind me, Hobbs rubbed my back through the blanket he'd settled over my shoulders hours before.

"Can we stay one more night?"

The soothing motion stopped momentarily after I asked, then started again; Hobbs knew the question wasn't for him.

Jazz stood in front of me, her arms crossed over her chest. "You know the answer to that."

"But I had a dream. Babka said something would happen on Saturday." I consulted my calendar to be sure. "That's today."

"Something is going to happen today, all right. We're going home," she said, and I clenched my jaw. "It's going to take me a week to recover from the mosquito bites I got last night, which will make a real nice look for my first day of work as it is, and I won't—"

"Oh, of course you won't," I said. "I don't know why I bothered to ask."

For all we'd shared over the last few days, the moments of closeness and new understanding, you'd think we wouldn't have been able to argue with such easy ferocity. But a mouth says things it shouldn't after a night without sleep, and as I rose to my feet the blanket around my shoulders fell away like a boxer's towel before a fight.

I couldn't tell you how the argument evolved to encompass everything, from Jazz's job at the funeral home ("All you care about is that horrible job!" "Maybe I'm sick of being around people who don't know how to shut their pie holes!") to Mama's book ("You don't believe in anything!" "It's a fairy tale, Olivia. Grow up!"), but it ended on the topic of the sleeping dog lying between us since yesterday: the letter I'd found the morning Mama died.

"I think you have that letter you found with you right now, don't you?" said Jazz. "I think it's in your suitcase, and that's why you don't want me to look in it, why you've been so careful not to let me so much as—"

I lifted my bag, opened the latches, and overturned the whole thing in front of her. Out rained shirts and shorts, socks and underwear, a toothbrush and paste, and an empty water bottle. And then I dropped the case itself, let it fall like a gavel. It hit the tarp in a blood-red splat.

"Turn out your pockets," she said, and I roared back.

"Stop obsessing about that letter! If you think for one second I'm going to hand it over to you, think again! I'm keeping it! I found her that morning! I miss her more, and I loved her better! You didn't even like to be in the same room with her when she was alive, you didn't—"

"You're making it really hard to be sensitive!"

"This is you being sensitive? You missed your calling, Jazz. Maybe you should be working for world peace or something instead of working with dead people, because you're so very good at being sensitive."

"Oh, fling you, Olivia Moon! Fling you!"

"Nice curse that doesn't even make sense!" I yelled at her retreating back. "Hey, we're not through here!"

She stayed silent as she walked off across the bog.

"Wow," said Hobbs, still on the tarp. "Maybe I should be glad I never had sisters."

"Be glad you didn't have *her* for a sister."

"Um."

"What?"

"The ashes, Livya."

It wasn't clear at first, but then I realized: My suitcase had bounced on the bag of ashes when I dropped it. The bag's seal had broken. And most of what remained of Mama had spilled beyond the seam of the tarp to where the grass grew thick and long, bled into the soggy ground, and was gone.

Maybe it's what she would've wanted, I told myself. Maybe this was how she'd see her wisp one day. Still, I curled into a ball and wept, feeling the acute loss of my mother all over again.

Recovery was slow. Hobbs lay beside me, let me be, which was what I needed him to do. Jazz stayed away. In good time, the tears stopped, and my brain settled on something it hadn't before. Jazz's assuredness that the letter was in my bag might be a sign of how she thought. What she'd do.

What she hid. Where.

"Let's go," I told Hobbs, hopping to my feet.

"Where are we going?" he asked, but I didn't answer, already two steps ahead.

I ducked into the small tent Hobbs had erected the night before, and pulled my sister's bag out onto the grass—the old college pack that had once been my mother's, that my sister had adopted. I unzipped it; the bold black ladder reappeared for a moment, then was gone.

"You think that's a good idea?" Hobbs asked from behind me.

"Does it look like I care if it's a good idea?"

"Huh. You're kinda cute when you're mad, Wee Bit."

He sat beside me as I plunged my hand inside of the canvas. I felt them within seconds; my fingers grazed over envelopes lining the bag like coins at the bottom of a well.

"I knew it," I said, but pulled one out anyway and held it near my right eye. I could almost make out Mama's handwriting, but not quite. "She had them all along."

"What are they?"

"My mother's letters to her father, my Grandpa Orin. She never sent them, because he disowned her a long time ago."

"Sounds like your grandfather and Bill might be soul mates." Hobbs sat beside me when I made room for us at the tent's entrance, and then I returned to the bag, felt around a water bottle, then brought out a book along with several newspaper clippings and a folded sheet of paper. "Help me, Hobbs. I can't read these, and I want to know what they are."

He took the clippings and opened the closed sheet, as I pulled one of the letters Mama had written herself up to my nose.

"This here's a job offer from *Rutherford and Son Funeral Home*," he said. "Huh."

"What?"

"The others are obituaries."

"Obituaries?" I dropped the letter into my lap. "Whose?"

He went through them one by one, naming people I'd never heard of before: Janie Wolf, Carl Books, Seneca Fine, James Conover. Why would Jazz keep obituaries of people we didn't know?

"Beth Moon. Is that your mother?" Hobbs asked, another piece of paper in his hand.

I nodded.

"I'm sorry," he said, and handed it to me, as if he was giving me back a piece of her. I took it and put it on top of the letter in my lap.

"What about the book?" I asked.

He lifted it—"It's called *The Plague*"—then turned it over. "Story about rats. Death." He huffed. "Your sister sure likes light reading, doesn't she? Why doesn't that surprise me?"

Obituaries. Funeral homes. Plagues and rats and death, death, death.

"I'm worried about her," I said, and he laughed a quiet *ho, ho, ho.* "What?"

"You two are so strange together. You're worried about her, but you bit her head off and shoved it down her throat two minutes ago."

"I know." I pursued my lips. "I know, I'm just . . ."

Exhausted. Backed up against a wall. Finished. Sorry, too, for all I'd said to Jazz. Sorry, even though I hadn't been able to help myself.

"You'll be all right, Livya," Hobbs said, and I pulled more of my mother's letters out of the bag until at least a dozen sat in my lap like a giant puddle of loss.

"Do you know I'm going to have to leave you today?" I asked. "I don't want to leave you. I love you, you know."

Silence. It's not that I'd necessarily expected him to say it back, but I still felt disappointed when he didn't. I'd never told anyone other than family that I loved them before, never felt that way to say it. And now I wondered if I'd made a mistake, been wrong about . . . everything. Because there seemed to be something palpable in Hobbs's silence, almost as if it had formed a physical presence in the air, a hand, of sorts, that wanted to push the words back into my mouth. I wished I could look at his eyes, try to figure out whatever it was that he felt. But he gave nothing away, didn't move an inch. When he did speak, he avoided my declaration altogether.

"All those letters are to this Orin, from your mom?"

I hugged the letters to my chest, and tried to keep the hurt out of my voice. "Yes, he's my grandfather—Orin. There was a lot of pain between him and my mother. I thought maybe we could send all the letters to him now that she's gone, and at least we'd have some closure. Jazz disagrees, of course, and says I'm stupid to suggest it. But I think I'll—"

The sound of running feet filled my ears. Wet. Urgent. Streaking my vision with colors like a fresh bruise. Jazz.

I didn't even have time to zip the bag.

September 21, 2011

Dear Dad,

*Yesterday Branik did something for me. He took the
day off from work, an unprecedented thing in the
middle of a non-holiday week, and surprised me
with a plan. He wanted to take me to the glades.
He wanted to take me, because he's known that I've
wanted to go for ages. At some point he must've
decided to drive us there despite my hemming and
hawing, my usual response to him bringing it up,
because this morning he appeared with my purse
flung over his shoulder and said it with a huge smile
on his face: "Let's go, baby. Let's have an adventure.
The cranberries are ripe. Let's find the end of that
story of yours."*

*Do you know what happened? I had a panic attack,
and we stayed at home.*

*Maybe I should try again, force myself to take the
trip. But this was something we were supposed to do
together, Dad, and the idea of doing it without you?*

It makes me feel like that pathetic little girl lost in the wilderness all over again.

Which frustrates me so much, like I've been asked to walk forward into an empty space but keep hitting up against invisible walls. There is no sense here, and it makes me angry! Angry with you, yes, but even angrier at myself. I am stronger than this. And you may never agree, but I am <u>wealthy</u> in all the ways that matter, even if I don't have a lot of money stored away in a bank account, or a retirement fund, or stocks and bonds, or college funds. I am wealthy in better ways, because of my family and the love in my house, and the ability to laugh and dream and be accepting of people's differences. Yet something like this happens, and it's as if I've been asked to turn out my pockets only to find holes in the cloth. My family deserves better than this damaged-pocket woman I sometimes am, even if I don't know what more I can do to fix her. Even if I am angry, so angry that she needs fixing.

Beth

CHAPTER TWENTY-ONE

Regrets

✳ JAZZ ✳

The last conversation I had with my mother was nothing special. We didn't argue. I didn't tell her to close the kitchen door or anything dramatic like that. Closing the door was what you had to do if you wanted to be warmed at all by the oven heat, and it was a cold February morning, I remember.

We didn't argue. It was worse than that.

She asked if I'd mind picking up a quart of milk on the way home. I didn't even answer her with words, just nodded and left her there.

That was it. Our last interaction. The last time I saw her alive.

I'd bought the milk before heading to Susie's to work. I thought to take it home when I saw and followed behind the ambulance later that morning. Nothing much mattered after that.

The milk curdled on the kitchen counter. Later, I emptied it into the sink in a solid clump.

I couldn't recall the last time I told her I loved her.

For maybe ten minutes after my fight with Olivia, I walked. Off the bog, past bushes that smelled of rosemary, until I reached solid land again. There I stopped beside a tree, a tall and twisted variety that I couldn't name, my head still full of my sister's words.

I miss her more, and I loved her better! You didn't even like to be in the same room with her when she was alive!

I wouldn't be mad at Olivia for what she'd said, even if she deserved it. My love for our mother was different, more complicated than my sister's, and not comparable because of that. Besides, I'd known Olivia would react emotionally as soon as she realized the glades weren't about to offer up a vision of enlightenment. I understood how a fusion of uncertainty and disappointment could settle into anger. Besides, an angry Olivia was preferable to a depressed Olivia any day of the week. Depressed Olivia was like being stuck behind a tractor on the backroads; you knew you'd get beyond it eventually, but Jesus Christ.

That didn't mean she hadn't cut me at all with her new sharp tongue. And that letter. How would I ever see it now?

If you think for one second I'm going to hand it over to you, think again! I'm keeping it!

Keeping it. But not in her bag. So where would she have—?

All my thoughts aborted as I realized that I'd left my pissed-off sister with *my* bag, home to all of our mother's other letters. But she wouldn't. Would she?

The obituaries. *Orin's* obituary.

I barreled with high inefficiency across the bog, panting as water splattered up my body and onto my face. And there they were, Olivia and Hobbs, just where I feared they'd be—beside the tent with my bag open between them.

"Get the hell out of there!"

I snatched up my canvas pack and stuffed the scattering of letters and the book back inside. But where were the obituaries? I peered inside the bag's yawning mouth and, after shuffling things around, saw them there at the bottom.

Relief. Olivia hadn't seen them. Hadn't seen *it*. Not that she would've been able to read it if she had, but still . . .

I avoided Hobbs's glaring eyes; this wasn't any of his business. Olivia—though I would've expected her to argue or at least
condemn me as a hypocrite for having those letters in my bag all
along—didn't say a word.

It would be the silent treatment, then. Fabulous.

"We should get out of here," said Hobbs, still staring at me.
"Before folks start showing up for the day."

Olivia turned whiter than normal and, despite everything, I felt
a pang of sympathy for her. But she'd have to say goodbye to Hobbs
at some point; it wasn't as if we were going to be able to bring him
home and adopt him like a pet. And we couldn't chase after foolish
fires forever. None of this craziness would erase what had hurt our
family the most. None of this would bring our mother back.

"Yes." I zipped the bag. "Let's go."

Describing things in vivid detail started as my version of a peace
offering to Olivia, as we began the hike back to J.D.'s truck,
walking through the field we'd stayed in the night before.

"I know things didn't happen the way you'd hoped," I told her,
"but Mom did want to come here, and I want you to try to see it—
really see it, and try to remember."

"I thought you weren't a tour guide," she said.

It started as a peace offering, but it became something else. In a
strange way, it seemed I was seeing it all for the first time as I relayed
the sights. The Christmas-tree evergreens, gray-barked beeches and
broken-barked black cherries, the thorny hawthorns, and tall oaks.
The penny-colored yellow birches, and the curved branches of the
sugar maples.

> Wild geraniums,
> and a cloak of buttercups.
> So much beauty here.

When Hobbs pointed out some bear scat, my lips curved into a reluctant smile. "Right," I said. "We wouldn't want to forget the bear scat."

Olivia didn't smile.

"Stop a sec." I put my hands on her stiff shoulders and made her turn around before we left the field, my eyes on the closest bank of hills. "There are layers and layers of green in the mountains, different from the way we see it at home. Vibrant, forest green, fading to a near-fog, like an overexposed photo. And there's a sort of blue-gray line off in the distance, before it fades to silver. After that, it just ends."

"Doesn't end," said Hobbs. "The mountains of West Virginia, they go on and on. Sometimes seems they go on forever. But I've been beyond that blue-gray and silver, and I can tell you there's plenty more to see. Somehow, though—" He gave a shake of his head, a wry smile. "Somehow this place gets in your blood."

We stood there for long minutes, as something like pride welled up in my chest. This state, this land, was mine, and I'd forgotten how to love it.

"Can't live with 'em, can't imagine living life without 'em," Olivia said.

I squeezed her shoulder, unable to find words to respond as I took it all in: how big the world seemed to be, how I'd forgotten that as well.

Later, when we passed the old prison grounds again, we stopped to read signs that we'd ignored the day before. The Mill Point Federal Prison, where you could still see the remains of stairs, had never been gated. Six thousand prisoners were able to roam free, and had rarely left.

"How the hell did they get away with that?" I asked.

"Prison's a state of mind," Hobbs said.

It was something I thought about the rest of the way back.

✳

The sleep of the dead had long been my sister's specialty, so it was no surprise to me that she not only dozed off on the return trip to Miner's Barren but when we arrived she was immovable. Unwakeable. Unshakeable. Beyond walking with her own two feet. Honestly, I didn't know if hers was a true sleep, since she hadn't slept all night, or a faked one, because I knew how desperate she was not to part ways with Hobbs. But it didn't matter; I'd let her have her nap. The time to take her home would come soon enough. Today. Finally, today.

Hobbs carried her inside and put her on the bed they'd shared the night before. I stood watching like a voyeur as he pulled a sheet up around her, kissed her forehead.

"You like her," I said. The idea didn't bother me as much as it had twenty-four hours before.

He didn't deny it, and even though he didn't confirm it, either, he lingered beside her and moved wayward strands of hair off her face, tucked them behind her ear.

"I'll miss her," he said. "Her and those big eyes."

"Eyes she messed up pretty good," I said, watching his face for a reaction. But he surprised me.

"She told me about that. Must've hurt like hell to stare at the sun. Tells me it hurt even more not to." He kissed her forehead one more time, then stood. "She says she doesn't even know why she did it."

He noticed when I swallowed hard.

"Do you know?"

I shook my head. There was no room in my head for that question just then. "I need to get to a phone."

"I'll take you."

It was well into the afternoon by the time we arrived at a gas station, which was more than thirty miles away.

"There has to be a closer station," I'd said when we first started to travel, and he'd given me an E.T.A.

"Welcome to the hills," he said. "You should've used the phone at the Visitors Center."

I didn't bother arguing, because he was right. I'd been wrapped up, thinking about prisons and West Virginia on the walk back. Living in Tramp had always seemed like my lifetime sentence, regardless of what my mother said or what she might've wished for me. But maybe what I wanted to escape was all in my head and not so much about West Virginia, with all its hills and layers. Maybe I wasn't so stuck. All those prisoners stayed put, after all, when they could've run. Because they were safe where they were, or because leaving was a risk.

I'd never spent so much time thinking as I had over the last few days, but I had to admit—as inconvenient as it was now—that maybe having all those thoughts was worth missing the chance to make a phone call.

When we arrived at the station, Hobbs donned his usual sweatshirt and pulled up the hood. Some of his tattoos were beginning to bleed through the makeup, enough that it might make someone look twice. He followed me inside to size up the junk food while I went to get change. I was ready to go back out and call home when I saw him filling a cup with coffee.

"You want one?" he asked when my gaze lingered on the rising steam.

"Sure," I said. "Thanks."

Whatever the hell this was, Hobbs and I were not becoming friends. We were just tolerating each other because we knew we'd only have to do it for a while longer. Still, I cracked a smile when he held the door open for an old woman a minute later, while I spoke with my grandmother.

The call started well enough. Babka was happy to hear from me, and to let me know that the bus had been repaired and was ready to take me to my job. My father, too, had been doing much better, she said, though I'd believe that particular report when I could see evidence of it with my own eyes. When I told her that we'd be coming home later today, that we'd found someone to drive us, that we'd visited the glades but hadn't seen anything and that Olivia wasn't all that happy about it, her voice turned heavy.

"This is going to be a *thing*, I just know it," I told Hobbs on the ride back to J.D.'s. I couldn't shake my grandmother's disappointment, even though I should've felt good about it all—that I'd done what was expected of me, and that I could finally go home again.

"What do you mean, a *thing*?"

"I mean the sort of thing that keeps coming up every damned day for the rest of the year." My chin settled into the palm of my hand as I leaned against the door. "About how Olivia made it to the glades, fulfilling one of our mother's lifelong ambitions, but was unable to see a wisp. There will be dreams and wishes and all sorts of bullshit my family insists on when things don't happen the way they want. My grandmother will be right in the middle of it, too, maybe even my father."

It began to drizzle.

"You know," Hobbs said, turning on the wipers, "I used to see ghost lights all the time up at my old house."

I turned to stare at him. "What?"

"Not a bog up there, it's swampland," he said. "But the lights are common in the summertime as long as you're looking for them with peeled eyes. I never bothered to mention it because Livya stressed how important it was to go to Cranberry Glades in particular, because of your mom's story. But if it's lights she wants to see, well . . . I could take her. Take you both."

"By *old house*, do you mean the one you shared with your father?"

"Yeah." He squinted, and I wondered about his thoughts, which horror he might've been remembering. Then decided I didn't want to know.

"I haven't heard the best of things about him," I said, with as much care as I could muster.

"There's a neighbor, Betty, whose land butts up against ours. You can see the lights as well from her place, and Bill would never know we were there. Trust me, she hates him, too."

I ran my thumb nail along the foam cup in my lap. "I don't think it's a good idea."

"No?"

"We're delaying the inevitable. Better Olivia deal with her disappointments now. She may not like it, but she needs to face reality."

The truck buzzed when we rolled over the edge of a rumble strip, and I realized that he'd been looking at me.

"What? Watch where you're driving."

"You feel that way, do you?" he said, turning his eyes back toward the road. I was unable to read his expression.

"Yes," I told him. "I do."

We traveled down one road, then another, on the way back to the cabin. Soon we'd veer off these roads altogether, and onto rutted paths. Reaching a place wasn't always a neat undertaking.

"Besides," I said as an afterthought, "I have important things coming up next week, and plans to make."

"Yeah, I know. Congratulations on your job with the funeral home. I'm sure the competition was stiff."

"Hysterical. You could have a career as a stand-up comedian."

I turned away from his smirk and back toward the window, as we passed a mail-delivery truck, a man blowing leaves across his yard, and a child selling stones alongside the road.

J.D. met us on the packed-dirt drive behind his place as Hobbs shut down the engine, his hair ruffled and his jaw set.

"Something's wrong," Hobbs said, and we leaped out, my first thoughts on Olivia.

But this wasn't about Olivia.

Red Grass was gone. Sometime between breakfast and lunch, he'd freed himself and left through a cracked window, J.D. explained, digging his hands into the pockets of his jeans.

"You've got to get the hell out of here, man," he told Hobbs, his thick brows furrowed. "Disappear for a few months. I don't know how long Red Grass has been out or what he's been doing. Bill could be on his way right now."

A guilty heat swept through me. Though the situation with his father was real enough, Hobbs didn't have all the information. Not yet. Maybe some prisons were, as he'd said at the glades, a state of mind. I didn't want any part of that. Not when I might hold the power to set someone free from their own personal Oran, point out the absence of bars.

This. Was the right thing.

"He might not be working with Bill," I said, and their attention locked on me.

I spilled it all. How Red Grass had come up with the plan for me to arrive on J.D.'s doorstep with the gun in his side. How he'd forged that plan so that I could be with Olivia again, and how I hadn't cared about his personal motivations then because I'd wanted my sister back. How it was Red Grass's phone number on the poster, not anyone else's. I pulled it from my pocket and showed them.

Hobbs snatched it from my hands. "This picture didn't come from my old man." His eyes flickered between us. "This was me at a coin shop a few months back."

He described that brief visit, how he'd brought the coins there after taking them from Bill, which had mostly been an act of defiance. He'd long suspected that his father had stolen the coins once upon a time, but he'd never understood his refusal to sell them; it wasn't as if each one was labeled with a UPC code. But that day Hobbs began to understand. The shop owner disappeared behind a door for a few too many minutes after asking a few too many questions. Hobbs knew a setup when he felt one; he took the coins and fled before the cops showed up. Everything he'd imagined about the coins changed after that. If his instincts were right, they were more than stolen goods. They were linked to a graver crime—something that could land Bill in more trouble than he'd ever seen before.

And Hobbs, too, if he wasn't careful.

"You think Red Grass is working with the law?" J.D. asked, and I remembered the older man's flashlight; Red Grass had said it was the kind used by the police.

"I asked him yesterday if he was a bounty hunter. I asked him if he was working with your father," I told Hobbs. "He said no."

"Means nothing," said Hobbs. "He could be anything, be working for anyone as well as himself. He's a liar, sure as I'm standing here." He threw his head back, and I thought he might howl at the sky. "I should take those coins back to where I found them—right back up to Spades Hallow. If anyone should go down for this—"

J.D. nodded. "Don't just think about it. Do it. Keep the truck. Take the girls home, then go and get rid of those coins once and for all."

Hobbs pinched at his chin, pinched off his makeup, and left a smear of color in its wake. A day ago, I had a different feeling about those tattoos. Now I knew what they hid, and what they stood for. A badge, of sorts. A badge of survival. Maybe he shouldn't be so quick to hide it.

"I could do that," he said. "Or I could drive up to get rid of the coins, and show Livya her ghost lights before I take them home."

Before I could think to respond, I noticed Olivia a few feet away.

"What ghost lights?"

CHAPTER TWENTY-TWO

Right Tree, Wrong Dream

✳ OLIVIA ✳

Mama and I talked about death sometimes.

What do you think it's like? I'd ask, and she'd tell me the same thing every time.

Her father believed there was a big tree on the other side of life. When you died, it was your job to find that tree. Maybe you had to journey to reach it, maybe it took a long time. But when you succeeded your whole family would be there waiting for you. Not just the people who'd already died, either, but everyone. Because time was immaterial on the other side.

Will death hurt? I'd ask.

No, she'd say. *I don't think anything can hurt more than the hardest parts of life.*

Mama had built her story around a tree, but it wasn't a place of joy and reunion; it was a site of entrapment. It wasn't anything I put together until after she was gone. But as soon as I made the connection I decided not to wait for Christmas to make a wish. I took out a slip of paper and wrote:

> I wish Mama finds the right tree, a good
> one, and that it's better than anything
> she ever dreamed. I wish I'm hugging her
> there, right now.

It's been under my pillow ever since.

Betty was crazy, I learned after we arrived at Spades Hallow. Not that I meant to hold that against her.

"Get outta here!" Her yowl shredded everything around us after we pulled into her drive and Hobbs turned off the ignition. In the shadows before us, I was able to make out the hulking form of a person. "I got me a gun and I'll be damned if I won't enjoy using it to splatter that melon on your shoulders all over the yard. Dogs haven't had a snack in a while," she said, then added, "haven't humped nothing in a while, neither."

"What the hell?" said Jazz. "Please turn around."

"Betty, it's me, Christopher," said Hobbs.

I nudged him in the side. "Christopher?"

"Hush." He nudged me back. "That's classified."

"Christopher doesn't have normal skin," Betty said. "Who are you really? Mafia? Russian spy? I don't know the codes."

"It's me, look." He mopped a hand across his face, and I realized he was wiping off his makeup. "I covered up the art so Satan wouldn't recognize me."

"Well, why didn't you say so?" said Betty.

"Satan?" Jazz seemed to sink more deeply into her seat when Hobbs opened his door. "Why am I not liking this?"

"It's her name for Bill," he said, and we slid across the seat after him, as Betty warned us not to step on her fairy rings.

The pebbled path that wound its way to her house was hard to distinguish in the evening light, and I faltered a few times, too wound up maybe to attend to the business of walking. Hobbs had been optimistic about seeing will-o'-the-wisps there, even as Jazz warned me to keep a tether on my hopes.

Be careful, Babka had said in my dream, pointing toward Saturday.

Everyone asked that I hold back in some way, but I couldn't help my excitement. I felt sure that tonight would bring good things, and that I could be careful enough without needing a tether at all. Jazz hadn't even complained about making the trip, which in and of itself was a small miracle, a fateful sign that things were on the right track at last.

"Take off your Mafia shoes before you go inside," said Betty, as we walked up a set of narrow wooden stairs. "You'll ruin my soup."

"We can stay out if you want," Hobbs said. "I'd like to show off the dog house before I head to Bill's."

"You'll go and eat some soup while I talk you out of whatever fool idea you have rattling around in that skull of yours," said Betty. "Don't argue about it, either, Mister Skin-and-Bones. Got hemorrhoids bigger than you." She poked him in the side.

"Dog house?" I asked.

"Wait and see," he said.

The orange crescents that showered over me when Betty creaked open her door reminded me of the art on the novel in Jazz's bag— which, I noticed, she wore as always on her back.

"You need surgery to detach yourself from that thing." I nudged the pack. "It's like a growth."

"Don't hassle me," she said. "If I don't trust that people won't paw through my things when I leave them behind, you have no one but yourself to blame."

I wasn't interested right then in Jazz's backpack. I had everything I needed in my pocket—the salvage of Mama's remains, all that I had left of her after the spill.

It would be enough.

*

M y first thought when we stepped inside Betty's house was that it was funny she'd asked us to remove our shoes. I'd seen pictures of houses being renovated before. Mama used to get a lot of magazines, and one that she sometimes picked up was a home-builder sort of thing—as if we might someday add on or update the kitchen or whatever. Never before had I seen a house torn down to the bone in person, but Betty's place had been stripped to beams, bare bulbs, and concrete floors, and looked as huge and white as heaven. Her husband had died a decade earlier, as it turned out, and he'd been in the middle of a remodel when it happened. Betty never finished the place. She decided that since the kitchen and the bathroom were functional, and because there were fewer hiding spots for the Russians with the house wide open, she'd leave it the way it was.

The faint scent of wood married with the stronger smell of good cooking, as Jazz and I sat at a green laminate table. Soon we were shoveling spoonfuls of garlicky, buttery, lemony mushroom soup into our mouths, while Hobbs and Betty debated who would go near enough to Bill's—or Satan's Outhouse, as Betty called it—to find out if he was at home. Hobbs didn't like mushrooms, he whispered to me at one point, but neither did he like upsetting Betty, so he pretended to eat and poured soup into my bowl on the sly.

"It should be me," Betty said, ladling more soup into Jazz's bowl. "That man's been afraid of me since the time I got him drunk and burned off half his arse hairs."

"Let's pause the debate for a few minutes." Hobbs took the spoon out of my hand, set it on the table, and encouraged me to my feet. "I want to show Wee Bit something before it gets dark."

Together we weaved through beams, before Hobbs took us onto what seemed to be a porch.

"Careful, there's a loose nail there," he said. "Gotta fix that."

Again, we stepped out into the warm summer air, but this time a new excitement wound through me as I took in the gloaming. "It's almost dark."

"Almost," he said. "But light enough to make it out. Here, take off your socks. It'll be better this way."

"There aren't any bees out there, are there?"

"No bees," he said.

A minute later, he guided me sockless up a small hill. I took careful steps beside him, my mind still on bees.

"Hearing about your mother's story made me think you might like this," he said.

"This must be one impressive dog house."

"Just wait." He stopped at the top of the hill. "All right. Do you see it?"

I scanned the ground for something stubby and full of fur. "Look up, Olivia," he said, and pointed.

Nestled in a tree before us was what looked like a tree house. "Is there a sun fairy up there, gagged and bound and needing our assistance?" I asked with a wry tone as I tried to take it all in—the angles of the slim structure, the way it sat with surety in the crook of the big tree.

"I built that when I was, I don't know, maybe twelve, out of old slabs of wood that Betty's husband, Jake, had hanging around. He helped me build it, too, knew I needed a place to go to get away from Bill sometimes. Most times. That shelter survived plenty of storms, so we must've built it well enough. Saved my life a time or two."

"Things were that bad?"

He didn't answer. I could tell him then what I thought I knew, what I'd guessed from the dark needlework through his voice. But that would be a cheat. Hobbs would have to tear those particular walls down to the bone for me himself, when he was ready. In due time.

"You can see over his land from here, right out onto the swamp-land," he said. "You'll be able to sit up there all night if you want, look for those lights of yours. That is, if you want to go up, if you're not afraid of warlocks and steaming cauldrons."

There was no question. Once upon a time, I'd been a monkey child, climbing trees all over town, even climbing to the top of St. Cyril's Church one day. I liked to see the world from up high, get a bird's-eye view of things—a different view, but real all the same.

I let him direct me up the tree one step at a time—my bare toes resting in old notches, on old slats, his body warm and sure behind me—until we stood together inside the small structure. He drew me to the solitary window, where I skimmed my fingers along the frame, then described details that my eyes missed and the growing dark obscured. The scrubby brush of the land, a scattering of boulders. Tall reeds poking out of the swamp water that lay between Betty's house and Bill's. An old beaver dam.

"Wish I could stay with you the whole night," he said, and settled his hands on my waist.

"So you're going to do it?" I asked him. "Go to Bill's and leave the coins there?"

"I'd be stupid not to. For all he's done, my piss-poor excuse for a father deserves everything coming to him. But do I want to set him up and send him to jail? Is that what I'm doing here? I've been asking myself that since we left J.D.'s, and I don't know the answer, Wee Bit, now that I'm here." I locked my hands over his and pulled them forward. He rested his chin on top of my head. "I'd be a fool to come up here, just to turn around and keep those coins on me, though."

"Maybe you could get rid of them another way." Once more, I thought of my mother's letters—the ones she'd stowed under her altar, and the one I'd pocketed in my coat. The words felt ripe in my mouth. "Maybe you should set them free."

"Yeah? Cast them out over the land?"

He made a wide sweep of a gesture with our conjoined hands, like a farmer tossing seeds, before he turned me around. I first noticed it then, with my eyes closed and lost in a kiss. A light, shining behind my lids.

My eyes fluttered open, and I glanced back toward the window. "Did you see that?"

"What?"

"Maybe it was a wisp." There was still a hint of color in the dusky sky, but no sign of the flash I'd seen.

"Wait till it gets dark-dark. If they decide to come out and play, you'll know it. One summer I saw them out here every night, I swear."

"What do you think they are?"

It returned when I closed my eyes again—a golden light, floating, blinking in long, slow drags like a lazy firefly.

"Betty used to say they were the ghosts of Alice's babies out there, dancing around a fire and looking for their mama," he said. "Jake thought they were barn owls. My old man said they were ball lightning, come to burn me up if I didn't listen to him."

"What do you believe?" My tongue felt strange—thick and woolly. "What do you believe now?"

"I don't know what I believe, but I'll tell you, they're not predictable. They might show up, they might not. I hope you're not disappointed if you don't see anything."

I opened, closed my eyes two, three times more, testing and testing. But the light remained after that, even with my eyes open, small but as brilliant as a star in the center of my not-so-blind spot. Dancing there like a grin.

"Your sister didn't want me to bring you here, you know."

"No?" I asked, entirely distracted.

"She didn't want me to tell you about the lights at all. Thought you needed to face reality, that that would be best."

"She goes on all the time about how she doesn't understand me," I said. "Makes it sort of ironic that she'd then claim to know what's best for me, don't you think?"

"Livya—"

The curve of his voice thinned as my blind spot shimmered.

"What's wrong?" I asked him, asked myself.

I could see less of him than before. My blind spot had grown bigger, expanded like a screen. The light was still there, but it had morphed, too, turned stark white and glossy, showed a hint of silver lettering.

"Your grandfather is Orin, right? You mentioned his name once or twice."

"Yes, he's my grandfather."

It was our family's stove—that's what it was, the white, the chrome letters. The light was the pilot light. How was this possible? I gripped Hobbs's arm. "Something's wrong."

Before I could explain what I saw, Hobbs said, "He died."

"Who?" I shook my head.

"Orin. I saw his obituary in your sister's backpack. He died this past February. I don't know why Jazz didn't tell you."

"February?"

I stopped thinking about the stove, and about the warm scent that seemed like my mother, like sunlight in the dark, and focused on Hobbs's words.

February was when it all happened. February.

"When in February?" I asked, and held my breath.

Not before she died. Not before February 19th.

Not suicide, suicide, suicide.

"February twelfth. I'm sorry, Livya, but I thought you should know the truth."

A bell clanged in the distance.

"Shit," he hissed. "That's the Bill bell, which means trouble somewhere. Don't move. I'll be back."

He pulled away, left me with a growing darkness.

Then . . .

a puff of breath

and the pilot light on the screen disappeared altogether.

May 30, 2012

Dear Dad,

I woke up this morning with a strange feeling in
my stomach. I didn't understand it until later,
after I'd seen Branik and Jazz off for the day,
after Olivia and I played a game of hearts. I
looked at the calendar and realized that it was
your birthday. Today you are seventy-three
years old.

Seventy-three.

It's startling to realize how many years I've missed,
and how many you've missed with me—and with
your granddaughters. I've found myself wondering
for the first time if I'll never see you again, as time
burns and burns, down and away, like thin sticks
of birthday-candle wax.

The phone just rang. When I picked it up, no one

answered, but someone was there, on the other end. I said, "Dad?," and the line went dead.

God help me, I wish it was you.

Happy birthday.

Beth

CHAPTER TWENTY-THREE

Mushroom Soup

∗ JAZZ ∗

I missed things about my mother, all the time. I missed the funny loop she used to make when tying her shoes. I missed watching her pet the cat with her bare toes sometimes in the evening, lying down on the couch. I missed the way she ran down the hallway after a shower, because she didn't want any of us to catch a glimpse of her in her towel. I missed the way she'd loop her apron string, tuck it back into the tie around her waist. I missed her occasional stupid joke, even though I'd never laughed at them; I hadn't wanted to encourage them, I guess.

I missed my mother's soups. She made good soup, maybe because they were rarely ruined and possibly even improved by her impromptu naps. All that stuff simmering in a pot, growing more complex. Carrot soup with curry. Pea soup with ramps. Chicken soup with celery and thick noodles. Minestrone with kidney beans and sausage, chunks of tomatoes, onions. The scent of soup had a way of filling the house as few other things could. It had a way of saying *home*, saying *here, things aren't that bad*, saying *breathe, eat, and know that you're loved.*

I missed seeing my mother bent over her typewriter or staring out a window, lost in thought. Working hard on something that would never be finished.

It's crazy that I miss that.

My last thought before I heard the bell was that I was pretty sure there was something wrong with Betty's soup.

Right after Betty left, intent on learning herself if Bill was at home or not—and who was I to stop her?—I tucked one of my arms onto her table and rested my head there. I felt a little sick. Dizzy. Closing my eyes did nothing to improve the situation: a twisting helix formed behind them, made my stomach churn. It was easy enough to blame the pace of the last few days: the lack of sleep, food, and quiet; the miles of walking; the physical and emotional stress; and everything I'd seen and learned. I opened my eyes again and found that the room had turned purple.

Mushrooms.

What was it about mushrooms? They could be hallucinogenic. That had to be it. This was a mushroom thing. I should sit still until it passed. But, hallucination or not, as soon as I heard the bell—*saw* the giant Newton's cradle that formed in my head when I heard it, with enormous metal balls swooping toward me, clanging too near me for any form of comfort—I was up out of my seat. I bolted for the door I'd seen Hobbs leave through earlier. Went outside to trample an untold number of Betty's fairy rings with my socked feet. Ran across a land dotted with boulders and tall trees. Realized with no small amount of horror that the ground was expanding and contracting like a lung.

"Olivia!" I shouted, and my voice took form in the air, like foam peanuts spilled from a box.

Hobbs appeared out of nowhere, running toward me, then past me. "She's in the tree house," he shouted, and I looked up the hill he'd run down. "Stay there!"

A giant lit tree lay at the top, jeweled stairs spiraling around the outside of it. I blinked hard—*not real*—but didn't care just then. The ground was breathing.

I took the stairs two at a time, and when I reached the platform at the top I could hardly believe my eyes. This was a delusion. A grand, mushroom-inspired hallucination. But Jesus Christ, this looked like my family's kitchen in Hobbs's tree house. The blue-clothed table with its scuffed pine legs to match the chairs. The old refrigerator. The small window, its curtains, the L-shaped counter and the chipped basin sink, a few colored bottles on a shelf. The typewriter. The stove.

I squeezed the strap of my backpack, surprised that it was with me, that I'd hauled it along. It felt strange, cold and bumpy beneath my fingers.

A note appeared in thick block letters on the refrigerator, like a rainbow of alphabet magnets: DON'T LOSE YOUR MARBLES.

The *A* was red.

A glass on the table reflected the image of a person behind me, and when I spun around I found my sister lying on the counter I'd just seen empty. Her left hand dangled toward the floor; the other rested alongside her head.

"Olivia?" I adjusted the bag on my back.

Her angle confused me. No matter how I tried to approach her, I ended up facing her bare feet.

"Leave me alone," she said.

The floor shifted restlessly under me; I sat on the table and lifted my feet to the chair, not wanting anything to do with it. "Olivia, something is messed up and I—"

"I can't talk to you right now! Will you go?" This time her voice reverberated off the walls in waves.

"Keep it down." I glanced again at the agitated floor, sure now that it was trying to take a nap and we were only making it angry. "What's your problem, anyway?"

"Why didn't you tell me Grandpa Orin was dead?"

I dug my fingers into the blue cloth, felt the splintering of wood beneath my nails. "What?"

"Why didn't you say anything? Why are you carrying his obituary around like your private dirty secret?"

"You're one to talk," I said, scrambling. "You didn't tell me about the letter you found, did you? You were hiding that, weren't you? And you still are."

"Leave me alone about that letter!"

The sound she made—a gasp or sob—distorted as if thrown into the auditory version of a fun-house mirror. This was not the rational conversation I'd hoped to have with her, and I still wanted that letter. As hard as it might be under normal circumstances—not to mention circumstances in which the floor snored—I'd have to try not to push her.

All right. I took a breath.

"At first I didn't mention the obituary because I'd promised Mom that I wouldn't. I saw her just after she found out, and she didn't want anyone to know."

I rubbed my fingers along the straps pressing into my shoulders. Marbles. The bag's straps felt like marbles.

"After Mom died, I didn't say anything because it didn't matter," I said. "Because her being gone took priority."

And everything was falling apart, I added silently. You were falling apart. Staring at the sun. Losing your eyes. Dad with his booze.

"I didn't think much about him after that until yesterday," I continued, "when I realized the truth might hit you hard."

"Why did you think it might hit me hard?" she said, with a voice that seemed—looked, somehow—clumped. Like curdled milk.

"It's such a clear connection, Olivia."

"That she killed herself, you mean?"

"Yes. That she killed herself."

Her cry grew blue tentacles that dribbled down the counter and puddled onto the sleeping floor. "It's my fault."

"What? That's not—"

"I knew she was in one of her up-and-downs that morning, and hardly tried to help," she said. "I knew it, and I left her anyhow. It was my job to pull her out of her funk and be there when she needed to—"

"It was *not* your job, it was—"

"Before I left, I told her to stay warm, Jazz. What if she turned on the stove because I told her to stay warm? I can't remember if it was on before I left or not, and I told her—"

"Olivia Moon, you stop it right now, do you hear me?" I got to my feet, strained to get a glimpse of her face, connect with her however I might, but again I couldn't see past her toes. "You can't believe what happened is your fault!"

"I saw the way her voice looked, so low down, but I told myself she'd be okay because I had plans and . . . Why did I ignore what she said?"

"What did she say?" Why had I never asked that?

"She said, 'If you live your whole life hoping and dreaming the wrong things, what does that mean about your whole life?'" A spiderweb sensation crawled over my arms and up the back of my neck. "Maybe Hobbs is right. Nothing brings on pain like a dream. Grandpa Orin was the dream. He was everything. She knew he was gone that morning—that's what she meant, why she was so upset. She was in pain, and I—I left her!"

She gave another blue-tentacle cry, and I met it with one of my own.

"I left her, too—the day she found the obituary, I left her in the kitchen!" I said, and felt something dark and dormant crack open inside of me, like my own private tomb. "Don't think it doesn't slay me to remember that, because it does."

That I hadn't made her talk to me, hadn't dug any deeper.

That I hadn't told anyone.

That, if I had, maybe none of this would've happened.

It was all there, under my own loose floorboards—my slow-boil pot of water.

"You're not the only one with regrets, Olivia Moon. You're not the only one with grief issues. You're not the only one who misses her, either, even if you think it's true," I said, and I swear I felt dirt on my tongue.

"I didn't mean that," she said, her voice quieter than it had been. "I shouldn't have said that."

"It doesn't matter. I'll never know if Mama and I might've been friends one day. And now I have to figure my shit out alone."

"Is that why you took her letters?" she asked. "To figure things out?"

Maybe. Maybe that was the reason.

The letters on the refrigerator changed colors; even the *A* turned purple.

"Those notes are tied to my life," I said, as I blinked back at the message. "They're what she wrote because I was conceived. That's why he disowned her, you know, because I existed."

"I don't believe that."

"Believe it or not. It's true."

"Have you read them?"

"No." I corrected myself, focused again on my sister's toes. "I read a few, but that was years ago."

Why hadn't I read them already? All of them, start to finish?

The answer shot through me with a stunning suddenness: I was afraid to read about all the ways that I might've ruined my mother's life—turned her into a person who couldn't complete things, who slept too much and couldn't face her days with any regularity, who'd left her children an inheritance of abandoned dreams. Not opening those envelopes left me with the slimmest hope. . . .

It'll taste like hope, Olivia had said. *The will-o'-the-wisp.*

Olivia needed hope because she feared what the letter she'd found would say, too, that it would prove that our mother had committed suicide.

Mama's life meant something—dreams and hopes are worth something!

Of course Olivia would want to believe that, because if your own mother decided life wasn't worth living, and dreams and hopes weren't worth having, what did it mean for you? What did it mean when you were just eighteen? If you thought it was your fault? If you felt that fear confirmed in your grandfather's obituary?

The room gave a little spin.

Olivia wasn't on a counter at all—of course she wasn't!—and the reason I faced her feet was that she was laid out on a branch. I was not standing on a table; I straddled a wooden tree-house window—one foot on the floor, the other on the same branch as my sister's body. Behind me was a simple tree house. Gone was the intricate staircase. Gone were the stove and the typewriter. The refrigerator and its letters.

Gone, finally, were my marbles.

"Olivia, what the hell are you doing out there?"

"The light was here earlier. I saw it. I thought I smelled Mama, but now everything tastes like ashes again."

"Olivia, the soup we ate is making us sick," I said as evenly as I could while my heart beat triple time in my chest. "It's making us see things that aren't there, do you understand me? You're on a limb, an actual tree limb, and the ground"—I looked down, felt even more nauseated—"is not close. For God's sake, be careful!"

"The light was in my blind spot. It was—" She lifted her arm, then slapped it back to the limb when her body slipped.

"Careful!"

"I can't hold on," she said. "The tree's made of butter."

"Yes, you will fucking hold on! There is no other option than you holding on!"

This was not going to happen. I would not lose more family. I tested the weight of the branch under my foot, but didn't dare try it when the wood turned to water before my eyes.

It's just the soup, I told myself. *There's still a branch there. It's not water, or butter.*

"Olivia, you need to move back slowly, okay?" I said, trying to keep the panic out of my voice. "Move little by little, and I'll help—"

"Mama's out there somewhere."

"If she is, she'd want you to come over here right now." I felt a surge of anger, of desperation. "Right now, Olivia Moon. Do you hear me? Move."

The pressure in my chest eased when her feet began to edge toward me. One inch. Another. I did my best to ignore the green things above her head, buzzing around her like dragonflies on mushrooms.

"That's so good, Olivia, keep doing that," I said as she made her way closer. Branch water splashed my arm when she gave a small kick. "Careful. Careful. Keep coming."

It happened when I tried to stretch a little more, to latch on to her ankle or any available part of her. My bag caught on something. I reached behind me until I felt the marbles, and then I pulled off my bag. Let it drop. Fall toward grasses that seemed a hundred miles down.

A huge blast of energy rose up in waves of light and Olivia reeled back, let go, fell and fell and fell away from the tree to follow the bag.

I screamed.

The ground stopped breathing.

And whatever was left of the sun went dark.

FIFTH STAGE:

ACCEPTANCE

Life is hard. Then you die. Then they
throw dirt in your face. Then the
worms eat you. Be grateful it happens
in that order.

—*David Gerrold*

CHAPTER TWENTY-FOUR

Hope Chest

✳ OLIVIA ✳

Goodbye wasn't as simple as packing up clothes and furniture and deciding in your head that that's the way it was going to be. Goodbye wasn't a *thinking* thing; it was a *feeling* thing. Goodbye was hard. Goodbye took time.

Sometimes the best way to say goodbye was to say it as if it wasn't forever. Goodbye, I'll see you again soon. Goodbye, see you tomorrow, maybe—or next week, or next year. Goodbye, see you at the tree.

Mama never said goodbye, not ever. Instead she'd say, *There's a long way to go before the end.* That made it easier, somehow.

Chicks, chirping. Yellow birds, full of feathers, fluttering around their nest. They surrounded me, noisy. I shushed them with my eyes clenched.

"You're awake! Good," someone said. This was a voice I didn't know, a tunnel with streamers hanging from the top.

I tried to open my eyes, and failed. Sank back into the darkness.

The next time I heard the birds, I realized they weren't birds at all; they were squeaky wheels.

I willed my eyes open, heard the tunnel-streamer voice again.

"There you are." She leaned over me—a plump dark-skinned woman. "Don't be afraid, sweetie. You're in the hospital. You've been asleep for a good long while—half a day. You had a nasty fall and broke a rib, but try not to worry. We're going to take care of you."

Warm blankets covered my body, and it felt as if there were a few stuffed inside my head, too. Something tightened around my arm, and I jerked back.

"That's just a machine taking your blood pressure. I'll take it off in a minute," the woman said. "You'll be able to see your family soon, once you do a few things for me. Can you follow this light with your eyes?"

"No," I said, "I can't." And then I started to cry.

A short while later, Papa, Babka, and Jazz came to see me. Jazz cried, said, "I've never been so scared in my life. I thought you'd died!" Babka kissed me a hundred times with her dewy lips and draped rosary beads over my chest. Papa leaned his head against mine, said, "I can't believe I let you go . . . could've lost you both . . . was such a bad father." His voice curled through the air like smoke rings from a pipe, and he smelled like cut grass again instead of vodka.

A nurse poked her head around a curtain, asked if I'd like some ice chips. I nodded. My throat hurt. My chest ached. Light streamed around me. How many hours had I lost?

"What happened?" I asked my family. The last thing I recalled was kissing Hobbs in the tree house.

"I couldn't get to you in time," Jazz said.

"Get to me?"

"You were so far away. I tried, but—"

I noticed Babka reach for my sister. "There, there, little *macka*. It is not your fault."

"Jazz? Just tell me," I said.

"You were on a tree limb," Jazz started. "Do you remember that?"

I didn't remember.

"My bag dropped," she said. "You fell right after it, right off the limb. You really don't remember anything?"

I didn't, and said so.

"It's all right, Liv. The important thing is you're safe now." Papa sat on the bed beside me. "We're lucky you weren't hurt a lot worse. We're lucky you're both all right after what you've been through. So lucky."

"You could've died," said Jazz. "You could've broken your neck or spine. We were so far up, and it looked farther at the time. It looked like a mile-long drop, though I guess that was from the mushrooms. I will never eat mushrooms again."

My skin prickled as pieces of the night before returned to memory. The soup. The obituary. The lights. My despair. Everything Jazz had told me. The slick-butter feel of the limb under my hands. And then I remembered what had come before even that: the *Bill bell*. Danger at the house. "Where's Hobbs?"

"I think he's still with the police," Jazz said, resting her hand over my shoulder when I struggled to pull myself upright. "Trust me, it's better to hear this lying down."

The coins Hobbs had taken from Bill *had* been stolen goods, she said, and when Hobbs tried to sell them he triggered the long memory of one West Virginia shop owner. The theft, though it happened more than a dozen years ago, had been big news because it also involved murder, arson, and the kidnapping of a young boy.

"The boy was Hobbs," Jazz said before doubling my shock. "Red Grass is his grandfather."

Reginald Guthrie was his real name, a retired insurance salesman who'd never given up hope that his grandson, whose body hadn't been recovered from the fire that had killed Reginald's son and daughter-in-law, was still alive somewhere. When the shop owner saw the coins Hobbs brought into the store in April—the combination of rare treasures too unique to be coincidental—he contacted not the police to share his shop's footage but the man whose grief and well-publicized frustration with the authorities had touched so many of them: Reginald. The kid, the shop owner had told him, looked like a train tramp. And the shop, as it turned out, was close to the rails.

"Red made posters out of that footage, plastered them in train towns across the state," said Jazz, as a nurse settled a cold cup in my hands. "Finally, a train worker called to say he'd seen Hobbs. That's when Red knew he'd do anything to make contact with the kid who'd tried to sell his son's coins. Anything."

He read two books on train hopping, grew some scruff, and adopted a less polished vocabulary. He bought light camping gear, a dependable flashlight, and a tracking device. It was May when he infiltrated the train community, and he admitted that he nearly killed himself on his first few runs. He thought it would take a week, at most, to find Hobbs; it took a month. Harder still was trying to get a look at the coins, proving the link to his son's murder. And because of some confusion about Hobbs's real birthday—and the fact that he used to be a plump, blond child and not a thin, dark hopper—it wasn't until Reginald escaped the outbuilding that he knew for certain that Hobbs was family.

"I don't have all the details," Jazz said, "but after we left, Red contacted that expert we met with, to verify that the coins matched the set stolen from his son. When he learned they did, he drove back to J.D.'s in his own car to find out where we'd gone. That's when he saw the coat."

"Coat?" I asked around the ice in my mouth.

I leaned close as Jazz explained how J.D. had pulled Hobbs's baby coat from a trunk of Alice's old things while looking for a pair of sweats for Jazz. It was still out when Red went back to the cabin—a link to Hobbs's old life that he recognized. J.D. found Red crying with the coat in his hands, and after hearing the story he led the way to Bill's place himself.

"No one was hurt," said Jazz, as I crunched through my ice. "Bill was asleep when they got there, so I don't know, maybe Red sat on him. However it happened, it sounds like there wasn't even a fight. Hobbs learned it all after Betty rang the bell, and he ran to the house."

"Poor Hobbs." My fingers dug into the cup. "He must be so overwhelmed."

"He wasn't exactly open to what Red had to say, I guess. He walked out after hearing the story, even though Bill didn't deny any of it, then minutes later found you lying like the dead at the bottom of a tree. What a mess he was for a while, holding you before the medics arrived, threatening you with beyond-the-grave curses if you dared die. I thought you were already gone."

I pictured this: Hobbs rocking me back and forth, so like Papa with Mama before the ambulance took her away. The memory of falling from the tree came to me then. The fear that I might die. The absolute recognition that I didn't want to, regardless of how I'd felt minutes before, when I learned a truth that had made my insides wither and ache.

My grandfather was dead. Dead before my mother by a week.

He had to have been on her mind as she sat with her pages that morning, when she'd spoken about wrong hopes and wrong dreams and alluded to a wasted life. Had she been steeped in regret over not sending those letters?

Maybe Mama never sent the letters not because she feared that her father might not forgive her but because she knew—with ninety-nine percent of herself—that he never would. *That's* what she believed, believed, why she never could bring herself to take action and why it might have hit her so hard when he died—when that one percent chance dropped to zero.

If she'd felt such a loss of hope that there seemed no other option . . .

Could she have?

Would she have?

Did she imagine, even for a moment, that a world without her parent in it was too bleak a world to face? That he was waiting for her at the tree? That the oven was there, right there, and all she needed was an absence of light, of fire, to make the pain go away? It took just one desperate moment to do something permanent. One desperate moment when everything felt black, when it seemed all hope was gone.

And what if it had happened—this worst thing? Did that mean she didn't want us? Didn't love us? That we weren't, never had been, enough?

Hadn't she wanted more for her life than to reconcile with her father? I knew she had. She wanted to learn how to speak French. She wanted to send one of Papa's songs to Nashville. She wanted Tramp to set up a town newspaper, even if it came out only once a month, and she wanted to help run it. She wanted to get her license back if she could. She wanted Jazz to go to college. She wanted Babka to start baking pepperoni rolls. She wanted to paint the kitchen pink. She wanted grandchildren someday. Lots of them.

I wish I could go back in time and tell her that maybe hope was no more than a foolish fire, but that maybe it could lead you to your heart's desires if you took a chance. I wish I could tell her that she could believe in her dreams with one percent of herself or ninety-nine percent or any percent in between, and she could believe whatever she needed to about her parent's last thoughts before dying.

So could I.

I felt it inside me like a flame, a pilot light that would never go out. Hope. Felt, too, the tingling of my feet, ready to climb me back into a tree, even if it meant I'd fall out of it again.

"I hope Mama knows she made it to the glades," I said to my family. "I hope she's happy, that she knows we love her no matter what. And we'll miss her, and never forget her."

Babka squeezed my hand.

"I can't believe you live in that mushroom-soup world all the time," Jazz said, her voice a wobbly line. "With all those shapes and colors flying around in your head. I don't know how you get anything done at all."

I would've said something about all of that, but the squeaky wheels came back. Chicks, chirping. Yellow birds, full of feathers, fluttering around their nest.

And I wanted to listen.

I t was late in the afternoon before Hobbs arrived, and I knew right away that something was wrong, because he wouldn't come close. Maybe he didn't want to hug me because he was afraid he'd hurt my rib. When the nurse came in to check my blood pressure and talk over my discharge instructions—there wouldn't be any tree climbing for a while—he stood at the window with his back turned. And, after she left, he said what we were both thinking.

"You're going to have to go now. So am I."

But everything had changed.

I slid out of bed and stepped beside him, my feet covered with blue hospital slippers. It seemed that it might be a chocolate coffee day outside—the sky was bright, the sun shone—but the glass was cold under my fingers.

"It's not goodbye," I told him.

"Maybe it should be," he said. "I'd be no good for a girl like you. Your sister sees that, has from the start. And you'd get over it—that taste in your mouth."

Once upon a time, Stan had pulled away from me, too, when things got hard. But I hadn't cared enough to fight for that relationship. Now I cared. Now I'd fight.

"Stubborn hopper." I took his hand, made him face me. "I won't get over it, because I don't want to. And you can't scare me off with talk of damage or whatever you've done in the name of survival or however much ink you've put on your skin, either. That's love. Tastes good, doesn't it?"

He tipped his head, and I thought I might've noticed a flick of his tongue, a lick of lips. When I hugged him, his fingers settled on the seam of my gown, spread against my back.

"What is it that you want?" I asked. "I mean, deep down."

He pushed his face against my neck. "I don't even know what I'm *supposed* to want anymore."

I knew he must be thinking about the kidnapping and who he was in truth—Christopher Guthrie. Hobbs didn't want to talk about any of that, he'd said, or about Bill or Red Grass, either.

"Forget about wanting, then." I pulled back enough to set my face just beside his, and looked at him as best I could. "What do you hope for? Not just the hopper who wants to find dragons but all the layers that you are, Hobbs and Christopher both."

"You know I don't hope," he said, but the upturned edges of his voice cracked and I knew he was thinking about it. Thinking *family*, thinking *a home*, thinking *someone I can trust*, thinking *love*, thinking *someone to wait for me to figure it all out*.

"Well, I do. I hope you see you have a choice now." I put my right hand over his left eye. "You can focus on the past"—then shifted it to his right—"or the future. It's up to you. I've already made my choice, and I can wait for you to make yours. Just don't make me wait too long. I know we're young and all that, but I'm not so good at waiting."

"I'd never guess that about you."

He let loose a sound that might've been the start of a laugh, or a cry. I kissed him after that—a kiss so full of want that it was like a hundred slips of Christmas Eve paper.

"Livya," he said. "Don't attach."

I shook my head—*too late*—though I knew already I'd set him free if that's what he needed, and hope he'd come back around in time, like the sun. But I wouldn't say goodbye. Instead, I borrowed a line from Mama. "There's a long way to go before the end."

AUGUST

CHAPTER TWENTY-FIVE

The Undying

∗ JAZZ ∗

At one point when the soup was still in my system I thought I understood all the secrets of the universe, but once the mushrooms wore off all that knowledge evaporated out of my head, which just figures. What I did know—what took me twenty-two years to learn—was that life was what you made of it. Perception was everything. And lying to yourself wasn't always a bad thing.

I guess I should be glad it didn't take fifty.

Our family doctor confirmed that my sister was "fit as a slightly fractured fiddle" three weeks after she'd fallen from a tree. She was lucky, he said, that she hadn't broken her neck in that fall. The light Olivia said she'd seen shining like a will-o'-the-wisp in her blind spot that night in the tree—the one I'd hoped was a sign of her vision coming back—was a photism. All the visuals created by Olivia's synesthesia were photisms, too—things forged by her brain that only she could see—and they were exacerbated by the mushroom soup. Dr. Patrick, who might've become West Virginia's expert on the matter, said that synesthetes with partial loss of sight often reported seeing things in their blind spots. I couldn't believe that finding a synesthete with a blind spot was common enough to generate this knowledge, but what did I know? Maybe they all stared at the sun.

Olivia, though, wasn't interested in science, and insisted she knew what that light had been and didn't need a doctor to tell her what she saw. I let it go. Despite her bill of good health, she'd been tetchy in the last few weeks—probably because she'd given Hobbs our phone number before coming home and he hadn't called.

Last I'd seen of Hobbs was at the hospital. My father and sister were busy with discharge paperwork and instructions, and so I'd taken a moment to steer him into a private corner for some instructions of my own.

Don't mess with her head, I told him, as he shoved his fists into his pockets and evaded my eyes. *Don't call unless you're sure. I mean it.*

He looked beyond me then, and when I turned I knew why. Reginald was clean-shaven, and wore a pair of plaid shorts and a blue polo shirt to match his eyes. He looked like a golfer. A far cry from a train hopper, in any case.

Red Grass, I said. *You clean up pretty well.*

He flashed a grin at me before sobering again and regarding Hobbs.

Come on, Hobbs, I thought. *Give the guy a chance.*

I know you have a lot to think about, said Red, *but I want you to know I'll take whatever you're willing to give, be it a punch in the head or a shake of the hand.* He extended his hand to Hobbs, whose expression was unreadable.

I may do both, Hobbs said, but he took Red's hand.

Red broke down then, clasped Hobbs close, and cried right there in the hall of the hospital. I could tell by the stiffness of Hobbs's shoulders and arms that he wasn't comfortable, but he didn't pull away, either.

Maybe Hobbs hadn't called because he was getting adjusted to being part of a real family again. Or maybe he hadn't called because he honestly wasn't sure what he wanted. Maybe there was no such thing as *sure* in this life. Maybe there was only doing the best we could, hoping that whatever choices we made would land us on the right road in the grand scheme of things. I'd warned Hobbs not to mess with Olivia's head, but maybe I'd messed with *his* head, and maybe I was starting to wish I hadn't. Maybe Hobbs deserved a second chance from me the way Red deserved a second chance from him, even the way my mother had deserved a second chance from her father.

Other than that, family life had been calm since our trip. Olivia and I hadn't spoken again about what happened between us at the tree, what we'd revealed to each other—probably because we were both still processing it all. Our father was doing much better— keeping regular work hours, eating normal meals again, not drinking. Maybe the shock of everything that happened changed all of us. I know I'd never been as appreciative of my rusty bucket since being back home, and looked often at the odometer, grateful not to be walking the 41.2 miles to *Rutherford & Son Funeral Home*, where I worked Monday through Thursday from nine to five.

I was in charge of the paperwork, and answering the phone, and setting up appointments in an office no bigger than a closet. I typed details into a computer. I printed out forms after filling them in electronically, then stored them in locked metal cabinets down the hall. (Emilia Bryce didn't trust computers, even though she wanted to use them.) At lunchtime I'd walk to the bagel shop I liked, and look at the paper. Sometimes I'd read through the obituaries, but more often I'd fill in an empty crossword puzzle or doodle. Nothing special. Shapes, a stray flower. Once, I caught myself writing out a poem. I left it half-finished.

Sometimes I heard weeping at the funeral home, and edged my way out of the office to bear witness. The other day I saw a couple kneeling before a corpse in a private room full of comfortable green chairs. The kneeling woman was daughter to the woman in the casket, lamenting the fact that she hadn't seen her mother in seven years. She'd been trying to save money, she said between sobs, so that she could travel out from her home in Hawaii, but there'd always been something. A broken car. Loss of a job. A dip in the stock market. She went through an entire box of tissues.

I might not know much for sure, but I do know this: Life at a funeral home was as real and honest as it got.

The night after Olivia's appointment with Dr. Patrick, I had the most vivid dream of Oran. The city gates were open. The rats gone. The streets scrubbed. The casket I'd seen in my prior dream was there, though, the lid lifted. I approached it as my mother sat upright, rubbing her eyes as if waking from a long sleep. When she saw me, she waved me forward. I stepped so close that I could see her freckles and the star shape of her pupils.

I forgot about the coat, she said, and reached to where a small trunk floated in the air beside her like a cloud. She opened it and peered inside. *And this. How could I have forgotten?* I recognized the orange scythe on the cover when she lifted the book from the trunk with a smile. *It's a good story. You should finish it.*

I did, I told her.

She set the book aside, then reached into the trunk again and pulled out a long cloak of gleaming gold. *No, Jazz*—she settled it around her shoulders—*you should finish it.*

She placed her right hand over her right eye, and I placed my left hand over my left before the huge burst of light came, not unlike what I remembered seeing after Olivia fell from the tree. My mother disappeared.

I awoke to find that it was just dawn but couldn't fall back asleep, my mind on the dream. My mother's book might end like that, with something revelatory involving the sun fairy and her stolen gold cloak. I should write down the idea. It hit me then how my dream had probably been inspired by Hobbs and his baby coat. How Hobbs and the kidnapped sun fairy were similar—both stripped of their identities and left without memories of their prior lives. Yes, the cloak could be the key. The cloak, the coat, the coat, the—

A teasing flash of memory blinked to life, beckoned like a will-o'-the-wisp.

Barefoot and in my nightshirt, I padded over creaky floorboards to find my mother's wooden trunk where it had always been, in the small space under the stairs. A yearning came over me when I lifted the lid, the same feeling I'd had months ago when I took *The Plague*. Inside were her old college books, layers deep, no room for anything else. But then I moved them enough to find an unexpected depth, and my veins rushed with adrenaline when my fingers brushed over something plush. I pulled books from the trunk three at a time until I caught a glimpse of a rich black *something* below a layer of scarves, and then I lost any form of patience and reached down with both hands, let books spill onto the floor with unquiet sounds as I hauled out the coat.

Gleefully, I tugged it over my nightclothes, ran my hands over its fur. I *remembered* this coat, though details evaded me.

Footsteps on the stairs above my head pounded out, and I cringed. My father appeared in boxers and a T-shirt. He gripped a tread, sighed when he saw me. "I thought we had a burglar."

I almost laughed—what did we have to burgle?

"Sorry, Dad, I didn't mean to make so much noise," I told him. "I had a dream, and then. . . . Well, I found this." I gestured to the fur.

"I forgot about that coat," he said, so like my dream. "Your mother loved that thing but felt a little guilty for it, I think. Looks like you might, too. You can have it if you want."

"I can?" I smiled wider than inheriting a faux-fur coat should warrant. "You don't think she would've minded?"

The lines across his forehead deepened when he grimaced, his whole face saying *no* when he shook his head.

"Funny how we don't let ourselves take hold of the things we rightfully should, sometimes," he said. "And how we hang on to other things long after it's time to let them go."

We stayed as we were for long minutes.

And then we removed all the covers from the mirrors.

Over my bed, I laid them all: dozens of my mother's letters to my grandfather. My fingers grazed over them as Olivia appeared in the doorway.

"Papa's going to make pancakes," she said. "He's talking about trying to grill them outside."

"Grill pancakes?" The neighbors would love that. "Should we try to talk him out of it?"

She shrugged. "A pancake is a pancake." She, too, was still in her pajamas—a yellow nightshirt that flounced along her calves. Her hair dangled in soft ringlets to her chin. She reached up, twisted a strand. "Are those the . . . letters?"

"Yes. I think I finally know what I'm going to do with them."

Her big eyes went bigger still, and she surprised me by not asking any questions. I glanced down at my open backpack, and a familiar something caught my eye. "I have a present for you."

She scrunched her cheek, then stepped into the room and sat on the bed beside me. "What?"

I dragged it out, settled the poster Red Grass had made into her hands. "It's a picture of Hobbs."

"Oh," she said in a small voice, as her eyes darted to the page.

Finally, bait she wouldn't be able to resist.

"Why don't you get your glasses? You can see him right here and now in a proper way."

Though the glasses would never fully correct for Olivia's vision, they could magnify details to a viewable level for her, details that would otherwise be lost.

She curled the page at the edges until it resembled an Old World scroll, then said, "I can't," in a rush, as if she'd been holding her breath. "I'm not ready." She stood and walked across the room with the poster in her hand.

I talked to her back—"If you run away from this when you have the ability to do something about it, if you take that picture and leave it on Mom's desk beside your glasses, I swear"—but she didn't turn.

I pushed the heels of my hands against my eyes, so hard that dots of light appeared beneath my lids.

"A little early for a cookout, isn't it, Dad?" I stepped off the back stoop and into our yard to find my father stoking flames in the stone fireplace he'd built. The day was supposed to be a scorcher, but the morning air still held a chill.

"I'd say it's late for a cookout, if anything," he said, and I knew what he meant. He'd spent many months last summer and fall, even up to the first snow, grilling out there, but the pit had been unattended since my mother's death. And even though pancakes over an open fire seemed like a bad idea, I was glad to see him there again and wouldn't try to talk him out of it.

I sat at the brown and splintery picnic table we'd had for longer than I'd been alive, put the letters before me, and waited for him to finish setting a pan up over the pit, balancing the ends on two tall bricks.

Finally, he turned, a smear of ash along his cheekbone, and saw the letters. "What have you got there?"

He sat across from me, listened as I explained what they were—letters that Mom had written to Grandpa Orin, starting way back. I admitted, too, that I'd read a few. I expected to step away after that, leave him with those memories and truths, but he invited me to stay, so I stirred embers for him as he read.

Sometimes he'd share a letter's details—*Jazz likes apples, and blowing bubbles; she says no even if she means yes. Did you know that* bog *means God in Slavic? It also means* fortune *and* destiny—and other times he'd keep a letter to himself. Sometimes he'd laugh—*Olivia Moon, if you're reading these letters, you should stop right now and mind your own business. Love, Mama.*

Only once did he cry. I stepped to his side when it happened, and slid the letter from his wilted hand. It was dated just last year:

December 25, 2012

Dear Dad,

It is evening here, on Christmas. I've spent most of the day with my family, at Drahomira's home. It's traditional that we all write wishes down on a piece of paper at some point during the day. For the first time, I found that I couldn't do it. Nothing would come.

It struck me while sitting there with a limp pen in my hand how much self-blame I've felt, like I've deserved punishment from you, Dad, because I had done the "wrong thing," according to you, so many years ago. Then I looked around at my wonderful family and realized that I could never think of them that way. They were the perfect thing.

What's wrong? they wanted to know when I left my paper blank. Nothing, I told them, but I don't need to make a wish. I have everything I need right here.

Beth

"I always wondered if she regretted keeping me," I said before I could think not to, then felt the swift rush of blood to my face. We'd never discussed this, not any of us, because it had never been acknowledged that I was conceived before my parents were married; that I was, possibly, the reason they were married at all. That I might've been the reason my mother had lost her father.

"Oh, baby, no." Dad pulled me down until my shoulder collided with his, and when he wrapped his arms around me, I let myself be held. "What she regretted was having to make a choice at all. But that wasn't her fault, and it certainly wasn't yours."

I nodded along his arm. "Why did she miss him so much, for so long? I never understood it."

"I never did, either, except to imagine they had a powerful strong connection because of the way her mother left them both. They had nothing but each other for most of her childhood. I still feel winded by what he did to her when I think about it, how he could cut her out of his life the way he did."

He went on to tell me things I didn't know—that Mom had tried to contact her father after the break, but that he'd threatened legal action if she continued to bother him. She'd tried, at least in the early days. It meant a lot to hear that.

"I wouldn't care what you'd done," he said. "I'd never do that to you girls. A father is a father, for better or worse. I'll give you two more of the *better* from me from now on, I promise."

"We'll give you better, too, Papa," Olivia said.

She stood on the stoop with a letter in her hand, half in the shadow of a tall oak, half in sun.

"You have another one, Liv?" my father asked her. "Let's read it."

"I can tell you what it says." She held the letter to her chest. "It says, 'Dear Dad. It's cold today. I'm going to put the oven on to warm the room, and close the door to keep the heat in so I can write this letter in private.'"

I closed my eyes.

" 'But I feel sleepy,' " she said. " 'And the pilot light . . . The pilot light . . .' "

Her voice drifted off. The fire crackled.

" 'But I feel sleepy,' " my father continued, and I opened my eyes again, centered myself on him—my parent—and his sturdy gaze. " 'And the pilot light just went out.' "

Olivia walked over to us, her quiet tears a reflection of our own. "I don't want this anymore," she said. "I haven't wanted anyone else to want it, either, so I kept it to myself. That was wrong, and selfish, and I'm sorry. You should have the choice, if you want to, if you need to read it. . . ."

Dear Family . . .

Olivia laid the letter on the table before us, still sealed, and I noticed what else she held: her glasses.

My heart felt bruised, as if I'd been flung from a tree, made to see the grass up close. The reason Olivia wouldn't wear her glasses was that she didn't trust herself not to read our mother's letter, feared what she might learn if she did.

"I didn't mean to hurt either of you by keeping that," she said. "I don't want any of us to hurt anymore."

Must've hurt like hell to stare at the sun, Hobbs had said. *Tells me it hurt even more not to. She says she doesn't even know why she did it.*

Blind people couldn't read pen-written letters. Was that why Olivia had stared at the sun in the first place? Would she have done that? Had she wanted to hold to hope so desperately that she would have? I thought of everything I'd learned about my sister, her fears over having a hand in our mother's death, her strong sense of responsibility for her mental wellness, and knew that it was possible, whether Olivia realized it consciously or not.

"I don't need to read that letter, Liv," my father said. "I think you're right about what she wrote that morning. That's what I want to believe."

He looked at me with new spine in his expression, and for the second time in my life the earth seemed to falter on its axis. We could choose this—how we would remember her, how we'd think about the way she'd died—and embrace the uncertainty of this bag-of-marbles life.

And maybe it wasn't impossible.

It had been a cold winter day, after all, and the stove was old. If Mom had been tired, might it, could it have happened the way Olivia imagined?

Some of the anger I'd carried over my mother's death loosened in that moment, and I knew then that I could let it go. Honestly. Completely. Not just for my sister and my father, to avoid becoming the boot that could crush their hope, but for me. Jazz Marie Moon. And for Mama. Maybe especially for her.

I slid a hand up to cover my right eye, grateful for a gesture that spoke enough for me just then.

Olivia's glasses were firm on her face when she fed my mother's last letter to the fire. Together we watched the paper curl and turn feathery, until wisps of solid ash floated above it all like gray ghosts. My father added other letters, too—not all of them, but some. Dropped them into the flames, until the fire consumed them, greedy as a starved child.

If they noticed when I stole away into the house, they didn't make mention of it. And when I returned with my grandfather's obituary in hand, I added it, without a word or a second thought, to the fire.

Minutes later, when my father went inside to make up a batter, Olivia pulled the poster of Hobbs out of her pocket. I sat across from her at the table, watched with anticipation as she smoothed the paper out, print-side down, and then turned it over.

"Well? Change your mind about him now that you've seen that mug of his?" I asked, and surprised myself by holding my breath, rooting for Hobbs and his face full of art and scars.

"He really is beautiful."

I nodded, despite myself. The photograph, and the negative.

"I dreamed about him last night," she said, looking again at the poster. "It was so real. We were in bed together and—"

"Okay, stop."

"We weren't *doing* anything," she said. "He was by my side, telling me about cranberry season, how the berries were ripe now and we should travel again to the glades. How he missed me and wanted to see me again so bad he could taste it. And then he said—he said he was . . . attached. That I was his missing part." She flicked a tear away. "I used to think I could be satisfied with a pizza shop, but now I can't imagine life without Hobbs. I really thought he'd call, but now . . . What if he never calls?" Tears streamed in earnest now, and she let them go, pushed her fingers against her nose as she shook her head, the very picture of doubt.

I walked to her side of the table and drew her face up with my hand on her chin. "What are you saying, Olivia Moon? What happened to *believe, believe*?"

"I don't know what I believe anymore. Why? Do you believe?"

"I believe in you," I said. "I also believe I just gagged from saying that, even though it's true. Now you'd better stop with the waterworks, because as far as I can tell you don't have windshield wipers on those things."

We giggled together, as my father returned with his batter and ladle.

"I guess we can't control life, or the people in it," I said, settling on the bench beside her. Not how they might or might not read a letter, or what they might feel or do about it if they did. Not who might have a heart attack while holding a pan of warm brownies, or get kidnapped in a robbery gone wrong, or drop from a buttery tree thanks to a tangle of events you never could've foreseen. Not death, not most of the time. "But we can control ourselves—right now, in this moment. That's something. Maybe it's everything."

Olivia clasped her hands together and sniffed. A breeze blew through the branches above our heads, and sunlight flickered over the table.

"I still see the light sometimes when I close my eyes," Olivia told me. "When I do, I catch her scent. I think it's her way of telling me that it's okay to move on and that she'll always be with us. Do you think that's stupid?"

She turned to look at me with her bespectacled eyes, the blue of them magnified in her glasses, her long lashes damp with sadness but prettier than ever. No glancing down to the ground. No blinking. Just one sister connecting with the other.

"It's not stupid," I told her. "I think you're right."

"I wonder if . . ."

"What?"

"It's terrible to think it, but if Mama hadn't died, I wouldn't have met Hobbs at all. I'm so glad that I met him. I guess I'll just have to take this waiting and wanting thing one day at a time."

"That's it." I nodded. "One foot in front of the other."

We sat together, watching our father burn pancakes.

"Why am I waiting for him to call me?" Olivia said, already out of her seat. "I can call information today, right now. I can track him down."

"Of course you can," I said, as my imagination cracked open.

I could stay at the funeral home or not stay. I could stay in West Virginia or not stay in West Virginia. I could follow an impulse. Me, Jazz Marie Moon. I might like that.

"Dad?" I said, as my sister stepped into the house. I noticed that his cakes had drooled all over the pan before burning, and he was using a stick to push at the bricks, attempting to make them a more even pair, I assumed. "Would it be wrong—I mean, would you mind—?" I cleared my throat. "Would it be strange if I worked on Mom's story?"

He turned to me with a wondering expression on his face.

"I sort of dreamed about it last night," I said. "I think I might be able to work up an ending. I mean, I know I won't be able to replicate her writing style, but maybe I can tell the story in a different way."

I was stammering, I realized, like an idiot. Oh, good; it had come to this.

"I mean, would that be wrong?" I continued, seemingly unable to help myself. "Do you think she would've—"

"I think she would've loved that," he said.

"Really?"

"Really."

I smiled back at him. These minutes were mine, right now, and there were so many possibilities, I felt anxious over them. Not in a closed-casket kind of way, either, but in a when-do-we-leave kind of way. And maybe writing about everything filling my head would help me to sort it all out.

A clatter and a hiss drew my attention back to the fire, where my father's makeshift griddle had toppled over completely, taking his charred cakes with it.

"Well, that's that," he said, adding his stick to the flames. "I give up."

"It was a valiant effort," I told him.

He crossed his arms over his chest, then turned with an eye on the roof. I hadn't seen that look on his face in a long while.

"You want me to go get your fiddle?" Who cared if it wasn't even ten in the morning? Our neighbors would have to deal.

"In a bit," he said, as black smoke billowed behind him. "I've still got to feed you two, and myself. I'm starving."

The phone rang from inside the house. Olivia shrieked.

"You think it's Hobbs?" His crooked grin added, *This could be interesting.*

"It might be," I said, thought, *I hope so.*

A quiet minute passed as we stared at the door, and then my father's stomach growled.

"Let's go." I nudged him in the side. "I'll make you a peanut-butter-and-jelly sandwich."

ACKNOWLEDGMENTS

I'm glad for the opportunity to thank some of the many people who helped to bring this book into being.

To my editor Christine Kopprasch, for her unfailing support, wise guidance, and kind encouragement; I am more grateful than I can express. And to Kate Kennedy, for an early and important critique that helped to shape this novel.

To my agent, Elisabeth Weed, for her many editorial contributions, for never losing faith in this story—or in me—and for negotiating a two-book deal with Crown in the first place. You rock.

To leading synesthesia researcher Jamie Ward, Ph.D., professor of cognitive neuroscience at the University of Sussex and author of *The Frog Who Croaked Blue*, and to James Sheedy, O.D., Ph.D., director of the Vision Ergonomics Research Laboratory at Pacific University, for answering questions that helped to define the mannerisms and experience of the most unique character I've ever imagined, Olivia Moon. And to heath-care providers Gary Dean, M.D., and Walid Hammoud, M.D., for other medical guidance.

To Sean Day and his superb Synesthesia Listserv. Thank you for letting me snoop about, and for all of the inspiration.

To Cindy Butler, executive director of the West Virginia Department of Transportation's State Rail Authority, for answering questions about trains and distances, and for providing railway maps; and to both Cindy and John Smith, president of the Durbin and Greenbrier Valley Railroad, for a fun ride while pointing out details that helped to make this story come alive.

To followers of my author page on Facebook who leaped in with suggestions when I requested ideas for fictional West Virginia towns, and especially to Rebecca Bussa Saunders (Spades Hallow) and Leah Welsh Lowe (Jewel) for their appealing suggestions.

To all of my friends, and especially my colleagues at Writer Unboxed. To Kathleen Bolton for her unfailing support, and to Jeanne Kisacky for being the first to understand what this book wanted to become. To Marilyn Brant, Keith Cronin, and Jael McHenry for thoughtful observations, suggestions, and encouragement that made an impact. Your perspectives helped to make this a better book and me a stronger author.

To my most beloved readers—my husband, Sean; my sisters, Heather and Aimee; and especially to my daughter, Riley. Riley, your understanding of both human behavior and storytelling is insightful beyond your years, and your tolerance of your indecisive mother—"This word better, or this one?"—is truly commendable. I have no doubt that you will one day take over the world, and your brother will be there to capture it all on film. (That's you, Liam. Go, New Hamsterdam!)

And finally to my mothers and my fathers. Thank you for all your love and support. You can read it now. (xo)

ABOUT THE AUTHOR

THERESE WALSH is the author of *The Last Will of Moira Leahy* and the cofounder of Writer Unboxed, an award-winning website and online writing community. She lives in upstate New York with her husband and two children. She loves haiku, photography, and tormenting her characters. She has a master's degree in psychology.

A NOTE ON THE TYPE

This book was set in Berling Roman. Created by typographer and book designer Karl-Erik Forsberg for the now defunct Swedish foundry Berlingska Stilgjuteriet in 1951, with additional weights following in 1958, Berling is an old-style typeface characterized by a small x-height and ascenders taller than its capital letters. Although influenced by Weiss, Berling has more contrast in the thick and thin strokes of its letterforms.

GUNNISON COUNTY LIBRARY DISTRICT
Old Rock Community Library
504 Maroon Avenue P.O. Box 489 Crested Butte, CO 81224
970.349.6535
www.gunnisoncountylibraries.org